BONEDALE

13 TALES OF THE SUBLIMELY ODD

PATRICK QUINN KITSON

SOPRIS
— PUBLISHING —

Paperback ISBN: 979-8-9928929-0-1
eBook ISBN: 979-8-9928929-2-5

Cover Art and Illustrations by Daniel Kelley
Edited by Christie Moreton

TABLE OF CONTENTS

SPRING-HEEL...11

CONFESSION..31

SHERO..53

SHREDDIN'..89

SOIL..112

POTATOES..126

FLICKER...149

RELATIVISM..176

HARVEST...206

PITCHBLENDE...248

REPOSITORY...273

YUM-YUM..304

HEADLINE...328

FROM THE AUTHOR......................................341

ABOUT THE AUTHOR...................................357

This book is dedicated to my mom and pops who did the very best they could with the raw deal that is yours truly.

"Here come the blue skies, here comes the springtime,
when the rivers run high and the tears run dry.
When everything that dies, shall rise."

— The The, "Love Is Stronger Than Death"

CARBONDALE, COLORADO

SPRING-HEEL

DO NOT DESTROY THIS REPORT

–Recovered from the site of the former Carbondale Police

Department on December 3rd, 2024–

*T*he following is a transcript of an informal interview between CPD Officer Lance Downey, 34; Principal James Weddock, 59; and Damon Tribbs, 17, a student at Roaring Fork High School in Carbondale, Colorado, as taken into record by registered town stenographer, Susan Fisher, 61, who arrived several minutes into the meeting. Said interview is dated December 1, 2024, commencing at roughly 10:40 p.m. in Interrogation Room Two at Carbondale Police Department. Any other persons involved in the interview are listed below.

This record is to serve as the initial written account of the reported incident.

Officer Downey (First officer on scene/detaining officer): Let's hold on for just a moment so that Susan can get her steno up and running.

10:41 p.m., Susan Fisher, transcriber of record, writer of this testimonial, and registered stenographer for Carbondale Police Department as well as the Carbondale Municipal Court, enters and sets up the stenograph machine. All discussion before 10:41 p.m. cannot be attested to on the record. Dialogue continues.

Susan Fisher: Thank you. Please continue.

Officer Downey: Thanks for the hustle, Susan. His parents will be here any second. So, as you were saying, Damon—not a bear or anything like that? It isn't possible you saw a bear and mistook—

Damon Tribbs: I don't know how many times you want me to say it, sir! It was a human, not an animal. It was a man. Just like you and butt-boy here—and just like me. Flesh and blood. Only difference was that, where you and I aren't able to leap from one goddamn building to another, this crazy bastard was. That, and the helmet thing.

Officer Downey: Well now we're on the record, so we're gonna roll through it one last time. This all happened just outside the school?

Damon Tribbs: As I've said again and again, right out in the parking lot, yeah.

Officer Downey: But you can see how, no matter how many times you've said that, it remains hard to believe.

Damon Tribbs: Lucky for me, it also remains the truth. Squaring it with what you want to believe is your problem, not mine.

Principal James Weddock: Cut the cute shit, Damon. He can make it your problem pretty fast if you don't—

Officer Lance Downey raises his hand to silence James Weddock.

Officer Downey: James, if you don't mind, I have this in hand. Now, son, we aren't here to do anything but figure out what happened this evening.

Damon Tribbs: I told you and butt-boy here that—

Principal Weddock: Goddamn it, stop calling me butt-boy! You...you will not—

Officer Downey: Hey!

Officer Downey shoots Mr. Weddock another look.

Officer Downey: Once more, James, and that's it. Another warning and you'll have to head on out, catch me? I'm trying to help you out here with the—

At this point in the discussion, 10:44 p.m., there is a knock on the door. Three persons enter the room : Mrs. Genevieve T. Tribbs, 44; Mr. Scott A. Tribbs, 51; and one Eric Landrush, 34, attorney with the law offices of Billings, Beecher, Landrush, and Associates of Rifle, Colorado. Damon stands up from the chair he was sitting in and embraces his mother and father.

Genevieve Tribbs: Are you okay, honey?

Damon Tribbs: Yeah, yeah; I'm okay. But it took Keith, Ma. It took him!

Genevieve Tribbs: What took him? What do you mean?

Scott Tribbs: The hell do you think you're doing here, Lance?

Officer Downey: Serving and protecting, Scott. How about you?

Scott Tribbs: Without any legal representation? I'd think you'd know better than—

Officer Downey: It's an informal chat, Scott. His friend is missing.

Genevieve Tribbs: Is that supposed to pass for amiable and down-to-earth, officer? 'Cause to me it reads as avarice. I swear to God that if you have done anything that isn't—

Scott Tribbs: Honey, honey…stop. Just stop, okay? Stop. We need— I mean, let's just…let's give the man a chance to speak before we come down on any side of this.

Genevieve Tribbs: What sides? I see no sides to this. It's our son who he's—

Scott Tribbs: Okay Genevieve, please. Let's just figure this out.

Officer Downey addresses Mr. Landrush.

Officer Downey: And how about you, bright boy? What's your end in all this?

Eric Landrush: Eric Landrush, of Billings, Beecher, Landrush, and Associates.

Eric Landrush steps forward and hands Officer Downey a business card.

Eric Landrush: I am here on behalf of this young man and the family. Unless you plan on charging him right now, I really must insist that he be immediately released to the custody of his parents, pending any further investigation into the matter.

Officer Downey: Maybe you'd like to hear what the matter is before you start spouting slick legalese to me, bucko?

At this point, Officer Downey points his right index finger at Mrs. Genevieve Tribbs.

Officer Downey: Mayhaps you wanna ask your baby boy why his shoes have his friend's blood spattered on 'em?

Principal Weddock: Or why he was standing in a pool of said blood when I found him next to the school? Hmm? You wanna explain to them where Keith is, Damon? Or should I regale everyone with your unbelievable yarn? Is that blood all over you from your so-called friend?

Damon Tribbs: That fuckin' leaping dude got him! I said that, and you damn well heard me! Get the wax out of your ears, butt-boy.

Principal Weddock: Goddamn it! Don't fucking call me that!

Genevieve Tribbs: Whoa, I know you did not just say that, you classless piece of—

Officer Downey: Stop! James, I need you to leave. Now. I'll make a transcript of this interview available for your records. Skedaddle and you'll be updated as soon the info is in hand.

Principal Weddock: Are you serious?

Officer Downey: Yep. Now please leave.

Principal Weddock: Did you hear what he just—

Officer Downey: I heard him. And you heard me. You bring tension and stress to a situation already brimming with too much of both. I'll call you back if and when I need you. Please, go.

At approximately 10:50 p.m., James Weddock leaves the room.

Officer Downey: But— See, Damon, this is the place where your little tale starts to leak big water from all the bulkheads. It's a mighty hard pill to swallow, and so far, I can't get it down my gullet.

Genevieve Tribbs: Jesus Christ. Do you think for one second that I can't or won't have you removed from your position if you stomp on my son's rights for much longer, Officer Downey?

Officer Downey: Oh, I do, ma'am. I do. But I would remind you that regardless of what your maiden name might be and who your family is, our lady of the steno over yonder is taking down everything that's said here tonight for the record. Extortion, or blackmail, or whatever heavy-handed shit your eyeballin' might fall under, is something you don't want hanging around your neck when it comes time to—

Eric Landrush: Mrs. Tribbs, perhaps you'd step outside for a moment while we—

Genevieve Tribbs: Oh get fucked, you tucked and tidy little pinhead. I barely even know you! You're a Christmas party acquaintance. Come to think of it, where's Theo? Why are you even here?

Scott Tribbs: Genevieve! That's plenty, really. He's here because I called him. Mr. Billings is hunting black bear in Alaska this week and we needed someone from the firm over here ASAP.

Genevieve Tribbs slams her hand on the nearby desk, knocking over a small, mostly empty cup of coffee. It falls to the linoleum floor and breaks into several pieces.

Officer Downey: Mrs. Tribbs? Are we okay here?

Genevieve Tribbs: Oh, yeah. No— I just… Yeah, no, I'm sorry. I'm sorry. I apologize. I'm not— I wasn't trying to sound crazy, I just don't know what this is. What is this? What actually happened?

Scott Tribbs: Yeah, first thing goddamn first. Damon, tell us what happened.

Officer Downey: Well don't clam up now, young man. Tell your parents what you've been telling me.

Damon Tribbs: I don't… It didn't make any sense really. It was crazy. All of a sudden, a man-type thing in a pinstripe suit jumped to where we were and we tried to run but it stabbed Keith in the chest with…something. A knife or something it had in its hands. I didn't see what. But then this thing—this guy, whatever—he laughed in a fucking horrible way and flew off with him. And it was—

Scott Tribbs: Whoa, whoa! Just wait. Now, that's…a lot. For starters, where were you?

Eric Landrush: Mr. Tribbs, I suggest you leave with your—

Scott Tribbs holds up his hand to silence Attorney Eric Landrush.

Scott Tribbs: That's plenty, Eric. I've got this for the time being. Damon, finish what you were saying. Everyone just let him goddamn speak!

Damon Tribbs: Thanks, Dad. I'm just uh… I'll try to explain it, but it's crazy. Really crazy.

Scott Tribbs: Explain yourself, Damon.

Damon Tribbs: So, yeah, we were on the roof of the school and we were about to jump down—

Scott Tribbs: Forgive me, I know I just said…but why were you on the roof of the high school?

Damon Tribbs: It was a senior prank thing. We were just scouting it out. Later tonight, Keith and I—and if I'm being honest, the rest of the football team—we were gonna use a key we copied from the janitor and then we were going to put all the principal's furniture on the roof.

Genevieve Tribbs: That's not very smart or funny. Why, Damon?

Damon Tribbs: Because it is, in fact, both smart and funny, actually.

Officer Downey: Damon—

Damon Tribbs: I don't fucking know! It wasn't my idea, okay! I was just…

Genevieve Tribbs: Just what, Damon? Just trying to be the big man on campus again? Like with that bullshit during homecoming?

Damon Tribbs: That wasn't my fault! I didn't know any fireworks had been stashed in the base of the bonfire until I was fleeing from it just like everyone else! One hundred percent not my fault!

Scott Tribbs: Damon, focus, please. What are you saying? That some man flew onto the roof and then what?

Damon Tribbs: Like I said already, we were about to climb down, then we see this thing in the distance. It's hard not to notice because it's like coming in our direction really, really fast. It looked like a white spot hopping from rooftop to rooftop. But once it reached those apartments on the other side of the parking lot, we got a better look at it. And this dude with a crumpled jacket and burning white eyes leaps all the way over to us. Just right there, boom! We jumped down off the roof and not three seconds later it's right on top of our heads—or, you know what I mean. Then it grabbed Keith.

Officer Downey: And one more time, for the record, this wasn't an animal that you saw attack your friend?

Scott Tribbs: What kind of animal leaps from one building to another, Lance?

Damon Tribbs: He thinks it's a bear, but it wasn't. Also, bears don't wear metal masks!

Officer Downey: I never said that, Damon. I asked if perhaps a larger animal like a bear could've been what you saw.

Genevieve Tribbs: Bears can't leap from roof to roof.

Officer Downey: Far as I know, neither can any human, ma'am.

Genevieve Tribbs: Honey, he has a point. Are you saying he had a flying machine or something?

Damon Tribbs: No.

Genevieve Tribbs: Then give us something better than that.

Damon Tribbs: I'm serious, mom. It was the most terrified I've ever been in my life.

11:04 p.m., Damon Tribbs starts to cry. Genevieve Tribbs comforts him.

Genevieve Tribbs: I'm sorry baby. It's okay; I'm here. We're gonna figure this out. Okay?

Damon Tribbs: It killed him, Ma. He was screaming when it carried him off and it sounded like it stabbed him a bunch of times. I heard his ribs crunching. It sounded…fucking terrible.

Scott Tribbs: Damon, it's extremely important that you be as honest about what happened tonight as possible so that we can protect you. Do you understand?

Damon Tribbs: I didn't fucking kill him! And butt-boy knows that shit!

Genevieve Tribbs: Who?

Officer Downey: He means the Principal, James Weddock. Though that particular joke, if ever funny at all, has long since stopped being so. He isn't wrong, though. James did attest to as much.

Scott Tribbs: Why haven't you charged him, Lance?

Officer Downey: I'd prefer Officer Downey at the least, Mr. Tribbs, though it hardly matters at this point. Honest opinion—I don't think your son killed his friend.

Genevieve Tribbs: Of course he didn't!

Eric Landrush: Mr. Tribbs, I must insist that we abstain from discussing this matter any further until we—

Scott Tribbs: I appreciate what you're saying, Eric, truly. But I'm aware of any and all risks and I prefer we hear what the officer has to say. Go ahead, Officer Downey. Please.

Officer Downey: Between two former Rams, Scott, I've known your son for many years now, and he's maybe fibbed to me a few times here and there, that I can recall. Boys being boys and all that, nothing unusual. But this sure doesn't feel like a joke. Also, James said he heard the boys on the roof and then came out to find Damon on the grass next to the west side of the building, right near a pool of blood on the ground. I saw it when I got there. So I'm wondering now, if James came out that quickly, and I got there a few minutes after that, then where is the body? There's no evidence of it being dragged, carried, loaded, or anything else. No body at all. Enterprising though Damon may be for his age, hiding a corpse in a couple of minutes without leaving a trace is beyond even his skills, I'd suspect.

Genevieve Tribbs: You suspect?

Scott Tribbs: Gen, please. That's a good thing, though. Right?

Officer Downey: Not sure I would call it good, per se, but it certainly bodes well for your son's claim of not being the assailant. The rest of his story is a tall pile of shit I sure wish he'd give me a cleaner version of, I don't mind sayin'. But that's probably gonna be the purview of your legal counsel moving forward. As for Keith, we've left a message for his father but I've been told he's out of town and won't be back for several days.

Genevieve Tribbs: So, we can go?

Officer Downey: Well, as I said, I'd sure like a better take on what happened than this story about some joker in a hand-me-down tux and welder helmet. I'd really prefer to round up a better turn of events to inform his father of and because I want to find Keith, son. And frankly, you telling me over and over that some guy who can fly is responsible is just—

Damon Tribbs: I didn't say he flew! I said he jumped.

Scott Tribbs: Jumped?

Damon Tribbs: Yes, jumped, Pops. Jumped. He fucking jumped over to us from the apartment across the street! And it made a loud metallic sound when he took off each time.

Genevieve Tribbs: So he had long legs or something?

Damon Tribbs: No, no—that's not what I mean. I mean he jumped far, and there was like a spring popping sound. Like something…it sounds dumb, but it was like something from a cartoon. Impossible shit. I dunno. He looked like a normal dude, but tall. A bit taller than other dudes. And he didn't have a jetpack. The shoes were doing it. I don't know how; it all happened so fast. What are we going to tell his dad? Oh, Jesus—

Genevieve Tribbs: Calm down, baby. Calm down. It's… Don't you for a moment worry about any of that, hon. We can—we will—handle all of this.

Eric Landrush: Mr. Tribbs, may I ask the officer a question?

Scott Tribbs: Yes, you may.

Eric Landrush: What else aren't you telling us, officer?

Officer Downey: Caught that, did ya, bright boy?

Eric Landrush: As you imply, I'm not that dim. And it comes with the trade, I'm sure you know. What is it? Is this the only incident or have there been others? There have been, haven't there?

Genevieve Tribbs: Is that true?

Scott Tribbs: Officer?

Officer Downey: About a week ago, we got a call from Gertrude up Thompson Creek Road. Said she was feeding her sheep when she got eyes on someone or something leaping around, sorta like you're describing. From roof to roof. Same thing about the eyeballs in a mask too. Gerdie said they were glowing white. Even said he nabbed one of her flock the following evening. So, one supposes there's that.

Scott Tribbs: Jesus jumping Christ, Lance. Why wouldn't you tell the town about—

Officer Downey: What, Scott? What? Tell the town that the cranky ol' sheep-herdin' buzzard by the Beaver Ponds spun a yarn about a spring-footed devil prancing about her shingles at all hours of the evening? What, say, I told you that one, Scott? What'd be your first response?

Damon Tribbs: Nobody would have believed you. Bet that shit for real though.

Scott Tribbs: Damon, just—

Damon Tribbs: He's right, Dad. I saw it. Gerdie's nutty ass must've seen it too! It's not bullshit. This isn't bullshit!

Scott Tribbs: Okay, Damon, okay. I hear you.

Eric Landrush: Has there been any formal report made about this matter, Officer Downey?

Officer Downey: Well, no. Since this is all just now coming together, we haven't yet. And if we did—

Officer Mike Brower, 27, knocks on the door to the room and enters.

Officer Mike Brower: I was told you wanted to see me?

Officer Downey: Yes, but it's just gonna be… Well, damn, yeah…I should just— We've got some trouble brewing this evening and I need you on point with this.

Officer Mike Brower: Alright. Okay, so what's going on?

Officer Downey: In a nutshell, all hell breaking loose. But literally we may have a homicide on our hands.

Officer Mike Brower: What're the specifics?

Officer Downey: Too few so far, but a guy hopping from building to building and stabbing teenagers is what we've got to work with right now.

Officer Mike Brower: What, really? Where?

At this point, several phones begin to ring in the adjacent room.

Officer Downey: The high school.

Officer Mike Brower: What do you want me to do?

Officer Downey: Go and take those calls, but when we head out shortly, you're my man. Less than five, good?

Officer Mike Brower: Sounds good.

11:10 p.m., Officer Mike Brower leaves the room.

Officer Downey: Where were we?

Scott Tribbs: Why do we need to remain, Officer Downey?

Officer Downey: The situation is still in motion, obviously. I'd count myself a fool not to ask once more. So, Damon— last chance saloon. If there is anything else you could tell me about what happened this evening, it will only help us help Keith.

Damon Tribbs: I told you everything, Officer Downey. Everything. I don't know what you want me to say.

Officer Downey: Something just like that, Damon, actually. Something just like that. I know you didn't hurt Keith. You understand that in my role as an officer of the law, I have to push for info when it's still fresh in the mind of any witnesses. I would be lying if I said that—

A loud knock on the glass door, and Officer Brower enters. His tone and face are more serious than before.

Officer Mike Brower: Excuse me, but Lance, I think this might be something.

Officer Downey: What is it?

Officer Mike Brower: We have two callers on the line reporting similar occurrences over by Bert 'n' Ernie Park.

Officer Downey: Go on.

In the adjacent room, several of the phones ring.

Mike Brower: They've been saying that someone or something is leaping from rooftop to rooftop, setting off car alarms and causing the whole damn neighborhood to wake up. We need to get over there.

Eric Landrush: Whoa—

Scott Tribbs: That means that Damon is clear of any suspicion, doesn't it? Now that you got someone to go chase down?

Genevieve Tribbs: Of course it does!

Officer Brower starts to leave, but Officer Downey stops him by waving his hand.

Officer Downey: Yeah, go grab Clement and Diggs. You three can go handle that for the time being. Marbury stays. I need to hang back too until the chief comes, if we have an active situation across town. Keep sharp while you go. As for the rest of us, well, I think it's best if we all stay right here in this interrogation room for a few minutes until they get on site and give us an update. You head out, Mike. I'll be on your tails if need be. Bring the heavy artillery.

Officer Mike Brower: From the lockup?

Officer Downey: Oh yeah. Don't risk being under prepped when this is the state of it all.

Eric Landrush: Officer, may I ask why you would need to detain this young man any further when your suspect is at large and spotted miles away at—

Officer Downey: Pump the brakes, Yale Law Review; I'll be with you post-haste. Mike?

Officer Mike Brower: Yeah?

Officer Downey: You're looking for some joker with a mask and glowing eyes—possibly some sorta electronic device and knives or something like that. Get rolling and take firepower.

Officer Mike Brower: Seriously, Lance?

Officer Downey: Deadly serious. We don't have the luxury of time—go.

Officer Mike Brower: Going. Gone.

Officer Mike Brower leaves the room and the door shuts.

Genevieve Tribbs: We don't need to stay a moment longer.

Officer Downey: Scott…can you—?

Scott Tribbs: Gen, just… Lance, what's the reason you want us to remain back?

Officer Downey: So we can clear your boy, that's why.

Genevieve Tribbs: How's that?

Eric Landrush: He's right. We should stay just a few minutes. If they can confirm the suspect and you at two different places then that might help to clear you of suspicion in case they're unable to detain the suspect.

Officer Downey: Detain him we shall, rest assured. And see there, bright boy? I knew you'd earn your name at some point. Also, since I'm not sure I've made it clear enough, I'm sorry, Damon. I'm sorry about Keith.

Genevieve Tribbs: Are you?

Officer Downey: Yes, Ma'am; I truly am. Good kid—great kid. I'm sorry. That's what we're doing this for.

Damon Tribbs is sobbing and hugging Genevieve Tribbs.

Damon Tribbs: Doing what?

Officer Downey: Tracking down this lily-paddin' sonofabitch, tossing him in a cold cell, and seeing what the hell this chaos is all about.

Eric Landrush: Has the chief been notified?

Officer Downey: At a conference in Denver, but he's been briefed and is hauling ass back here. For the time being, I'm on-site command. That's also why I need to stay put.

Eric Landrush: Good. That's good. So now what?

Officer Downey: So now we wait.

Genevieve Tribbs: For how long?

Officer Downey: Just a few more minutes.

Scott Tribbs: Gen, Damon, let's—

11:15 p.m., Officer Downey stands up and motions his hand for the others to sit. The Tribbs family walk to the interrogation room table and take seats. Eric Landrush stands nearby. Several minutes pass as they whisper amongst themselves.

Officer Downey: I'm getting waved at. I'll be right back.

Officer Downey exits and walks to the nearest deputy, Amanda Williams, 31, who hands him a radio. He holds the radio to his ear for a few moments, speaks into it, and his face contorts into fear. He rushes off, and all those inside the interrogation room watch as he disappears around a corner. The three other deputies start to move around the surrounding office area of the police department. One officer disappears around the same corner as Officer Downey.

Genevieve Tribbs: What's…what's happening?

Scott Tribbs: Susan?

Susan Fisher: I don't know.

Damon Tribbs: Some shit is going down out there.

Genevieve Tribbs: Does that mean we can go?

Both officers come back around the corner carrying several firearms that they rapidly hand off to the other deputies in the room. Officer Downey, holding a shotgun and several pistols, approaches the door to the interrogation room and enters.

Eric Landrush: I'm thinking we should stay put.

Officer Downey: I have to leave. You should all stay right here for now.

Sounds echo from the Officer's radio on his belt. Officer Downey reaches down and pulls up the radio, turning the volume knob.

Officer Downey: Say again.

Through the static of Officer Downey's radio, voices, screaming, and what sounds to be Officer Thurston Diggs, 33, calling in from the site of suspect contact.

Officer Diggs: *Over here! We need backup now! Hurry the fuck up! He's on top of the car, and I can't shake this sonofabitch! I'm coming down 133 heading south, and I should be able to—*

Through the radio, the distinct sounds of metal screeching and glass shattering, followed by a muffled explosion. Then silence.

Officer Downey: Thurston? Officer Diggs, please respond! Michael? Michael! Somebody, please respond!

Eric Landrush: What the hell is happening?

Genevieve Tribbs: Is this a goddamn joke?

Officer Downey: No joke. We need to batten down the hatches.

Scott Tribbs: Lance. What the fuck?

Officer Downey: I don't know, Scott! But Ted and I are going to head out and bring some much needed sanity to this colossal shit storm. I know it's…whatever, but you can't leave just yet.

Genevieve Tribbs: Oh come on now!

Damon Tribbs: Did it take out your homies too?

Officer Downey: My homies? Oh no, I doubt it. But—

Eric Landrush: Didn't sound good from what we just heard, Officer. We should be reaching out to the CBI or whomever at this point, shouldn't we?

Officer Downey: We do. Or we are. Lacey has them on the line. But I'm going.

Eric Landrush: Are you sure that heading out is the best bet?

Officer Downey: No, I'm not. But I can't not go. So, you stay put and if you need to—

The lights in the police station go out, as well as all other electronics. Several flashing green emergency lights come on, filling the room with enough light to continue typing. A loud, metallic sound strikes the top of the building. Everyone looks up.

Officer Downey: It's here. Take these.

11:29 p.m., Officer Downey hands a shotgun to Scott Tribbs and a pistol to Eric Landrush. Both men take the guns without hesitation.

Officer Downey: I know you're good, Scottie, but how about you, bright boy? Can you handle that thing?

Eric Landrush pulls the clip out from the gun, checks the load, pops it back in, and cocks the slide.

Eric Landrush: I'm good.

Officer Downey: Good. Don't hesitate, now. You catch sight of this fucking guy, you empty your clips into him. Get me?

Genevieve Tribbs: This is insane!

Damon Tribbs/Officer Downey/Eric Landrush: Shut up!

Genevieve Tribbs goes silent. Both men nod. Officer Downey looks at…me.

Officer Downey: Susan, time to wrap that shit up and get your ass under the table. You too, Damon. Now!

Susan Fisher: Okay, I'm packing it up.

11:30 p.m., I pack it up.

****END OF REPORT****

Patrick Quinn Kitson

CONFESSION

In the dirt parking lot outside of St. Mary's of the Crown church—which stood at the crest of White Hill in Carbondale, Colorado, overlooking the former high school/current middle school's football and track field—the congregation, numbering a little over hundred or so, began filing into their automobiles while the midday sun shone down brightly upon their Sunday best. A well-mannered, post-glad-handing smattering of the town's more demurely dressed denizens had spread out among the parked vehicles. Soon black Tesla's, navy blue Rivians, souped-up white Toyotas, as well as more than a few sporty red Audi's, began to whir to life, commencing the brief run down the hill and back to the town proper.

Since its dedication in the late seventies, the modest church had sat adjacent to sweeping fields of green in which the local farmer families planted their yearly potato crop. Past a corral of hay bales and several rolling center pivot sprinkler tracks, a small cemetery lay just half a mile down at the other end of the same dirt road which led into town.

Having adjourned the Sunday mass and engaged in the ritualistic shaking of said congregation's hands, leaving his flock to seek out their midday meals, Father Eric Pearson had thus set upon his usual habit of straightening up the church before heading down into his residential quarters, generally for a spot of light afternoon reading. Since the service itself created little mess or trash in the bins, he decided to first do something which he'd been putting off for weeks: polishing the varnished wood of the confessional booth. It was there he now stood, inside said booth, ready to give it a quick once over before moving onto the task of taking out the waste bins.

Clean shaven with a crop of short brown hair and standing nearly six foot five, his head all but touched the roof of the small nook. Sleeves rolled up, and dabbing the top of the bottle holding the solution with a rag, he had begun to run the wet spot of the cloth along the long brown arcs of the wood grains on the interior wall when he heard the sound outside of someone entering the church. He quickly placed the cap back on the bottle and gently laid the rag over the top, then set down the bottle on the floor by his feet.

The light trot of hard-soled shoes clicking in the entryway fell silent as the person hit the carpeted aisle between the wooden pews and made a beeline for the confessional. It wasn't cause for any alarm, as it was common enough for one of his parishioners to stay afterward and seek confession once the crowds had largely departed.

Before he could properly situate his black cassock to sit down, the person who'd entered made for the compartment to his right, pulling the curtain closed behind them and kneeling on the stoop. He could only vaguely see their form through the intricate, wooden lattice work separating them, yet he knew the voice the moment she spoke.

Making the sign of the cross before her, the young woman's voice was cheery and bright as she said, "Bless me, Father, for I have done it once again."

Wincing, Father Pearson replied, "Are you— Is that you, Darla?"

The shadow beyond the lattice nodded. "From your lips to God's ears, *Padre*. And a good morning to you too. How goes the weekly fleecing of thine sheep?"

"Oh Christ," he murmured, head slumping.

"Yeah—hey—hi." The young woman cleared her throat then continued, "Look, I know you said I should wait a while before I came back but—"

"Yes, Darla, I did say that. That is precisely what I said."

"Yeah, and I would've, but...you know, you were sorta rude about the whole thing, so I only sorta half-took it seriously. And anyway, this is really important."

Rolling his eyes, the priest replied, "You always say that."

"Well yeah, sure, because it usually is. But for real, this is actually, truly, one hundred percent *muy muy importante*. No kidding, *Padre*. And I figured we could also bury the proverbial hatchet after how harsh you were last time. Unduly so, one might be so inclined to think."

Sighing and slowly sitting down on the hard wood of the confessionals seat, the priest nodded, unseen by the woman in the adjacent stall. "Yes. Yes, of course; you're right, as a matter of fact. Upon reflection I don't feel I was particularly kind to you the last time we spoke. And for that I do apologize."

"It's okay. I forgive you."

"But still, you must understand that this isn't a position I usually find myself in."

"What's that?"

"Well, to be candid… You insist, week after week, on utilizing the sanctification of this holy rite as your personal repository for the sinful deeds that you brazenly commit upon your fellow townsfolk. And you know I don't enjoy being in a position where you are effectively admitting felonious behavior to me. That puts me in a difficult situation morally, you understand—and as I've explained to you more than once. To say nothing of any legal complications that may arise should your offenses become any more brazen."

"Yeah, well, that's fair. Pretty fair. But you're conveniently leaving out half of the equation, aren't you, *Padre*?"

Another audible sigh from the holy man in the cassock. "Well, if by that you mean the self-absolution you claim to glean by way of undertaking all these other ostensibly righteous acts you do, then yes. Yet you yourself conveniently forget time and again that if you're doing such good deeds merely to offset the bad ones, then they remain, at their core, selfish and therefore somewhat sinful in nature. Furthermore, you regularly dodge the fact that penance is something to be assigned by one's spiritual leader, not self-administered like some next gen party drug. It's not as simple as checking or unchecking a box, young lady."

The unseen woman's head shadow nodded through the latticework. "Hard enough to argue with that, though I truly believe that any objective look at what I do that's good would surely outweigh and therefore offset the bad, no?"

"That's certainly debatable."

"Well, sure, okay. But then *everything* is, theoretically. Right? So—"

"Darla—" he began.

"*Padre*," she interjected, echoing his derisive tone.

Eric shifted uncomfortably in his seat while keeping his eyes trained forward on the dark void of the confessional booth's black velvet curtain. "I'm simply saying that your morality—and more importantly, your immortal soul—are not balance sheets, Darla. You need to commit to being less sinful, or dare I say *sin free* in the future. Otherwise your personally prescribed penance is essentially a zero-sum game. Faith isn't about you keeping score; it's about developing into a better person and preserving your immortal soul."

"Sure, I totally agree with the sentiment there. One hundred percent. And I certainly don't have to be reminded of how bad of a girl I've been lately. Just rotten to the core, truly. Shoot, I spent the other night prank calling the homes of the girls in the Aspen cheerleading squad using a VPN voice over connection so that it couldn't be traced."

Shaking his head enough for her to see through the perforated booth wall, he sighed and asked, "Why would you do that, Darla?"

"Because those well-funded little glam-rats were of the mistaken belief that they were gonna be functional at the state cheerleader meet the following day. And I gotta say, not on my watch. By virtue of my well-timed machinations, neither I nor they were at our best. As a result they got knocked out in the second round of eliminations, which ultimately led to our ladies securing the win. The girls on my squad were totally jazzed. So one could argue that that instance was a bit self-canceling where penance is concerned. My squad benefited, and all is well."

"It doesn't work like that."

Scoffing, she quickly shot back, "And where do you find the instructions on the minutiae of such moral quandaries anyway, *Padre*? Where in the good book lies the equation which says that X amount of good deeds cancels out Y amount of bad shit? Hmm? Is there an appendix in the Bible that I'm not yet privy to that covers this sorta dilemma of recalcitrance?"

Stifling yet another aggrieved sigh, he simply stated, "You're doing things you know are wrong."

"Sure. Maybe a few. A pinch here and a sprinkle there... But I gotta say, I must've done enough this time around to keep the ethical scales balanced. Why, I even did something this morning to offset the whole cheer meet thing."

"Which was what?" he asked solemnly, rubbing his eyes with his hands.

"I went out and bought some girl scout cookies."

"Cookies?"

"Girl scout cookies."

"Cookies?" he repeated.

"Yes, cookies. Of the girl scout variety."

"Darla, that's not how this works and you know it."

"But it was, like, a *lot* of girl scout cookies, *Padre*. I got like five boxes of thin mints. That shit's delish."

"That doesn't... That doesn't somehow diminish the horrible things you keep doing to those in your peer group."

"But if I do more good than harm, and I have Christ in my heart—which you know I totally do—then I'm good right? As long as a person has got that solid gold Christ Love pumping through their veins, then they really don't have shit to sweat, headed off into that sweet, sweet afterlife, do they?"

"You don't get extra credit for—"

"For what? Seriously, *for what?* I volunteer at the nursing home. I'm active in student council. I do my dishes after supper, keep my bedroom tidy, studiously practice the piano, and do my homework more readily than nearly a hundred percent of my dead-eyed, technophile contemporaries. I also come to church every Sunday, for the most part. I don't skip a beat, Father. That's gotta count for something."

"Now you're the one leaving half of the equation out."

"*Padre*—"

"Darla," he said with a raised voice. "You cut off your sister's hair in her sleep."

Cracking a devilish smile, the young woman mused, "Yeah, yeah, I did do that. But honestly it looks much better now, seriously—"

"You confessed to planting marijuana all around your high school's track and football field—"

"Well, *sure*, but that was just *funny*."

"And planted the same at nearly every single family park throughout town?"

"Still funny."

"You withdrew how many thousands of dollars from your father's debit card so you could go on some drug-fueled weekend jaunt to the mountains with your friends?"

"Several thousands, and much drug-fueled debauchery was to be had. But he never found out about it. So I figure, no harm no foul."

"Except *yes* harm, and *yes* foul. And lest we forget, Darla, you've spoken of trying to hit people with your car."

"Always gotta make it seem worse than it is, don't you?"

"This isn't funny."

"And yet it seems like it would be damn funny if I ever managed to nail one. Am I completely nuts for saying that?

You can level with me father—you've never thought the same thing?"

"No, *Darla*. Never. Not once."

"Okay *Eric*. But I'm sure that isn't true. I bet you've been a bad boy too, imagining all manner of lurid end results, hmmm?"

"Darla, for heaven's sake, this isn't—"

The girl through the grill suddenly straightened up. "About what? You're gonna repeat that this isn't about our failed attempts to offset the sins of our past by trying in vain to walk in the light of the Lord? Like you do all the time?" She paused for a moment to let that last line hang in the air before finishing. "Like your whole façade over the last who-knows-how-many years has been? In vain, I might add. 'Cause you simply can't outrun some misdeeds, can ya, *Padre*?"

The man in the cassock remained silent in the stall as frightening, yet familiar, specters of past memories threatened to bubble to the surface of his psyche.

Darla's tone suddenly shifted, now low and menacing. "But you already know that right, Father? You know that only too well. Hell, you could say that I'm preaching to the choir on that count, couldn't ya?" A barely perceivable smile traced the hidden outline of her lips as she finished.

Brow furrowing suspiciously, Eric cleared his throat, then replied, "Yes, I suppose you are. That's…that's very clever. And at the risk of belaboring the point at hand, you obviously understand that you don't nullify nor negate the wickedness of your more sinister deeds by simply stacking up positive ones. I don't think you appreciate how bad the whole thing is."

"Oh I get it's bad. You get it's bad. We both *get it*. Though I'd be remiss if I didn't ask one thing…"

"And what's that?"

"Just who the hell do you think you're kidding?"

"What?"

"Well, didn't you used to have a penchant for the macabre yourself there, Father? Huh? Maybe a little love for bloodletting? A little compassion for chaos? You can tell me. I won't spill the beans."

A pregnant pause filled the air between them. Then—

"What do you mean?" Eric asked, his voice notably shakier than before.

"Well…" she paused for a moment, then shocked the priest by saying, "Haven't you ever wanted to just rip a human body apart using rusty metal implements, then leave the bloody, fly-ridden entrails strewn up like party decorations for investigators to agonize over in the following decades without ever finding answers?"

Making the sign of the cross before himself, the priest closed his eyes and calmly spoke, "Holy Father, please forgive this woman, for she knows not what she does." Then to the young lady in the adjacent stall, "Darla, what in the blazes are you talking about?"

"I'm talking about *you*, Padre. Those horrors I just described, have you no such skeletons in your closet? Skeletons of your past?"

Patrick Quinn Kitson

A flash in the priest's mind—again a maddening *tap-tap-tapping* at the back window of his recollection. And once again, he was able to fend it off, pushing it back down. Eric shook his head inside the dark booth. "No! No! God Almighty, forgive you for such blasphemy inside His house, young lady! I don't know what you are speaking of, and I don't believe I wish to hear any more of it on this day of our Lord! I believe you to be even more troubled than I had initially suspected, and as such, I think that for now you should leave. Hopefully you go in the light of God. Heaven help you, Darla."

"It usually does, in fact, no doubt about it. And I can go, no trouble there; but how's about you come outside with me? I do believe that there's someone out there who needs to have a word."

"No— Wait, someone is with you?"

Conveying her grin through her voice, she answered. "Yeah, sure, you could say he is always with me, bub."

"What do you mean?"

"Should we stop playing games now?"

Eric looked down at his palms and saw that they were shaking. He rubbed them vigorously to dispel the tremens. "I'm not playing games."

"Oh yes, you are. Every day you play games, *Padre*. You even play little name games, don't you? Because your name isn't really Eric Pearson, is it?"

Silence.

Darla continued, unabated, her tone increasingly more pointed. "Your name isn't even the name you had before that, is it? You've had a whole bunch of names. Loads of 'em. Shoot, didn't it used to be, like, Reginald Oslo at some point or something?" she asked, chuckling.

"I-I have not been that man for many, many years. I have lived in the path of His glory for decades."

"More than that. Almost a century, in fact. You've been convincing yourself of your own righteous piety for about one hundred and fifteen years, by my count. Which should've struck you as odd, right? Being around that long? Or longer, maybe? Sort of an extended stay for a mere mortal, don't cha think?"

Stammering, he managed to eke out, "I can't— I-I don't remember."

Darla nodded knowingly from the dark of the confessional booth. "Granted, you are a great deceiver. So it's not crazy that you might have done the same to yourself. Maybe, like your brother in arms, your greatest trick was finally convincing yourself that you don't exist. Makes sense. Lord knows I wouldn't wanna be you. But before this little spell, you made quite the mess all over the place, didn't you? Like that shit in Whitechapel I was just mentioning? All that careless carnage in South America?"

Still rubbing his hands together, the priest spoke softly, uncertain of his own words, "I–I don't know what you mean."

"Sure you do. What about your guiding hand with all that messy shit in Jonestown? I may have my facts wrong, but didn't I hear that you are the one who started the Chicago

Fire? Didn't you kill a Pharaoh with some sorta asp venom, and poison the water wells of the Sumerians?"

"I don't..." He took his skull into his hands and whispered, "I don't— I don't..." he trailed off.

"You know who you are. But you haven't been thinking about it lately."

"Please stop. I didn't—"

"Ah, but you did! All of it. What was it that Shakespeare said about good wombs creating bad seeds?"

Beads of hot sweat now ran down Eric's forehead, and he used the sleeve of his dark robe to blot it from his brow. "I've done all I could to— To try and..."

Standing up in the booth and seemingly gazing down upon the still seated holy man through the wooden latticework, Darla demanded, "What? Offset the bad things you've done by stacking up good ones? Even you just admitted that ain't the way this works, *Padre*."

Trembling, fear creeping up from the back precipice of his mind, Eric croaked out, "I don't wish anyone any harm..."

"Except for oh yes, you did. And oh yes, you *do*. You just forgot your name."

His arm muscles began to tense as his thoughts switched to ideas of racing out the stall and down into his residence, behind the safety of his triple-locked door. He managed to whisper, "I'm not an evil man."

"No, what you are is a broken record, skipping on the same beat line. Maybe one day someone will buy this big, fat, juicy burger of self-delusion that you're sellin' and call it yummy. Not me though. And possibly in a thousand lifetimes, you'll be forgiven by *His Grace*. Maybe that'll happen. I hope that for you, truly. However, until such a day comes, it's a dog-eat-dog sorta world, *Padre*, and I got orders from up on high to say nothing of a schedule to keep."

Before he could fully stand up to dash from the confessional, a whip of blue-hued electricity, unknown in origin, entered the small space he was occupying and coiled around his middle. Like a wrist flinging a ragdoll, he was tossed free of the booth, flying over the pews and straight into the double doored entryway of the small church. Smashing through the hard wooden doors, he tumbled out into the dirt of the parking lot, rolling end over end, cassock now lightly-browned with tan dust. Ground powder coated his face and mouth. He hacked and spit to clear the grime from his teeth.

Flipping over and with his eyes adjusting, he saw that the daylight which had earlier poured down upon him was rapidly diminishing, replaced instead by rumbles of distant storm clouds filling the sky. Gazing out across the town, he saw eldritch blue lightning bolts striking the ridge along the far western horizon.

Darla emerged from the freshly busted and ajar doorway. She strode out into the dimmed light of the now gray, cloudy day and straight to the downed priest. Her dirty blonde hair was nearly tied up with red ribbon into a small ponytail. Unlike his now fully departed parishioners, she wore more casual Sunday attire—blue jeans and a loose-hanging black shirt with

Depeche Mode printed in small white typeface lettering across the front.

As she drew near, he cowered and inched away from the building on his butt. Voice trembling, hands still shaking, he feebly whimpered, "Wha— What's happening to the sky? Are you doing this?"

Coming to a stop a few feet from him, she put her hands on her waist and scanned the sky. "Not me, *Padre*."

"Who are you? What are you?" He slid his butt backward along the now moist dirt, coating his trembling palms in muddy dust.

Eyeballs wide and full of blue-tinted righteousness, Darla croaked out in a boom that seemingly reverberated through the coalescing cloud cover overhead, as though the heavens were amplifying her voice. "Oh, me? I'm just another one of *His* children, don't you know. Incidentally—if, in fact, anything ever is incidental or coincidental within his grand design—I also happen to be the daughter of one of your old nemeses on the battlefield."

Shaking his head, he gazed up at her with eyes slowly filling with anger.

Leaning in a bit more, she calmly spoke, "Michael. You remember him don't you?"

And in that moment, for the briefest of flashes, he could recall that name, which instantly caused an unknowable and oddly visceral hatred to seize him from within. In his mind's eye, he rapidly spied fleeting glimpses of winged figures screeching through the heavens. Long trails of white bolts piercing the air, then finding swift purchase in the breasts of fallen comrades. A battlefield among the clouds with the righteous and the wicked warring in an ethereal landscape of light and chaos. Blood and feathers. Eyes numbering in the millions. Torn backs, dismembered bodies, and splitting heads.

Shaking, he coldly demanded, "What are you going to do to me?"

Rubbing her hands together, seemingly unfazed by the gathering storm, Darla smiled at the ground-bound man. "Just here to do the good work of the Lord—late though it may be. You, *sir*, sit in the direct path of *His* judgment.

The skies rapidly colored with gray, frightening the cowering man in the black cassock. Grey swirls of cumulus clouds moved with unnatural speed to occupy the whole of the sky, casting the earth below in a stormy shroud of half-darkness. His eyes lowered as he pointed one accusatory finger toward the young woman in the eighties darkwave band tee. "You are no emissary of the Lord! You are a minion of the devil made flesh—a child of no one but Satan himself! Even now it seems that you call forth the darkness of the Besieged One to change the very weather!"

Chuckling and shaking her head, she assured him, "Wrong again. I call forth nothing." She paused, looking up, then concluded, "That isn't me. If I had to call it, I'd say it looks like *our Father who art* just wants to stretch his arms before he finishes casting you down like the dirty-deed-dealin' demon you've been since time immemorial!"

The thing in the black priest's garb tensed up and twitched with subdued malice, grimacing and narrowing its gaze once more at the woman standing before him. Droplets of rain began to speckle his cheeks. "You are a foul, degraded witch! Nothing more than a heretic harlot by your own sin-filled admissions!"

"Yeah, uh, about all that… I wasn't really doing any of it. I was making all that stuff up."

"What?"

"For real. 'Twas all bullshit, I'm afraid—much like your whole tired schtick. See, I was merely using the subterfuge of said BS to keep tabs on you until I got the order from up on high to take you down. Or to help take you down, if we're giving credit where it's due. He's gonna do the heavy lifting on this one." She winked and pointed one finger up.

"You are just a devil by any other name!" he hissed through gnashed teeth.

"Nah, you got that wrong too, *Padre*. I'm no devil. You of all people should know that. The real guy is down in the abyss with your simpering cohorts. Rest assured, you'll see him again shortly. You'll be sure to give him my coldest regards though, won't you? Sure he'll take anything over that endless heat. Am I right?"

His tone now that of a pleading whimper, Eric cried, "You're crazy, do you know that? You don't know what you're doing. You're…you're making a mistake. I'm a man of the Lord." He stood up and tried in vain to dust off his black clothing with swatting palms. It only served to smear the now wet dirt into the fabric. Realizing this and straightening out, he hissed, "*I walk with the Lord!*"

Redirecting the single finger she had sticking his way, she replied, "You walk with the wicked when you aren't leading them. You made a mess of things for a while on Earth, and are personally responsible for the deaths of millions. Like, *literally*. I do not know—nor is it for me to know—how you ended up here or why our heavenly Father granted you a stay of execution. He saw fit to let you do a lot of nasty shit for a long time, but that is well and truly between you and him."

"You know nothing, young lady!"

"Sure I do. God certainly does. We're about to take out the trash, which means your dance card is all filled up, toots. High time you pay for some of those sins you've been stacking up."

Feverish talons of rising anger welled inside the ground-prone priest as he said nothing, but poured hatred from his eyes toward her.

Chuckling, she saw the look of malice and said, "You really don't remember? Is that what you're telling me?"

Shouting, the thing in the cassock demanded, "Remember *what*, goddamn you!?"

"Ha!" Darla suddenly spun around on one foot, two full rotations, ponytail whipping in an arc, before coming to a dead stop facing him and clapping her hands together. With a razor blade smile, she mused, "I guess it's possible you've been here for so long that maybe you eventually figured out a way to truly forget. Can't blame you, what with all the proverbial blood on your paws. But *He* doesn't forget. I mean, *obviously*. And you did forget your place, you bad, bad boy. You forgot that he meant for you to join your buddies in the deep hole. The really, really deep one."

"Fuck you!" he yelled, gripping the wet ground with taught fingers. "Why are you here?"

"Gotta do some grunt work before you get a seat at the big table, or so I'm told. This is just part and parcel with the path of the Almighty."

"Harlot. Heretic. Seething harpee of the—"

Seeming not to hear him, she quietly mused to herself, "It's your name, trust me. To hear your name again for the first time in millennia—that would surely break you of the stupor you've somehow put upon your own mind."

"My name is Eric Pearson! And I am a man who—"

The sky again boom-echoed with the reverberation of her words. Thunderous cracks of sound cut through the air.

"You are not Eric Pearson! You are one of the seven fallen, cast down after being defeated by my father, the Archangel Michael, who did so in the name of and at the behest of *your Father*—the Lord, our God. You're no mortal any more than I'm Taylor Swift! You are but a simple fallen angel in league with Lucifer, and your real name..." She paused. The clouds ran black, nearly blotting out the sun, and began to steadily rain down from above onto them. She took a few steps away from the man in the cassock, then stopped and lowered her eyes as she shouted to him, "Your real name...is *Moloch!*"

Splitting straight down the middle, the black robe of the priest shredded into two larger pieces and fell away as his chest swelled in size and his arms thickened. His face, now contorted, began to rapidly change color as he took on the appearance of a ten-foot-tall, muscular creature with sharply chiseled features. Two onyx black wings of torn tissue between a char-black skeletal framework slowly unfurled behind his now massive shoulders, the erstwhile priest's clothing now forming a damp puddle of fabric at his hairy, hoofed feet.

Eyes burning red with the vengeful heat of a thousand scorching suns, the now transformed husk of demonic malice and hatred—once called *Moloch*—inhaled, then exhaled deeply, taking in heavy breath and snorting out large tuffs of steam in the cold of the falling rains. He growled in a thick rasp at the woman before him, "I'll take you with me, daughter of Michael, and present you as a gift to the dark Lord below."

"Just can't see the forest for the trees, can you, bud? You don't seem to know when the house has you beat and is about to close your streak down. But I guess that's sorta what you and yours are all about—towering hubris, proud and fatal. You should ask Odysseus how that one worked out in the end."

A flash of purple light lit up the largely darkened area around the church, and as Moloch the Deceiver launched into a full run toward Darla, a single piercing cable of white hot lightning struck the top of the demon-angel, erupting his flesh into an explosion of red and black matter that shot out like a blood-filled balloon popped by a pinprick, covering everything within a hundred feet radius. Tiny, bloody bits of archangel muscles, tattered chunks of flesh, and oozing, viscous onyx organ residue coated the muddy ground, the front exterior of the church, and the first seventy-five feet of the road leading back to town. And it also covered Darla.

Closing her eyes, she could feel the blood and fresh bits of exploded angel covering every nook and cranny of her, head to toe. The rain, now coming down in sheets, increased even more, and soon a drenching deluge poured onto the land. The parking lot rapidly formed into a muddy flowing river which carried the bloodied earth away from the church and down the tree-dotted hill that flanked one side of the nearby school's football field.

Stepping back onto the concrete landing leading into God's house, Darla waited as the purifying waters slowly washed away the blood from her hair, face, and body. The red dripped down the walls of the church entrance, and within a minute, the white paint shone through. Every bit of Moloch's bloody remainder was carried away and down the side of the ridge.

Within minutes of the storm forming, it stopped pouring down rain. Not a full five seconds passed before a gale-force wind started to blow in from the north, rushing past Darla at such speed that she reached for one of the nearby entryway support pillars to steady herself. Not unlike a news anchor in a hurricane zone clutching at the nearest palm tree trunk.

Thirty seconds of hard winds whipping about, and the gusts diminished. As Darla's eyes peeked open, she beheld the front of the church. It was clear and clean, as was her clothing and the ground. Blown dry by the Lord's winds.

As she began to head down the dirt road back toward the town below, she pulled a small black case from her jeans and wiped off the outside with her hand. Opening it, she popped two earbuds out, then closed the case and returned it to her pocket. Putting them in her ears, she then fished her phone from her waistband, and was relieved to see that the smartphone's waterproof housing had been able to resist the torrent of rain she'd just endured. Clicking through her phone menus until her ears filled with the sounds of eighties-era goth-synth pop, she smiled broadly and began to put one foot before the other.

Skipping along the ground, she bobbed her head to the beat. Humming with the melody, she mumbled in tune with several lyrics, then raised up her arms and shouted aloud to nobody in particular, "Reach out, touch faith!"

Trotting along, she smiled as the skies cleared and sunshine poured onto the freshly cleansed ground surrounding the church at the top of White Hill.

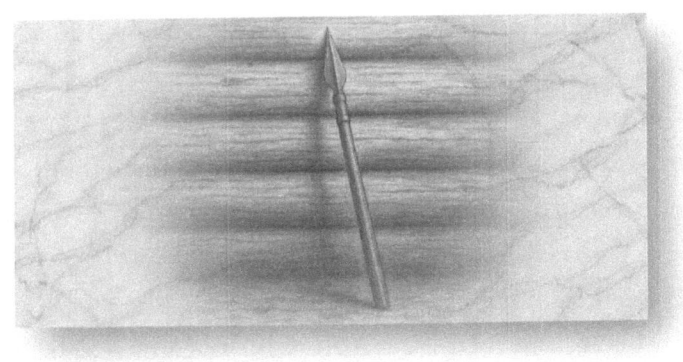

SHERO

O kay. Okay…situation assessment.

Fairly certain all my friends are now dead. Killed by that murderous freakazoid in the creepy skin-mask who's been stalking about for the last several hours. Badly injured foot from that fall off of the top of the main cabin's second story roof, after having jumped through the hallway window. Phones and power apparently cut to the whole area, providing visual cover for my stalker's sinister approach. And…I'm fairly certain that I'm also the last one left.

Pretty sure I'm the final girl.

And that's great, you know? Just friggin' perfect. Who asked for this? Not me, I can say that without much hesitation. It's a big burden to shoulder when all I really wanted was an easy, breezy, carefree, drug-fueled, nuclear-winter of a party with my raucous friends at the long-deserted campground near Dinkle Lake for the weekend.

The one they don't mark on the tourist maps, and that requires a four-wheel drive to ascend to. The one with the *stay out* signs that you won't see on Google Earth because of the dense overgrowth.

The one with the nasty past.

And sure, the many teenagers who had gone missing up here years ago were indeed part of the reason we all came up, but who were we to know it'd all go so massively fucked-up? We were just givin' ol' fate a little tempting poke in the keister. I really wasn't interested in becoming the sole survivor in the final act of a silly slasher saga. But *c'est la vie*; here I am.

For the record, my name is Tessa Maize.

Corny, I know. Did you catch it? Whatever.

The failing light of day is only faintly visible through the canopy of the lodgepole pine and old Aspen trees surrounding me on all sides. Nearby, a branch rustles and I spin on a heel, eyes feebly trying to adjust and scrutinize the dark void between the tree branches.

Shit! Is that—? No. That was…ah, just the wind. Maybe. *Hopefully.* But I shouldn't let down my guard. That's how they get you, isn't it?

It happens in horror movies all the time. People say you never suspect certain things could or might actually happen to you. You don't stress it much. Nobody worries about such trivialities until the day some skin-masked goober comes blasting into the cabin wielding a goddamn bloodstained ax and cutting your friends down in a fierce and fatal frenzy. And by then, it's already time to buckle down, nut up, and execute. There are no real dress rehearsals in life or death situations like these.

Yet unlike in the horror movies, my personal qualifications as a final girl are hardly textbook.

Not a virgin. Sometimes user of drugs. Godless blasphemer/fornicating harlot (according to my churlish and churchy cat-lady neighbor, Gladys), as well as being an all-around avoider of responsibility. My ex would say I also play fast and loose with the facts. Unreliable, even. But consider the fact that while he might be a male model—cut abs, gorgeous everything, a Greek God if we're taking a full accounting of it—he also possesses the same intellectual wherewithal as your average sedimentary rock. And a fucking weighty rock at that. One dumb, heavy, wildly fuckable but ultimately totally unmarriable goddamn rock.

Must admit, I do miss those firm abs, though...

Wake up, bitch! You wanna die!? You need to get a goddamn weapon in your grip, now! *Snap to!*

All around, the branches sway to and fro and the light begins to recede, leaving the spears and shadows of a fading dusk to illuminate the soft earth at my feet. It's just past sunset in the forest by the lake.

Or is it a pond? It's really more of a pond, right? Really, isn't a pond just a small lake—or vice versa?

Like that shit matters! Focus up.

What matters is that ol' fleshy face parading about unseen in the inky darkness with murderous intent. That, and I am still unarmed. Woefully without armament. And that's simply not how final girls usually do. Time to adjust and fit the part.

Sliding the hair tie from my wrist and swiftly pulling up my dirty blonde hair into a ponytail, I put a bit of weight on my foot to test it. And yeah, still a lot of *ouch* there. Should be good enough to seek safe harbor, though. Just gotta be extra careful.

I make an admittedly limping beeline for the nearest bush with thick branches and start to pull at the first limb I see. 'Cause surely it's better to have something to jab at a skin-masked face with than nothing at all. Pulling and twisting, it's much too thick and lush to snap easily, or even a little. However, I am quite effectively managing to stain my hands green with the chlorophyll from the mulched up leaves twisting in my palms. Sadly, I am not successfully procuring a weapon. So, I try harder and harder. Within moments I'm grunting and tugging and very much auditorily giving away my position to any and all masked murderers within the confines of the campground. I quickly realize this and go quiet, ducking; my eyes darting.

After a comically fruitless minute of wrenching and tearing at a shrub like a madwoman, the stark reality sinks in, and I reconsider my options. Wiping my wet green hands on my blood-spattered jeans, I look around, eyes landing upon a brittle stick about two feet long and half an inch in diameter on the ground next to my likewise bloodied sneakers. I snatch it up.

Gripping the crunchy, chipping bark tightly in my right hand, I do a quick 360-degree survey of my immediate surroundings.

Eyes piercing through the dark miasma created by the dense foliage hanging above, I scan the parking lot. I am granted some light by the silvery glow from the moon through an opening in the branches overhead. Nobody anywhere nearby. The owl's hoot and the rustle of the thicket brushing about in the cool breeze would surely mask the footfalls of anyone who might've heard my earlier antics and now approaches unseen.

Nestled along the side of the primary cabin, I'm kinda tucked away into the bushes, so it's also possible that I'm safe for now. That shit is fleeting though, best believe. Tippy-toeing on my injured right hoof and slowly creeping along a foot-beaten dirt path that winds around the building, I feebly brandish the dull stick before me. Careful to keep my ears up, as one cannot be too cautious, even as the final girl.

As I move, I am hobbling due to the aforementioned self-volley from the second floor. And sure, it might have been a bit premature to crash through the glass of the master bedroom window when I heard footsteps coming up the stairwell toward where I was. *Sure*. But discretion being the better part of valor, I seek to escape and now think I am onto something. Flight over fight might be the winning play here.

Sliding up to the peeling white paint corner of the cabin, I cautiously peek my peepers around it and to the large dirt parking lot where all the vehicles sit, effectively useless to me. I didn't bring my own car—cause I'm a moron, I guess—and therefore have no idea where any of the sets of keys are. Two trucks and two cars, not to mention the open-doored police car, crashed into the tree by the front of the building—but no keys.

I think that I might have an inkling of something. 'Cause I'm fairly sure that lying in the bed of the black truck about fifty yards away from me is my mountain bike. I guess I could make it, so long as the deadly dude is off doing killing stuff with other people. Hanging people in trees for later use as jump scares, or whatever they do.

What I need to do is hop on my two-wheel steed and beat a fast path outta dodge. Sure, I may be the final girl, but I shouldn't miss any opportunity to escape, if it's even remotely possible.

Trusting in that old sage wisdom that more is lost through indecision than wrong decision, I get as low to the ground as I can, then come out from the side of the cabin and hustle-hop my happy ass over to the big Ford pickup. I might be able to get my bike and get home before the ghastly goober gets me for good, I reckon. And if I manage to clear the kill zone and bring others back to assist in my greasing of the killer at hand, then I'll have done my duty as the final girl—*approximately*—and can rest easy knowing I righteously fulfilled my destiny.

Sorta.

And if there happens to be—

I stop mid-thought because I don't like what I see when I reach the rim of the truck bed and peer into it. The tires on my getaway vehicle are flat. Both of 'em.

Fuck me gently with a chainsaw.

That's no good, and somehow makes me nervous giggle because it implies a higher level of stratagem than I had thus far assumed my pursuer capable of. He's a clever feller, this one. I don't fully realize just how *not good* this development truly is until I hear a barely discernible increase in the white noise to my left.

My head turns, body following.

Standing across the twilight-dappled earthen floor of the parking lot stands the man with the gleaming ax. My foe. My predestined nemesis.

The Jason to my Tommy.

The Fred to my Nancy.

Funny thing though, he isn't as tall as he seemed when he was chasing me before. Like…he's actually pretty short. Almost comically so. Carrying a bloody ax and shrouded in loosely fitted weaves of fabric tucked in behind filthy blue coveralls, he has roughly the same physical carry to him as that bearded dwarf from the *Lord of the Rings* films.

Dude should've allocated more points to his physical stats, my inner LARPer thinks.

But who am I to judge God's handiwork where homicidal maniacs are concerned? I'm nobody's judge. Not me. No way. However, I am comfortable with going ahead and electing myself the jury and executioner for this mean muggin' bag o' bad intent, right over here. It's him or me, so like my boys, N'SYNC once said, *it's gonna be me.*

Holding little more than a wiener roasting twig as my only line of defense and shouting like an injured dope in my precarious position really shouldn't, I rely on the plot armor I've surely accumulated by this juncture in the narrative and holler, "I don't know how you evil bastard, but you are one dead bad guy!"

Skinface looks at me and waves the sharp blade in his hands my way. And it's terrifying. Really, just terribly spooky stuff he's doing with the damn thing.

I don't recommend it.

Before I can mentally quip any more or really even react, he pitches his shoulder forward and launches the ax across the lot—straight my way. It flies end over end, seemingly in slo-mo, right past my head. I feel the wind of it caressing my cheek at the same time the blade imbeds itself in the bark of a tree roughly ten feet behind me with a solid *thud.*

Stunned, I don't immediately move, even when the skin-masked marauder of my discontent stalks forward to close the gap between us. He doesn't come directly for me, but rather hovers over to the side of the house. On the cabin's outer wall, there are various wall-mounted hooks holding tools and random implements of the grounds-maintenance variety. He pulls free one particularly long javelin-looking spear thing— what the hell you do with such a thing in the real world is escaping me in the moment—and gives a half spin to reface me. Turning briefly to scan the truck, I spy some large metal object that looks to be a wrench or something and yank it free from the bed.

I sense his approach before I fully turn back to him and start to make my way around the truck to put it between us. As I do, he stalks in long, confident strides my way across the lot. Coming within forty yards now, he clearly doesn't realize I'm the fuckin' final girl and that his goose is likely cooked.

Dash-hopping around the other side of the truck bed, I use all the strength I have to hurl the metal tool at my attacker. Spinning in what seems like a perfect arc, it flies about a mile wide of him. So far in fact that he stops to watch it sail off to the right, missing him by no less than thirty feet. He turns his head back to me and cocks his head quizzically.

This is surprising.

With my survival mojo at an all-time high, you'd think that my many years of playing tennis and softball would have prevented such an egregious misfire. The bastard should be laid out with a welt the size of an orange on his friggin' dome. Instead, he slowly resumes his advance my way.

Sensing it as good a time as any to make my escape, I start to run. Moving from the truck and roughly toward the area between him and the cabin, I see him coming for me, all too rapidly. He's likely going to reach out and—

Whack!

My skull feels the dull impact of the javelin-thing's wooden hilt hitting my head, sending me sprawling. Collapsing onto the dirt-deck, I manage to escape full on cranium cracking by catching myself on my palms. Sharp rock points bury themselves into my hands. The same hands that immediately search for purchase to right myself, so I can stand.

Yet this is not to be, because now the bastard has reached one of my legs. My body lifts off the ground and flies away from my control for what seems like a slow-mo ten second count, but ultimately probably lasts less than a second.

Creepypasta-ass mofo has tossed me like one of those dog chew toys. I'm flung end over end, crash-rolling into the dirt like a disrespected gunny sack. I finally hit my head on the ground and spots of light dot my vision. In my mental fog, I can't help but wonder why he's doing so well against me. I guess even final girls gotta take their licks in the lead up to victory.

Lying prone on the ground, this ugly bastard makes haste to where I've landed with implement in hand. And he is looming, just positively looming over me with that big sharp stick he's been hoofing about with.

Suddenly, it doesn't look too promising for the kid. Not sure I can secure an escape from this buggy loon. In fact, with him mere seconds from offing me via impalation, I'm pretty sure we got curtains coming up.

Cover the kids' eyes, here comes a kill shot, and with it, a severe end to my final girl ambitions.

What the actual fuck? Seriously, I just don't get it. I'm the girl, damn it! *The final one.* Surely there must be some damn way for me to stay in the picture, as it were.

I move my limbs to escape, feeling as though my head is splitting like a watermelon on Gallagher's wooden smash block, and fall back onto the ground, dazed and confused.

And just as ol' Skinface raises the spear to bring the tip down on my cranium, and with it, prematurely end my (somewhat) innocent life, several shots ring out.

Suddenly, small bursts of blood pop in rapid outward spurts from his shoulders and upper torso, as nine millimeter slugs perforate his ugly ass. Leatherface's Colorado cousin over here flails backward, dropping the spear thing (gonna have to Google what the shit that thing is eventually) onto the dirt next to me as he tumble-rolls into a heap near one of the abandoned cars about thirty feet away.

I take the cue to reverse-scuttle on my ass a few feet like some retreating crab, then turn my body around to run away. It's then that I see the source of the gunfire.

It's Daisy. Daisy Dupree. Six foot two. Blonde, basketball, student council. Consummate theater geek. Black jeans and a snug black microfleece vest that both appear no worse for the wear. Landed a juicy scholarship on her ridic SAT scores, I heard.

She's holding the police officer's Glock 17 that she must have pilfered from his headless corpse sometime between now and when I last saw her, which was just before the harrowing attack on the main cabin. I think she was writing in her journal out back on the bench—waxing tragically hip as she is often prone to—so I'm more than a little surprised she hasn't been made into a mincemeat yet.

I stand up, snatch up the spear, and start walking toward Daisy. I can feel the pricks of pain afforded by all the little bumps and bruises that my night has thus far rend unto me, but I try to maintain a tough face.

Come to think of it, how isn't she even a little injured? Whatever, I'm just so glad to see her. I could always use a good sidekick. Strength in numbers and all that jazz. Helps to survive a—

"What's on your hands?" she asks as I reach her, careful to keep my eyes on the downed slasher. She still has the gun raised and aimed at him as well. My palms are now a gross mixture of brown and green smears with dots of red.

"Hey, Daisy! It's chlorophyll and dirt. I was tugging at a bush."

"Yeah?"

"Yeah, totally. But it was dumb, so I stopped."

"Understandable. Are you doin' alright, Tessa?"

"Yeah, totally. Dead friends notwithstanding, I'm peachy. Peachy keen. Here, hold this for a second." I notice my left shoe is untied and shove the weapon in her free hand, then say, "Who the hell hunts with a goddamn spear in the woods anyway?"

To my surprise, she replies, "Jason in *Friday Part II*, but I think it's a pilum, actually."

"A pilum?"

"Yeah."

Taking the hook-tipped javelin from my trembling hand, she looks at me holding my injured foot at an odd angle and asks, "Did he fuck up your hoof?"

My cheeks flush red as I coyishly confess that, "No, not exactly. I heard him coming up the stairs and bailed out the second floor window. I took a hard tumble off the roof and wrecked my shit."

"I think I heard you. But that wasn't him, it was me. I came in and started up the stairs then heard something crash through a window, and hit the ground outside. I figured it was him chasing somebody so I ran out the back and made my way around the cabin so I could shoot him."

"Oh. Well, okay," I mutter, a little embarrassed. My final girl Spidey sense is apparently such a broken, defective piece of shit that I should have exchanged it for one that works. What's more, I all but broke my foot running from my only remaining cohort. Where are my killer intuitions? Why isn't this going well at all? And, before I forget to ask, I toss Daisy a quick query: "What's a pilum?"

"Basically a spear. Supposedly it won the Battle of Telamon for the Romans back in 225 BCE. Not sure why it's up here though."

I nod, knowing little and caring even less about the impromptu history lesson she's laying down for me. Kneeling and tying my shoe, I watch as she deftly flips the pilum (spear) onto her shoulder, then pops the gun clip out and eyeballs it before slapping it back into the butt of the gun and racking the slide.

"I got four more rounds. We can't keep relying on running. Time for fight, not flight. We might need to end this fucker with a big rock or a steep drop into a deep hole if he gets up. But for now, both of those ideas are impractical as shit. What we really need is a death blow we can deal to this freaky creeper."

I give her a frustrated glance, and ask, "Then why not go and bury the remaining slugs into his ugly fucking dome? Let's finish this!"

"That would be a good idea, but for one lingering possibility."

"What's that?"

"We can't yet say for sure if he's alone. For all we know, he's got another inbred redneck homie lurking in the dark out there. Best to be prepared rather than being screwed if we happen upon the next member of the family. You know, like in *Wrong Turn,* or that *X-Files* episode, 'Home.' For now though, he looks like he's not going anywhere. And I wanna be properly prepped for another encounter. No offense intended to that ancient war weapon you got there."

"None taken." Though I do wonder why she's the one coming up with the better stratagem.

Standing up and holding out my hand for her to return the pilum, something finally dawns on me like the breaking sun over the eastern horizon, and I feel like I'm gonna puke. It's scary and heartbreaking and it doesn't seem to make any sense at the moment, yet remains true all the same.

I've been living a lie this evening. I am, in fact, *not* the hero here. I'm not the final girl.

She is.

Daisy is the real deal, and I'm just some lucky dipshit who has yet to be dealt with.

If intuition is to be trusted, I can now sense that I'm but a side character in Daisy's coming-of-age tale of survival and personal growth. I'm no invincible Ripley about to toss the queen alien out of an airlock. No, no, no. I am, in reality, the humble and hopeless sidekick who offers up dopey metaphors, quips nonsensical non-sequiturs, and provides ham-fisted exposition for the tried and true main character—the main character who is clearly not me.

What's more? This new development means I can die. Pretty fucking easily too, if your average slasher flick is anything to go by. How many sidekicks has Sydney Prescott burned through at this point in the game, anyway?

Too many. Way too many, that's how many. Nobody should hang out with her. Like my guys Bell Biv DeVoe once said—*that girl is poison.*

Shit. And here I thought I was rocking a nice, straight-off-the-assembly-line layer of plot armor, to say nothing of righteous purpose. Divine righteousness to keep my head above the rising tide of bloodshed. Now I feel I'm sinking in the mire, and hella fast.

Why does Daisy get to be the final girl? That's what you'd call a damsel in distress, right there, not a badass leading bitch. She's on the student council, for Christ's sake. Who's ever heard of a final girl who was on student council? Maybe that one chick in *Final Exam*? Betsy Russell in *Cheerleader Camp*, perhaps? Suppose Alicia Witt in *Urban Legend* might've been. I can't remember, but—

Wait…so, but they often have sidekicks, right? And those sidekicks survive sometimes, don't they? In fact, Gail Weathers made it out of plenty of *Screams* intact. And Alicia Witt managed to escape *Urban Legend* with Jared Leto's handsome ass no worse for the wear. Every other boyfriend of the final girls in the *Friday the 13th* films gets out alive. Shit, half the goddamn cast of *Freddy's Dead* is unscathed by the time the credits roll. You just gotta be half-witty, fire off inappropriately timed jokes that fall flat, take a few cheap cracks at the slasher, but above all, stick to your final girl like glue. Super glue. I can help her, and she can help me.

Daisy will be my plot armor now.

I just need to stay super-duper close to her and match her survival instincts, play for play. Back her up. Hand her fresh ammo clips, open doors, dress wounds with medic kits—be a good little helper when and where I can. Be integral to the survival of the final girl and you'll survive as well, right?

Right?

Shit. Who am I kidding? It's a roll of the dice either way. Nothing is assured in the postmodernist slasher era we now find ourselves in. But fuck it; it's the only play I have, so it's the one that'll have to do. Gotta try. And if things do go completely sideways, I guess I can always use her as a human shield like that asshole psychiatrist from *Friday the 13th Part VII* did with Tina's mom.

"Why are you staring at me like that?" Daisy suddenly asks, studying me with a cocked eyebrow of suspicion on her face, causing my reverie to break as I snap back into reality.

"Oh, nothing. Just, nothing really. It's just that I am so fucking happy I ran into you! We can easily survive this shit now that we got each other's backs!"

Her eyebrow remains unwaveringly cocked as she mumbles, "Yeah, yeah; I'm glad I found you too."

"I can be helpful during the final battle, you know. I'm certain that I can. I've got mad utility."

"What…do you mean, final battle?"

"*The* final battle. With our nemesis. Supposing Skinface there isn't entirely down for the count. We can tag team his ass! Encircle him in a pincer movement and pry out his eyes with our fingers!"

She looks around nervously as she replies, "He might already be done for. So I don't know about—"

"And then, when we finally have him dead to rights, we can pull off that damn mask, end the Scooby Doo mystery once and for all, then ride off into the sunset like Nancy at the end of *Nightmare I*. And I'll be Tina. I can be *your Tina*. Not *Friday* Tina of course, *Nightmare* Tina, know what I mean? I wasn't thinking about Friday *VII* or the psychiatrist. I meant *Nightmare* Tina."

"Are you feeling okay, Tessa?"

I chuckle and scoff 'cause, *Yeah, I'm just fine, actually.*

"Yeah, I'm just fine, actually," I say.

Fine and dandy, long as I got my lady-shaped plot armor over here.

I giggle for levity, which does not land. "Just a bit jacked up on Red Bull Jägerbombs, plus I got my fucked-up foot. And I'm more than a little worried about not dying. But I'm pumped. I'm jacked. Should I get another weapon?"

She nods, still eyeing me with a trace of suspicion. "I was thinking about that. We might want to—"

An audible groan comes from our ground-bound foe, startling us. Both of our eyes go wide, then meet one another's. Daisy clicks the safety on and slips the mostly spent gun into her waistband, behind her back. She shrugs and quietly admits, "Okay, so maybe he's got a little oomph left in him after all." Her voice lowers even more. "Let's go. We need to be out of sight before he comes around."

She turns and starts off toward the side of the main cabin that I just came from. I follow diligently without another word. Scuttle-scurrying like exposed cockroaches retreating from the light, we make a fast dash to the building. Reaching the corner, she slips into the welcome cover of darkness, and I stumble my happy ass along to join her. Rounding the bend, we slink along the wall and quietly cower toward the back of the house.

She holds out a hand to stop me and we crouch in the failing light. I can see enough to detect her hand holding up a finger to red-hued lips in the universal sign of "quiet". She leans in and whispers into my ear, "Isn't there a shotgun in that case upstairs?"

And of course she's right. Marking yet another missed chance for me to have flexed my non-existent final girl gravitas.

"I think so," I whisper back. "I mean, David mentioned something about using it tomorrow to go hunt ducks. But A: I think he was joking, and B: David is dead."

"Shit. That mad bastard got David?"

"Oh yeah. Quite deceased. He was one of the first to fall."

"How?"

"Skinface ripped his spinal column from his back."

"Skinface?"

"That's the impromptu moniker my brain randomly latched onto."

"Ah. Not bad."

"Thank you."

"Ripped out his spine?"

"Yep. And it was even less pretty than it sounds."

She runs her hand over face and clears the loose hairs from in front of her eyes. "Fuck. How is that even possible?"

"But for seeing it with my own two eyes, I wouldn't have thought it was. But I did, and he did, so yeah…it's a thing."

"Shit. That's too bad. I was kinda hoping he would make a move this weekend."

"You two had a thing?"

"No, but I was hoping for it."

I reach out to pat on her shoulder and say, "I'm sorry." But the truth is, I'm not entirely all that sorry. I don't wanna sound morbid, but with her prospective love interest off the board, my odds of coming out the other side of this mini-meta-movie we find ourselves in just went way up. His untimely demise likely giving my own survival stock a massive hop in value. Still, I resolve to keep this particularly grim appraisal to myself for the time being.

She runs her fingers through her hair. "It's fine. I'm fine. Or…I will be. No time to ruminate on it just yet. Let's go inside." She points to the back porch.

I follow her lead and we hurry to the back door. Daisy casts a cursory glance about, then cautiously pulls open the old screen door. I wince in anticipation of a loud sound coming from the rusty hinges. But, in true final girl fashion, she manages to silently pull open the door without the usual loud creaking, and we sneak in.

Entering the kitchen located at the back of the house, we see that the room is as dark as the rest of the cabin. No surprise there. However, even in the failing light, we can make out the body of, uh, someone lying dead on the floor. Might be Tony or Joey, but it's so impossibly dark that I can't tell for sure.

Daisy carefully steps over the fresh cadaver and makes her way to the door leading into the living room. I awkwardly step over the body, but my hurt foot hooks a toe on the dead dude's leg and I nearly go tumbling onto my face. Luckily, and somewhat unsurprisingly, Daisy catches me. Not sure how she saw me, but I suspect I know already. Final girl mojo. The kind I do not (and evidently never have) possessed.

As we hustle through the likewise dark living room, we both hear something stirring out front. No doubt our assailant coming to his senses and resuming his pursuit. I raise my pilum and hold it toward the doorway, but after another second, there is no sound forthcoming. I continue to limp-hobble behind Daisy as she crosses the foyer and makes her way to the foot of the stairs.

Climbing up, we hit the second-floor hallway with its several offshoot doors. At the end of the hallway, we can see the outline of the gun cabinet with its glass door.

Daisy points to the other end of the hallway and then at me. I take the hint. Skulking along, I hold my ancient weapon in front of me and take up position just around the corner of the stairway landing. Behind me are two doors and the same broken window that I stupidly jumped out of earlier. Still, I'm ready to do my part if need be, though secretly hoping it won't come to that.

The true final girl strides over to the gun case and pulls it open. She takes out the only weapon inside—a Mossberg, pump-action shotgun. Wrapping the sling over one shoulder, she half-kneels, snags a box of shells from the bottom shelf of the case, and starts filling up the gun.

Just as she pops the final round into the shotgun and gives it a pump, we hear the front door open and freeze in place.

Oh shit. *Shit.* I really don't want to do this. *Can I go home now?*

Daisy raises a hand to her lips and slowly shoulders the gun again. I take a cautious step back so that if (when) he comes upstairs, I can impale the fucker with the same weapon the Romans used to beat their foes back at the Battle of Telamon.

In fact, he might just be checking out the downstairs and hopefully won't come up here.

However, any hopes of that being the case are quickly dashed as my last step back creates the loud creaking sound that we'd managed to avoid when coming in the back door downstairs. And it *is* loud. Painfully loud. Loud enough to instantly notify Skinface as to our position. I hear him make a run at the stairs. His footfalls are noisy, as he likely gives little shit about letting us know that our demise draws nigh.

I hold up the pilum and notice that my hands are shaking. I think Daisy must somehow see this in the failing light of the hallway, because she motions for me to go into the nearest doorway.

And like the hapless, hopeless side character I am, I slither into it, poking my head out to see what happens next.

Skinface surely hears my retreat as he makes it to the stairwell landing and turns straight toward me. I can only stand, frozen in place and terrified beyond belief.

"Hey, fuckface!" Daisy shouts, causing my pursuer to turn and face her. I don't see this part as I swiftly retreat. Tucked back into the room, I hear a stomach churning *crack* as Daisy swings the butt of the shotgun at Skinface's thick skull. He takes a teetering few steps backward until I can see him.

And he sees me. Good golly Miss Molly, he sees me!

His head turns ever so briefly and his gaze pierces the darkness where I stand. I can feel his eyes burning a hole into me, but before he can do anything more, another swing of the shotgun butt sends him back toward the door. Rustling leaves don't shake as much as I am currently.

Daisy runs straight up to Skinface and gives him a roundhouse kick to the sternum, which sends him flying back into the window. Crashing through the remaining glass shards, we hear him roll along the same roof I had, then hit the ground with the same dull thud.

Daisy rushes into the room and sidesteps my trembling spear. She yanks at my sleeve. "We gotta go. Come on!"

As we hurry into the hallway and back down the stairs, Daisy stops short of the front door and pauses. She turns to me and says, "Look, honey, I think we should split up for a minute. I have a plan. You just need to—"

"What?" I ask incredulously, cutting her off. "No! That's a bad idea. I need to stick to you like glue. Plus only the dumb fucks in the movies split up."

"This isn't a movie."

"It sure as hell is! And if we part ways, I am totally gonna end up as a dead body hanging from a fucking tree! Then you'll find me that way and have to tell my parents about it! That's a bad beat. Not advisable."

And I'm right, you know. One thing I can count on is that if I get separated from the heroine, I'll likely turn up as yet another victim, right before Daisy steps into the proverbial ring for a final fisticuffs with the evil slasher-man. Any second he's gonna come in to finish the job.

"No time to quibble, sweetie. He's on the move again. I'm gonna lead him around the other side of the cabin, then I'll meet you in the back."

"I'm not sure that's a good idea. How am I gonna make it to the end intact if you bail on me?" I ask, wondering what she means to do for all of one second, before I hear the stalker of our discontent rallying his inner-unkillableness. Lest my ears deceive me, it sounds like he's rapidly getting to his feet. I can hear movement through the wall to the outside. Eight or so slugs and this fucking guy is still coming.

But they do that, don't they? Smug bastards that they are.

Daisy shakes my arms and hisses at me, "Tessa! Just do what I say. I'm not bailing on you. We can get this fucker, but we need to surprise him. Like you said, we're gonna pincer move his ass. But for now, just hide in that closet over there. Trust me. Count to ninety and then meet me in the back. We are gonna finish this. Together. Okay?" She gives my hand a squeeze and I know that time's a wastin'.

I shake my head no, but acquiesce, nonetheless. "Okay. Okay. I can do that." Though I don't think I can.

"Good girl. See you in ninety." She flings open the door, and without looking back she slams it closed, loud enough to let the bastard know where she is. She must have a plan.

Just do what the bad bitch with the big gun says. That's how you survive, you silly twit.

I slip into the nearby coat closet and pull it closed. Then I start to count silently.

One, two, three...

It's pitch black inside and impossibly cramped. Shifting silently, it feels like there is something in here with me. Something big and—

Ten, eleven, twelve...

I move my hand up and touch the bloodied face of some other dead somebody that has been stuffed into the closet with me, and oh *yuck*, my hand comes away wet.

Fifteen, sixteen, seventeen...

I don't know who it is, and frankly, I don't want to know. I'm stuck in a closet with a corpse and that's just a little bit more than I bargained for when the weekend began. I wipe my hand on my pants because they are already red with other people's blood, so why not add to the collection?

Twenty-four, twenty-five, twenty-six...

Oh Christ. I want to scream and flee, but I said I would do as the final girl asked, and so I shall.

Thirty-one, thirty-two, thirty-three...

Why do so many slasher dudes store dead bodies? There never seems to be any sort of rhyme or reason to it other than to provide the audience—and by proxy the heroine—some well-timed jump scares later in the narrative.

Forty-two, forty-three, forty-four...

I'm wondering if I run right now, will it look bad if she makes it out and then tells everyone that I flew off like a scared little bitch? Probably. More than probably. And so I stay where I am.

Fifty-six, fifty-seven, fifty-eight…

Still, if I'm gonna make it to the back door by the count of ninety, I need to go, and now. I slip open the door, praying that he, the killer, isn't waiting for me on the other side. Lucky me, as the door cracks open, he is nowhere to be seen. I step out into the living room and close the door behind me.

Sixty-nine, seventy, seventy-one…

I can hear commotion outside, but keep stalking through the dark and make my way through the living room and back into the kitchen. This time I easily avoid the dead body of, uh, whomever is on the floor there, and reach the back door just as I hit a count of eighty.

Eighty-one, eighty-two, eighty-three…

Taking one final deep breath, I slowly open the back door and, to absolutely no one's surprise, it makes a loud fucking sound as the metal hinges squeak. I'm like the anti-final girl over here.

Eighty-nine, ninety!

And the reason this is really bad news lies in the fact that as I come out to the back porch, I can see ol' Skinface just thirty yards away. He was just about headed off into the woods, but the noise from the screen door alerts him and he turns to face me.

Fuck, fuck, *fuck!* What now?

He cocks his head the way those creepy-creepin'-creepers always do at a moment like this. Pilum in hand, I consider my options. Should I break left, or right? Make a move to insert the spear-thing into his body, or scamper back into the house and hope my friend's plan isn't foiled?

While I'm contemplating the various avenues of effort, he starts toward me. Not moving very fast, because he really wants to see the terror take me over. And take over it thusly does as I again—vexingly, stupidly, frustratingly—freeze solid as a marble monument. Again, the curtains are threatening to come down.

He draws nearer, twenty-five feet, twenty feet, fifteen. Just as he reaches ten and goal, a rustle comes from stage right as the bad bitch babe with the buckshot belching barrel comes hard and fast out of the shadow-clouded tree-line.

Skinface pauses his pursuit of yours truly to turn toward this surprising plot development. Student council member and purveyor of destruction Dupree raises the gun to steady herself against the kickback.

"Not today, numbnuts!" Daisy pulls the trigger and sends the rag-covered body of Skinface flying backward.

Time slows and I watch in amazement as Daisy doesn't miss a beat. She rushes up to where the felled and fearsome foe of our collective despair has fallen, hesitates for exactly no seconds, and racks round after round, blasting at ol' Skinface with deadly reckoning. She obliterates his kneecaps with gunfire, pulverizes his fists with steel BBs, and perforates his chest and stomach with buckshot. He increasingly resembles an overly sauced, uncooked chunk of lasagna.

An oily, rag-covered lasagna.

But if this is indeed the fast approaching end of our night o' terror, I really should offer my assistance instead of just standing here like some gawky lookie-loo.

Rushing down the porch steps and up to where his probably now done for body lays, I barely look down as I use the tip of the pilum to jab at the bloody, mangled torso and barely attached limbs.

Daisy empties the gun and steps back. And that's when I start to really offer up my two cents. He's effectively (and clearly) a mashed meatball already, but poking is what you do best with a pilum (I guess?), so poke away is what I do. *Poke, poke, poke.* I go for the eyes, I go for the face, I go for the gold. Mashing up his head, I stab and stab and stab. Each hit elicits an icky little slurp when I retract the tip from the body.

This goes on for a while.

After who knows how long, Daisy winces with a look of abject disapproval. "You know, I think he's…I think he's dead, honey. For real. You can stop doing that, uh, whenever."

I stop, because, you know, my arms are getting tired and that's enough and all, then raise my eyes to meet Daisy's. She's givin' me the ol' evil eye something fierce.

"What?" I ask, red blood spatter dotting my face.

Like I don't know.

"Just, uh, nothing. It's fine. He's done for and that's what matters." She's clearly taken back, but she's putting on a strong face.

Staring down, I think about who our assailant might be, then realize out loud, "Shit! Well, it's gonna take more than a cursory glance to figure out who this guy was."

Daisy shoulders the shotty and uses her other hand to pump it, popping out the final spent shell onto the ground. "Yeah, I guess we can't really pull off his mask since you've pulverized his cranium into red Jell-O."

"Yeah, I sure did, didn't I?"

"Yes, Tessa, that you surely did."

"Fucking badass," I murmur, not realizing how low my voice is. And I mean it, truly. I knew that if we worked together like Gail and Sydney, we were gonna be tops in this whole thing. Absolutely top of the charts. And here we are. We done did it. We Dr. Loomis-ed his ass like it's the early morning hours of November first (the day after Halloween, you know?). I'm jazzed, I'm jacked, and I'm totally pumped. Just like my girls Katrina and the Waves once said: *I'm Walking on Sunshine.*

"And it's time to feel good!" I hum-mutter, not realizing it was out loud rather than in my mind until it's too late.

"What?" Daisy turns away from the puddle of reddish goo she has thusly turned Skinface's head into via a veritable volley of buckshot and faces me. "What?" she repeats.

"Nothing, it's just…we did it! Well, truth be told, *you* really did it. You're the final girl and I'm just glad you needed a sidekick. You're just…" I hesitate, but then just go ahead and admit what I've been thinking all along. "Daisy, you're one savage lassie. A total wrecking ball! In fact, you're sorta… you're kinda my…shero."

I wince, 'cause even I wanna retch at the badly worded sentiment, and I almost tip over. My goddamn foot is positively on fire. Not Daisy, though. In true badass fashion, she smiles, tosses the shotgun aside, and holds out her hand to me. I use her leverage to regain my balance, standing side by side with the true final girl.

"Sorry to sound so corny," I say, brushing dirt off my clothing, as if it matters at this point.

"No problem. Corny works, Ms. Maize. It's only fitting that the last lines of the movie be cringey as fuck as we head on into the credits. It certainly can't hurt our sequel potential!"

"Credits?" I ask, wondering just how fourth wall-breaky we plan on getting up in this mofo when the screen suddenly goes pitch black and…

Written and Directed by
Patrick Quinn Kitson

Produced by Daniel Kelley

A Sopris Films/Rusty Hoot Motion Pictures Production

SHERO

Starring (In order of appearance)

Hagen Weber – Victim #1 (Annoying Jock)

Tom Detlefson – Victim #2 (The Other Annoying Jock)

Daniel Kelley – Officer Harangue

Sean Smith – Officer Hassle

Scarlett Johansson – Daisy Dupree

Sophie Turner – Tessa Maize

Shero

Denzel Washington – Tony LaRusso

Christopher Simon – Joey Wilson

Timothy Chalamet – David Totty

Nicole Covington – Nicole Covington

Gina Tallman – Slutty Nursing Student

Cholla Eaton – Hapless Partygoer #1

Colette Armstrong – Hapless Partygoer #2

Colette Quattrone – MDMA-peddling Goth Chick at Party

Christine Hall – Unconscious Girl on Front Porch of Party

Jessica Moratto – Girl Trying Fruitlessly to Wake up
Unconscious Girl on Front Porch of Party

Brad Pitt – Boyfriend of Girl Trying Fruitlessly to Wake up
Unconscious Girl on Front Porch of Party

Michael Cera – Guy Silently Doing Cocaine off a Mirror
Balanced on His Kneecap in the Garage

Julia Roberts – Tessa's mom, Nikki

Patrick Quinn Kitson

Glen Close – Gas Station Attendant

Matthew McConaughey – Park Ranger Wooderson

Robert DeNiro – Old Man Curruthers

Chris Evans – Skinface

All cinematography, FX, set design, location scouting, makeup, wardrobe, gaffing, lighting, catering, pre-production, post-production, scoring, distribution, and editing were begrudgingly provided courtesy of Patrick Kitson and Daniel Kelley.

Soundtrack available on Casablanca Records

"Holding Out For a Hero"
Written & Produced by Jim Steinman and Dean Pitchford
Performed by Bonnie Tyler
Copyright 1984 Columbia Records

"Hero"
Produced by Suzy Shinn
Written & Performed by Weezer
Copyright 2020 Atlantic Records

"Hero"
Written & Produced by Enrique Iglesias, Paul Berry, and Mark Taylor
Performed by Enrique Iglesias
Copyright 2001 Interscope Records

"Heroes"
Written & Produced by David Bowie, Brian Eno, and Tony Visconti
Performed by David Bowie
Copyright 1977 RCA Records

"Jukebox Hero"
Written & Produced by Lou Gramm, Mick Jones, and Robert John "Mutt" Lange
Performed by Foreigner
Copyright 1981 Atlantic Records

"Short Change Hero"
Produced by Jim Abiss
Written & Performed by The Heavy
Copyright 2009 Ninja Tune Records

"My Hero"
Produced by Gil Norton
Written & Performed by Foo Fighters
Copyright 1997 Capitol Records

The filmmakers would like to thank the town and population
of Carbondale, Colorado for their inspiration and *relative*
cooperation during the production. They further acknowledge
and understand why said town eventually took up arms to
force the expedited departure of the aforementioned
filmmakers.

Finally, the makers of this macabre motion picture would like
to again apologize for the several innocent, frightened animals
that were *accidentally* sacrificed to the Babylonian God of chaos,
Tiamat, during the production of this film—the regrettable
and arguably preventable result of gross negligence and
misfeasance (wine-fueled bacchanalia) on set.

Rest assured, we've all been fined. *Heavily.*

The persons and events in this film are fictional. Any resemblance to any real person, living or dead, or any real-world event, is entirely possible, but really all done in good fun.

Shot in PANAVISION.

Please don't sue us.

SHREDDIN'

Once you've been shreddin' chords, bendin' boards, and rippin' frets for as long as this mother fucker over here has, you best believe you see the bigger picture, for better or worse. Bright lights, big cities—people, places, and the many, many proverbial *things*. A vast myriad of experiences and memories, all stained, smudged, and soiled through and through with varying degrees of human-born bullshit. No matter how far you travel, no matter how many faces blur past in the ephemeral time fog of existence, no matter how many books you read, or miles you ride, or pussies you fuck, or lines you snort, or pills you pack down, or stages you play, or sunsets you see, or sludge-brained people you kill off, absolutely nothing—and I do mean nothing—ever beats back the cold, ever-present knowledge that this tall, smelly waste heap/four-alarm dumpster fire we call life on planet Earth is just one stupid frat joke away from complete and utter annihilation.

And I'm being serious when I ask this question: What in the bug-eyed, god-damned smoldering fires of fucking hades is wrong with everyone up in this mother?

Well, before you even bother, just *don't*. I'm asking and I'm answering:

Everything. That's what's wrong.

Everything is wrong with everyone. They suck. And only too much. You probably do, too.

But take heart, 'cause it ain't just you that sucks. I mean, you *do* suck, and mightily at that. But really, we all do. Every last one of us. Even me. My seething, ever-simmering contempt for the unyielding flood tide of dimwits, dipshits, and dweeby, dumb-fuck dullards I must endure in my excruciating time festering here on this rotted shit bowl of a planet is an endless ocean with no bottom. I long for the murky mud at its end, though none is in sight and we are fathoms deep.

So you may then feel compelled to ask: "Well then, Mr. Anonymous Gloom 'n' Doom, if you're so goddamn miserable, why not take a flying fuck off some bridge and quit dropping your dark-cloud horseshit on my day, pal? *I'm* not all bummed out. I do Pilates, I ride trails, I listen to Taylor Swift, I eat seaweed chips from Sprouts and with my body mass index as it is, I feel just fine and dandy."

That's because we are different in this way, you and I.

I'm different this way.

I don't like sunsets or television or phones or dead poets or WiFi, or clickbait or higher education or religion or political apathy or Chinese takeout—or any of this other bullshit. Not me. You can have it. Frankly, that crap is for the blind birds and the bumbling bees.

The one thing I have ever been able to find any solace in, and the only thing I can enjoy in any tangible way, is the abject fear and confusion that seizes my hapless fuckin' victims when they feel the life slipping from their grasp as I pull it from them.

But I don't do it like others of my ilk (if any others even exist). Not like those serial killer guys do, mind you. I'm not so hands on as all that. I don't grip throats, choke necks, or cut up little ladies then leave the bloody remains along highways for the FBI to ponder over. No, I don't want to bring any suspicion. Suspicion brings scrutiny. Scrutiny brings coppers. And coppers can, among any number of other dumb things, bring a swift end to all the fun.

And believe you me, it's fun. I don't want that fun to end, fleeting though it may be.

So the million dollar question becomes: How do I achieve this seemingly supernatural feat of vitality osmosis from the hapless sheeple of the world without arousing unwanted attention?

Well, via the Devil's Hum.

That's what I call it anyway. A life-changing, life-extending, and ultimately life-sapping little trick of the spirit that I figured out a couple centuries ago. A couple of choice licks from me on damn near any stringed instrument, and I can drain years, decades, shit, even entire lifetimes from people. Soon enough, I realized that if you do it around large groups and only for a brief moment—as the backup guitar player for some band, say—then you can suckle out decades without anyone being any wiser.

To this end, it's good to be one of those background fellas. No need to go straight for the limelight like James Hetfield or Freddy Mercury. In fact, that's exactly what you don't want as the monster lurking in the mist of the fog machines. Nobody gives a solid shit about what the nameless rhythm guitarist or bassist at the back of the stage is up to.

And that's where I shine. That's where the magic happens. It's where the only fun is to be had.

My victims may not (and almost never do) know what is happening in the moment, but they sense the needle prick of their essence falling away all the same as I'm at the back of the room, or auditorium, or outdoor concert. At least, this is what I've been able to surmise from watching the expressions of so many who've unwillingly given me their time. Their life. Their essence.

I'm the little needle-nosed bug on your arm you'd love to slap, but for the fact that by the time you realize I've drained you, I'm already gone.

Hurry, hurry. Step right up! Jump right on into the swallowing drain pan of my melody's grasp, boys 'n' ghouls. There's plenty of space in the dank grotto of my blackened heart for your discarded youth to take root and help me grow. I am the tree, and you are the soil.

Right now, I'm warming up backstage at a place you've probably heard of before. Red Rocks Amphitheatre in Morrison, Colorado. A nifty little venue (actually, quite large) with stellar acoustics that's snugly nestled against a large sandstone wall just a little ways away from the capital city of Denver. Generally recognized the globe over as the world's greatest naturally formed outdoor amphitheater.

And I'm certainly no stranger to this particular stage. Been here a few times. Drained a lot of years into the ol' reserves on this stage. Still, to me it's just another set of wooden planks flanked by lighting grids. Another plate of grub to eat from, then toss aside.

But to the locals (and plenty others), it holds a semi-mythic status. To hear them yak about that stack of concrete steps in front of a big, dumb stone wall, you'd think the place was the fuckin' Rock of Gibraltar or somethin'.

Back in '64, The Beatles did a little concert here. And despite their already meteoric rise as rock 'n' rollers, the mop-topped quartet of Brit scrubs didn't even manage to sell out all the tickets—if you can imagine. Like the dead man said, *It's easy if you try.*

The air is somewhat thinner here within the foothills of the Rockies, and wouldn't you believe it, those dainty little pub pluckers couldn't handle the heights. Accustomed to the lowlands of the ocean wart they call their home, one assumes. They were sucking on oxygen tanks between every other song just to keep from passing out. Ringo especially. Mediocre drumming makes for wheezing exhaustion, I guess.

I was there, ya see, ostensibly to lend my hand at prepping the equipment. A bit of light roadie work can do just fine sometimes. A bit of income to square the ol' wallet. Even as an apex predator of the musical variety, sometimes you gotta make a little extra money, and sometimes you have to do a little grunt work.

Anyway, believe it when I say, those dainty mop-topped twats did less than an hour before their wheezy butts bailed back to Brittania, and henceforth headed off into the history books.

Submarine ridin', snaggle-tooth having motherfuckers.

Now this ain't neither here nor there, but *goddamn do I despise the British*. I mean, sure, I truly loathe everybody, everywhere, with the immeasurable heat of the brightest star in the night sky. But my baseline avarice toward humanity as a whole is especially (and inexplicably) elevated in the presence of those POME scum.

You know what *POME* stands for, don't cha?

Prisoners of Mother England.

That's right. Slaves of the Queen by any other name. A feisty slang term that the Aussies came up with, and an all too apropos one to boot. I'll tell ya, those croc-wrestlin', whizz-banging, boomerang-chucking kangaroo punchers might not be winning any Nobel prizes anytime soon, but they sure as hell have the Brits all figured out, alright.

Patrick Quinn Kitson

This whole world—England included—is just a greasy mudball covered in cluckin' fuckin' chickens, straight ripe for the pluckin'.

Not that I give a hum-diddly-ho who I pull from or how many. The more the merrier, I always say. I've done ten thousand at once. It's true. They bob their stupid little heads to the literal sound of their already fragile mortality shortening, with each and every plink of my sapping melody. They think it's groovy tunes and good times. If they only had a clue. But that's the one law of the jungle, isn't it? The cardinal law.

When the lion is hungry, it eats.

And so do I. When and who I want to. I drink the dreams, inhale the essences, and suck the soul-fed juices from any and all within earshot. Anyone who can hear the chords I use to drain them.

You wouldn't know this because you're you—a simpering dullard at best—but I can play one stroke of the Devil's Hum to an anticipatory crowd of chowderhead misanthropes and sack up a good thousand years in one satisfying gulp. When I lick my lips, tasting their saucy, succulent, somewhat sweet youth tickling my taste buds, I start to get hard.

To stay under the radar, crowds are always best. That way no one knows what just happened. Sure, every once in a while you get one of these make-a-wish kids in the crowd, rolled in by some teary eyed, doting parent hoping to give their progeny one last thrill before the inevitable end. And with how short their remaining life is, by the time you finish your set, they're dead in the same chair they rolled in on. Slumped over, aggrieved relative wailing. It makes people uncomfortable. Sometimes it can even stop the show. People care too much about the other appetizers on the buffet table. They're sentimental. And with their fleeting mortality, who can blame them?

But you know what I say about all that ol' bullshit right there?

I say fuck 'em, right in the keister. Kids get warned all throughout childhood, don't they? Metal music, jazz, blues, hip-hop, rock 'n' roll—this is all dangerous stuff, folks. It'll make you a dope addict and get ya pregnant, or didn't ya hear? Your parents must've cautioned you about the perils. Sure they did. But have you any need to heed their dire warnings? Nope. Not you. You're a rebel without applause. You're a unique *widdle* snowflake. You still listen to whatever you feel like, and I don't blame you one bit.

Parents just don't understand.

Back in the here and now, everything around me is abuzz with pre-game scuttling. Hazy noise and tuning guitars. Chord progs on the multi-synths. Taps on the cymbals and intermittent sniffing to clear drug-filled sinuses. The sun is rapidly fading over the Western horizon in Morrison, Colorado as thousands of people file into this stony grotto they call Red Rocks. Above our heads, a big, hot-pink sky is going deep purple, and fast.

I can hear that ever-evolving white noise of footfalls and clacking jaws emptying into the venue from where I am backstage. Back here in the blacklight. Behind the black tarp they string up as the show starts, so you can't see that the wizard is just some mustachioed dude yanking levers. Back here with the spandex-clad band members and their unkempt heroin-hungover roadies. The stage lights and black satin backup singers and awkward clingers-on. The managers with their dead-eyed drudgery. The press lackeys, pressing the flesh with their unimpressive prissy press lanyards.

You know what I mean. It's a beehive of activity.

So here I am, sitting on a chair by an amp with headphones on, and tuning my shit myself. Can't rely on some hopped-up roadie or anyone else to control the output—that might be dangerous. As for me at a glance, I'm rocking a tuft of black hair, a finely trimmed black goatee, a black Dio T-shirt, and a tight pair of black leather pants. Just a costume, to be honest—something to blend in with the herd—but it ain't half bad. You should've seen the shit I wore back in the early 1900s. Or mayhaps it's best left back there, beyond your view.

Tonight, I'm again lending my guitar shreddin' talents to the soiree. I need to make a bit of money, as I mentioned, so on this evening (it's someday in late July, isn't it?), I'm the third guitarist for one of these over-the-hill, downright geriatric hair metal bands from outta the eighties. Who gives a shit who, but you'd know them from their three hit singles.

The lead singer is a chubby bub with scruffy stubble and bloodshot eyes. He's got flowing lashes of fabric hanging from his arms and his long gray hair is dyed blondish, tied up in a ponytail. He's standing a few feet away, probably not even realizing that I'm behind him, tweaking my tunage; syncing up my sonic siphon.

At present, this formerly famous/currently crumbling tub of lard—who I've landed on calling Chunky McGee—is fawning over a gaggle of nubile young chickies who look like they've just barely crossed the legal threshold. He's gabbing them up about coming to his hotel room after the show. Presumably for sweaty endeavors of the sexually regrettable variety. Anything to make him feel young again. Anything to feel alive. Anything to ignore the fatal fact that the clock is rapidly ticking down to death for everyone.

No one here gets out alive, ol' Jimmy Morrison used to croon. This life is a one-way ticket for any and all.

Not for me though. I've racked up so many years that I ain't going anywhere anytime soon. Bad luck for the rest of y'all, I might suppose, if I thought about it. Which I don't.

Another half hour, and some local pricks take the stage on the other side of the towering curtain and start to warm the crowd up. Knuckle-dragging covers of eighties bands who aren't the dippy-dips I'm sitting backstage with reverberate off the time-chiseled, sandstone face of the amphitheater.

Everyone sings along. Everyone knows we're not gonna take it anymore. Everyone knows how to come on, feel the noise. Everyone knows that you give love a bad name. Everyone knows that every rose has its thorns. Everyone knows that money ain't for nothin', get your chicks for free. And of course, everyone knows that everybody wants to rule the world.

A few more toots from those small powder-filled plastic bullets you can easily order off the Internet these days, and this raggedy bunch of tired old rockers are drug-animated enough to take the stage. Lady Cocaine—still the belle of the ball after all these decades. The bassist hands me his coke-sniffer and I take a few liberal bumps before handing it back. By now, the last song by the opener is ending and the background crowd chatter is a symphony of swill and swine.

We are set back from the curtain, and a lot of our setup is on the other side. Pulling off the headphones and nodding to a nearby roadie, he scurries over, then takes my input and plugs into a small mixer behind the speaker stacks. I straighten out, slip a couple picks into the neck slots, and crack my knuckles.

The song ends and the crowd wails with the dopamine drop of nostalgia. I watch the rest of the band, maybe eleven others, getting ready for the curtain to be drawn up. Stage managers rapidly shoo-off the proximity-whore girls, the clingers, and all the press cunts dithering about.

I hang back with a couple other backups because they always want the illusion that it's the band that is still performing. But it isn't. It's us. The hired help to give the crowd the sound they remember from the dope smoke-laced memories of their oft-bygone youth.

These old geezers dry-humping their primetime glory can't play like they did thirty years back. They can't play for shit really. You ever noticed how many people fill the stage for older bands these days? Multiple drummers, guitarists, and singers. It's to carry the old bones across the finish line. Saw the Eagles (yet-fucking-again) a few years back and there were like fifteen people on stage. Funny, really. I mean, whatever it takes to hold onto your younger self. I get it.

Believe me, I get it.

Out goes the announcers call and up goes the curtain. The crowd sees these erstwhile rockers with their neon bullshit and fly into a fuckin' frenzy something fierce. The stage is aglow with a technicolor tapestry of spotlight beams. These rockers of yesteryear step out into the light and start to wave— pumpin' their fists at the crowd like they still got it.

Me and the others of my temp-job ilk come onto the stage last. Because we aren't the main attraction. I'm just some string-flicking hired gun, and really, I wanna kick back in the shadows when I do my thang.

The cheers fill the amphitheater just as the last slivers of daylight disappear over the edge of the world. Stars dot the sky, and fugly faces dot the rows and rows of seats that line the open space. Nearly all the mean muggers are on their feet and stomping about. I can feel the vibration in my toes like they're tuning forks.

And then the show begins.

Chunky McGee, the who-cares-what-his-real-name-is lead singer, rushes to the mic stand and wraps his gnarled digits around the metal like he wants to choke the life from it or something. He looks drugged-up, desperate, and drained, but he howls, "Gooooood evening Coloradoooooooooooooo!" nonetheless.

Waves of applause, shrieks of delighted spectators. A cacophonic chorus of clapping.

With an off-key holler of, "Are you ready to rock!?", the crowd goes even wilder.

This is gonna be a nice thing, taking the life away from this lot. Draining the nectar. The only thing that's worth anything to me.

The opening chords of their first big radio hit shoot from the stacks of speakers flanking the stage, and somehow propel the volume even higher. People pull out smartphones and start to watch life through a shield of screens.

Lights, camera, action!

Music, singing, shouting, screaming—rocking the motherfucking night away. And while I don't really get much from the actual act of playing, it isn't exactly torture, neither. Shreddin' ain't what it used to be, but it does the job all the same. My fingertips are a blitzkrieg of bopping flicks and scale-hopping string slides.

Rolling through track after track, this scene is the same as all the rest. Every so often, between songs—and while Chunky McGee is soliciting praise from the crowd by asking if they remember this or that about the bands short, albeit storied history—the older gents will walk to preplanned spots behind a speaker stack, under the ostensible pretense of picking up a freshly tuned guitar for the next song. But what they're really doing is re-upping their chemical reserves so their hands forget how old they are. So they can come back with at least a fragment of their former confidence intact.

The crowd doesn't see what it doesn't want to see. They wanna believe these suckers are still smooth and silky. Not a frail cadre of cranky coke-clickers.

Chunky gets his doses by sipping off a water bottle he's got on a nearby stack, so that when he turns away from the crowd, he can hoover up a bump from between his thumb and index finger.

This is precisely what Whitney Houston used to do. I was on tour with her for a bit right after *The Bodyguard* soundtrack blew the fuck up back in '92. That was one crazy fucking lady, I'm telling you. Rabid with the nose candy. Utterly voracious, the drug appetite on that hopped-up howler.

Cocaine in place, a few swigs of beer later, and we move into the song that will probably be the one where I make my move.

In front of the stage, a cluster of girls tear off their shirts and start waggling their titties about, much to the amusement of the band. Chunky McGee puts up two fingers and laps between them with his dry tongue in the universally recognized sign of cunnilingus.

The titties waggle more.

As we start the song, I see a bunch of muscly, yellow-shirted security bros storm over and tell them to put their shirts back on. The wild girls seem to refuse, and are summarily dragged out by their naked torsos.

It ain't as much fun these days, what with the social standards adjusting as they have. Too bad I can't target this shit like a sniper rifle. I'd pick off each of them muscled macho men one by one, so the titties could waggle more, unabated.

So, in lieu of that, I'm grooving and I'm shreddin' and I'm tickling these here frets a mighty bit. The crowd is singing along and the band of former chaos-makers saunter lazily about the stage so they don't risk a fall and a surefire hip-cracking.

I close my eyes, and without any other thoughts, I kick it over into the *Devil's Hum.* Just for a few fleeting moments, mind you. I don't plan on playing it for long 'cause it does its job fast, you better believe.

I play for a few seconds and watch those that have that extra bit of unexplainable perception rattling around those dense skulls of theirs. Eyes go wide. They don't know what, but something is wrong. Something they can't describe or even understand, but they feel it just the same. Something is changing. My invisible fangs are sucking away. The needle plunger is pulling back with fresh blood.

And it's nice. Oh *yeah*, that's nice. This is what I like. This is that good shit. Well, as close to good as anything can feel.

And that's when it happens.

I have no idea how exactly—I'm a melody-driven apex predator, not some geeked-up sound technician—but this pedal I'm using (it's a new one that I haven't really tested in a crowd setting) is not doing anyone in the crowd any favors. Nor is it helping the downright geriatric members of this formerly famous rock band.

It's exacerbating the rhythm in a dangerous way. I can sense the difference. Somehow this fizzy fuckin' pedal is not only amplifying the sound from my ripping thrash pad (courtesy of Ibanez, naturally), but it's taking way too much, way too fast.

When I pull from a crowd, I can roughly sense how much life I'm pulling. Usually it's a few hundred years, give or take. Doesn't take much of the hum to take a lot from a group of preening sheeple. And once you've been doing it as long as I have, you can see it coming at you in a thousand tiny strands of light, like strings of reddish, electric energy.

However, right now the strands are way too thick. They're more like ropes or cables of drained life heading my way.

Nervous of just how much I might have already taken in, I quickly switch my chord progression and the light trails stop within an instant.

Still, it's way too late. I done fucked up.

The gray/blonde-haired lead singer is the first one to drop. Gripping his chest like he's having a cardiac episode, the chubby bastard's body—as well as the microphone stand he was gripping onto—crash to their respective sides, causing everyone I can still hear to gasp and shout.

A whizz of harsh feedback causes the speakers to whine and shriek. In the audience, people are covering their ears. The whole place is now pointing at the stage.

As for us in the band, we slow and stop. But then as the music largely fades away and some roadie from stage left runs out and clicks off the overturned mic stand to kill the feedback, other people in the open venue against the stone wall of Red Rocks start to scream. Because several people throughout the crowd are tipping over like cows in a darkened field, crashing into nearby concertgoers.

The drummer—dipshit that he surely is—is still going, but soon enough notices what is happening. Dropping his tempo, he allows one final crack of the snare to ring out.

This single shot of drum, combined with the twenty or more people who have begun to fall over in the crowd, causes some members of the audience to shout, *"Gun!"* And then you know what happens, don't you?

Chaos erupts.

It absolutely jumps the fuck off in Morrison, Colorado. And hard.

A fear-fueled stampede of bodies begin to scramble for either side of the theater. Two long stairwells flank each side of the auditorium seating at Red Rocks, and everyone is heading for an exit. There is no civility in it. Not a shred. People are running over women and children and one another with reckless abandon, with any and all on-site security swallowed up by the tidal wave of mortal terror gripping the all-too-hip ticket holders. They're clamoring and crushing and cascading end over end down rows of hard plank seating. Probably not what they had in mind when they'd purchased their seats.

And just as it's getting good, another shot rings out, this one real. It's obvious that someone has actually been shot.

Likely as not by some police officer playing cowboy. In this mess, who's to say anyone would ever be found accountable?

The other band members have drawn back and are scurrying off the stage themselves. Soon enough, the curtain drops before anyone can clear Chunky's spandex-covered, free-flowing fabric festooned, very dead ass off the stage.

Security swarms the backstage area. Amid the rising chaos, I calmly walk over to where the bassist has unceremoniously abandoned the bottle he was swinging off of between songs atop an amplifier. I plug down a hard pull of some rotten, dime-store whiskey and cough. Then, as the flashlights and sirens and screaming people continue killing off more and more of their number with this mindless stampede they got going, I snatch up my guitar, unplug myself, and pop it into the case I got for it. A long black case with a rose along the side.

The noise is all encompassing. I nod as some dude to my left asks if I'm okay, but say nothing. He races past, searching for sanctuary like The Cult in '85.

The roadie who first arrived to tend to the lead singer appears from under the dense black fabric of the drop curtain and slowly drags the now-quite-dead fella out of what he must perceive as harm's way. Like that shit is gonna help undead the dude. He lets go of the neon spandex-clad corpse and steps back, like he's Forrest Gump dropping off another soldier from the jungle.

And the crowd catches on, presumably. With nothing but fleeing folks and wailing fucks all around me, people are now climbing onto the stage to escape the shooter that never was—or…might've been.

People are easily spooked in these violent times. Can't blame 'em. School shootings in some other state, concert killers on the upper floors of Mandalay Bay, and every silly little mass murder by gunfire that you'll easily forget by the next news cycle. It has alerted everyone to the horror of the here and now, while making sure everyone's as numb to it as they are comfortable with it. And it's almost enough to make this guy smile.

Almost.

But this whole scene might not be such a bad thing. This is pretty good cover for my literal departure via stage left. Plus, enough folks will have by now bypassed the barriers that it will be all too easy to slip out relatively unnoticed. I have a smaller scooter I rented in Denver, and I can drive around the sluggish lines of the automotive exodus quickly unfolding and make a beeline for the greener pastures of anywhere else.

This scene is beat. I'm out. Even the wise ol' lion splits when the hyenas start getting this riled up.

Shuffling past the mobs of swirling flesh, I am half dazed, but coke-alert. Shoulders smack against mine, but my forward momentum is undeterred. The guitar case becomes my riot shield. I taste the metallic, almost lemony flavor of the red electricity I just devoured as I bust through human barrier after human barrier. I can feel my pulsing pants, hot and heavy with blood from the utter fear and pain I just wrought onto this massive cluster of livestock, making my cock stand at attention. I could shoot at any moment.

I don't even realize I'm smiling until I stop because, the joy, if that's what it is, is nothing if not fleeting. I wonder if other killers have the same diminishing returns on the pure pleasure of taking life from others.

It only takes a few more quick swings of my elbow into the sides of a few deserving skulls and I'm largely free from the raucous amphitheater anarchy. A deluge of flesh spreading out like ants running from an overturned farm fill up the parking lots and turn on their cars. The vehicles are soon bumper to bumper, so I slide between them and break on through to the other side of each one. Just another hop, skip, and a jump away from the dirt-floored parking lot where my scooter is waiting.

I notice vehicles ramming one another, a couple of people getting run down in the chaos. It's all quite delicious, truly.

Bike-locked to a metal post, the scooter is easy enough to jimmy loose, then turn on with the key. As I roll toward one of the exit roads, I see a large woman with mammaries the size of Gallagher's watermelons break from the stampede. She starts careening my way, threatening to flatten me with her momentum. I use a hard side kick to stop her in her tracks, my right foot's steel toe boot slamming her in the sternum and sending her splaying onto the rocky road. Her head pounds the ground and she's out cold, if not worse. Had I not done so, she might have taken me off my feet and over the side of the winding road's steep drop to my left.

I don't wait to see if she gets up.

Scooting down the road past the escaping concertgoers, I pause long enough to pick up a baseball-sized rock in my left hand, then continue down the road as honking and bright beams and revving engines make the world a noisy mess of panic and fear. Gravel spins out from under my two-tire transport as I swerve like an action film baddie between fleeing sheeple who are howling and baying like madmen and women into the night sky. Crying out for solace from the deaf ears of one another.

I ready my arm for one last blast of funny on my way out. I pass a few more chuckleheads, and soon I'm narrowly squeezing out and beyond the boundary of the flesh cloud I'd just been weaving through. Cars have largely stopped the flow of escaping persons and the road headed back to the highway is now, but for my own high beams, dark and largely void of anyone.

Well, I should say, *almost* anyone.

This tall, gangly looking athletic type dude with a turned around mesh trucker hat and an oversized blue flannel button up straight out of a Nirvana music video is making like he's running the 500 meter at the Munich Olympics. A dead set, full-on sprint for the goddamn hills is what he's rocking in his socks.

I cock the hammer and let loose the stone in my grasp. Even through the orgiastic miasma of noise on all sides, I hear the satisfying crack of his temple caving in as I pass by and he collapses onto the dirt. Some bitch next to him screams with grief. Too bad I didn't have two stones.

I kick the odd fear-fueled fuckwit outta the way as I weave down the road, and finally I'm back out to West Alameda Parkway. Just a few more miles to the interstate.

Might've caused a bit too much chaos at this particular soiree. Not that I give two hoots. My ability to feel sorry for the life I live, the lives I take, and the grave choices I make is a colorless void. A negative-sum game. Double zero on a roulette wheel.

Truth is, they don't feel like choices at all. It's just what I am now. I take what I want because I can. Because I just do. Because when the lion is hungry, the lion eats. That's the only rule in the jungle.

I figure I might connect with I-70, then turn to head west, like manifest destiny. And eventually I'll head south, to the western foothills of the Rockies. Once I get good and clear of this shitshow, I think I'm gonna lay low for a while. But probably only for a week or two. Take a little break and maybe eat something other than the life force of my fellow man.

And I know just the place to rest my hell-bound heels. I could go back to the stomping grounds of my youth (the mid-1800s, if you're curious)—back to good ol' Bonedale. Back to my hometown, where nobody remembers me these days. Last time I was there was back in '91. I don't go there much anymore—maybe every few decades, just to hold off any suspicions about my eternal youthfulness.

Besides, isn't the Mountain Fair this weekend? Usually it's the last weekend of July, so it's a safe bet. I doubt I'll make it there for the Friday opener, but I can probably catch the last day or two. Maybe pick off a few homeless guys on the way. And I can always see if anyone needs a backup guitarist on the main stage.

I could be more cautious, it's true, but I'm fairly certain it doesn't matter. My hunger is my one true guide in this hollow shell of existence. And nothing else really matters.

Ol' Hetfield and Mercury had that much right.

Carbondale, here I come!

SOIL

This story was originally written for and read aloud as part of a special Halloween episode of The Witching Hours radio program on KDNK Radio in Carbondale, Colorado.
It aired at exactly midnight on October 31ˢᵗ, 2024.

On Halloween in the Roaring Fork Valley, hardly anyone knows of—nor actively engages with—any of the local lore. And really, why would they? This valley we love so dearly—an all-too-sweet expanse of ridge-nestled townships and picturesque communities that occupy the narrows running alongside the Roaring Fork and Crystal rivers—is chock full of legends and hauntings and various denizens of darkness which go largely unnoticed and oft-forgotten by the residents of today. Nobody dares dance with the ghosts of the valley's past on this fateful holiday. Your average valley resident hasn't the time for such dalliances.

Nay, they don't pay their histories any kind of mind on Halloween, and if we're shooting straight, they rarely, if ever, do on any other day of the year either. With the evolution of technology and the proliferation of its varied electronically facilitated distractions over the last few decades, not many folks spend a lot of time looking up from their screens long enough to spot the terrors that lurk behind the sun-dappled rocks and lush green swaths of the valley walls.

Our collective history fades concurrently with our diminishing interest in it.

At least, that's what usually happens. Not always though. Because sometimes there is something so bad, so heinous— dare I say, so *evil*—that it leaves a residue of the area's past sins in its stead.

Sins that seep deep, deep, deep into the soil.

Horrors so grave and ugly that they penetrate and permeate the very ground underfoot.

A psychic pox which festers and rots until eventually becoming the source of an invisible, unknowable contagion. One which, if left unchecked, can spread like a deluge of virus cells into the body politic, plaguing the surrounding area without any future generations of occupants knowing why.

Now I'm just gonna say this out loud, 'cause it's high time someone does. Crazy as it may sound, there is, in fact, such an ancient evil that soils the earthen floor under the very spot where the Redstone Inn and Restaurant in Redstone, Colorado currently resides.

Surely you've heard of such a place. It's a tale as old as time; haunted places and Colorado go together like peanut butter and jelly.

But what's different up in shady-all-day Redstone is that, on each and every Hallows' Eve, the horrors of the past come back like clockwork to haunt the present.

To be specific, the Redstone Inn chooses one person per year, and mentally draws them to the site of its past sins. Then, once said victim has arrived, the property does God knows what to the body of its victim, somehow absorbing their spirit and summarily depositing the skeletal remains into a subterranean grotto—the basement, if we're being generous—situated deep below the property.

But you won't read about it in the tourist brochure. Hotels.com conveniently won't mention anything about all the accumulated bodies in the basement below the inn.

No ghost hunter TV show is going to tell you that every Halloween, one person is psychically summoned to the grounds of the Redstone Inn to serve as a satiating sacrifice.

Not one travel agent is going to explain that, for each victim it takes, the building's time-worn façade is slightly repaired. A roof spire is straightened, a patch of latticework de-splinters, creaky stairs go silent, cracks in the concrete foundation seal up.

And one thing the general manager ain't gonna tell you is that their workplace is, on the sly, straight up dissolving and digesting human bodies whole, healing itself along the way.

And if the whole sordid affair sounds like something out of a Spielberg production of a Tobe Hooper film starring Jo Beth Williams and Craig T. Nelson, I get it. Sounds just as crazy to say as I'm sure it is to hear. But I assure you, with God as my witness, the Redstone Inn is most definitely eating people up. Like a fat man in an Olive Garden bib slurping down spaghetti and meatballs, so too does the hotel devour and digest its fleshy meals with reckless abandon. Tossing the sucked down skeletal remains into the hollowed out subterra below the hotel in much the same way we sports fans toss hot wing bones back into a red basket at our favorite watering hole. Every Halloween, somebody goes there, and every Halloween the hotel gobbles up their essence and craps their bones into the basement, not far from where the staff stores the wine racks.

And it's all because of that other wildly unoriginal time-worn marker of Colorado's checkered history with its indigenous population of yore: the all-too-common tale of the profiteering white man fucking with the natives for his own ends.

I wish it was something more original, but it ain't.

It wasn't the hotel that killed anyone back then, ya see. The hotel may have been constructed in 1902, but this was long after the Utes and several other nomadic Native American tribes had ceased to frequent the narrows of the

Roaring Fork Valley. They'd all but disappeared by the mid to late 1800s in response to the gross influx of nature shredding and land-defiling white men (and more than a few white women).

Pouring in and pushing them out.

Manifest destiny—westward expansion in all its bloody glory.

And the new arrivals made that destiny manifest by displacing, plundering, and often violently taking ownership of the land from the native peoples who'd made the valley their sometimes-home for well over 800 years previous.

One such surreptitious removal of the native population took place early in the morning hours of October 31st, 1894.

By that fateful date, It had already been quite some time since any Native Americans had frequented the Roaring Fork Valley, near modern-day Redstone. In truth, by the early 1880s, the writing was on the proverbial wall. The white man cometh and the white man taketh away. He *(the royal he)* cared nothing for the darker-skinned folks. And most of those tribes which traveled seasonally through the cross-Valley expanse had made their way west in a fruitless attempt to avoid the unavoidable stampede of Oregon trailers and mineral seekers. The money-mad barons and amoral land grabbers.

You see, on October 31st, 1894, it was a dark, cold, and frosty morning in the area now known as Redstone. A few settlers had begun to plant their flag along the Crystal River, but none as enterprising and wholly destructive as the nefarious Osgood Clan.

A ragtag assemblage of ne'er-do-well homesteaders led by Sir Timothy Cabbot Osgood the third—himself, the arch baron of some old generationally-held property back in ol' Britannia. Now emigrated to America and seeking their fortunes in the mineral rich hills of snowy Colorado, the unscrupulous clan had had their run of the land. If a small family were to set up shop nearby, they might be pressured to pay tribute to the scions of the House Osgood. Upon any ill-advised refusal, members of the new family might start disappearing until somebody signed over their deed, thus ceding all the land to them.

It's true that by the year 1900, the family's reign of territorial terror was extinguished by the brutish influx of wealthier, more resource rich bloodlines. But back in the late 1880s and early 1890s, the Osgoods were the big dogs on the Rocky block.

The tragic events of the day in question were never fully detailed by any local papers. The *Carbondale Advance*—its namesake's first regular press periodical—made no mention at all. As a matter of fact, the only thing *The Denver Post* wrote in reference to the death of some one hundred Native Americans near modern-day Redstone was a two-paragraph blurb at the bottom of the fifth page in their November 15th issue of that year. And despite a hundred lives being lost, not one death was mentioned in print.

Obfuscation and relativism, the coin of the realm.

The eventual headline read: "Savages vacated from beautiful area near Elk West Mountains. Groundbreaking on a new township is expected to commence in the spring."

And they got that part half-right. The ground got broken, no doubt about it. Not just by shovel and pickaxe, mind you, but rather broken in two by the sorrow and bloody vengeance of those so callously slaughtered. The innocent lives taken just after midnight had struck.

It was in those wee hours of October 31st that the Osgood Clan, plus a great many workers from the Colorado Fuel and Iron Company, made their move.

A group of one hundred or so Ute Indians making their yearly sojourn south through the resource-packed Valley had set up their elk-skin teepees not far down from what we modern folk would call the Penny Hot Springs. Just as a quick stopover. They'd even traded furs with some of the locals earlier that same day. They meant no one any harm, least of all the Osgood Clan.

And, truth be told, the Osgood Clan didn't much care about the native peoples either. Their massacre was merely a message—and a bloody one at that. To them, the early morning slaughter of nearly one hundred Native American men, women, and—*God knows*—children, was simply a bloody means to an ugly end. Mostly done to create the kind of carnage that would send a grave message to others in the surrounding area, letting them know in no uncertain terms who was at the top of the heap.

But, truthfully, it was also to satisfy a uniquely unquenchable bloodlust buried deep within the Osgood family line. They made no secret of their dirty deeds. The following day, sons of the clan would set out on horseback, making the rounds at many of the thirteen local saloons in nearby Carbondale, simply to regale any and all who would listen with the sordid tale of their bloody rampage.

To hear the wicked men tell their version, you'd be led to believe that the natives had aggressively asserted their possession of the land near the coke ovens that the Osgood Clan was using to make some of its fortune. Most historians would tell you otherwise. The beehive ovens of coal owned by the Colorado Fuel and Iron Company were as foreign to the natives as the wrought iron railways the company workers rode in on. The cover story, concocted by the Osgood Clan for public consumption, was a lot of lip service and hogwash.

Mind you, this was five years after the Meeker Massacre of 1879 had forced droves of native Americans into Southwest Colorado and Utah reservations. And it was a good twenty years before the Ludlow Massacre of 1914, the latter of which was also executed by the once Osgood-owned Colorado Fuel and Iron Company.

And so, to the everyman of that day, coal interloping and coke-oven ownership was certainly as good a reason as anyone needed to excuse the murder of dozens of so-called "*Injuns*."

Ugly deeds in the deep dark of the valley walls. Screaming women and sobbing children, their wails cut short by sharpened blades and pointed metal implements.

It was the sort of event that leaves a scar on the land. The kind of scar that never fully heals. Hasn't to this very day, in fact. Its fury is still locked steadfast within the soil lying underfoot, just below the Redstone Inn.

Most would have no reason to know such a thing, but mud born from the unholy union of blood and soil has a copper hue; a metallic smell, and all the bad will one could reasonably expect from a single shovelful of dirt.

The spilled gore was enough to turn the future grounds of the Redstone Inn into a muddy quagmire for weeks after. And just as the blood mixed with dirt grew colder with each step toward winter, so did the blood of the general population grow cold toward the Osgood Clan. There might have even been eventual local reciprocity for the family's misdeeds, but for the fact that fate had other plans.

Because a funny thing happened a few years later, when the fortunes of the Osgood family took a hard turn for the worse and they lost ownership of almost all the property they once held between Carbondale and modern-day Marble. The Colorado Fuel and Iron Company was sold off to pay accumulating debts. Whole branches of the family begin to die off due to mysterious illnesses, incurable diseases, and more than an uncomfortable amount due to sudden suicidal impulse.

The locals long suspected that the Hallows' Eve Massacre might have been at the heart of their troubles, but all it amounted to was suspicion.

Nowadays, the only trouble that the property ever sees is an ever-increasing accumulation of bones in the dank, musty pop-up ossuary that nobody asked for, lying beneath the hotel.

And the staff knows to keep their mouths shut, by golly. Oh yes they do. Legend has it that those who learn of the hotel's dark secret and deign to speak of it are quickly added to the pile of bones below by the specters of the slaughter.

Is it true?

Nobody knows for certain, or at least nobody is saying. Most employees would never learn the truth, and those that might possess a vested interest in keeping their knowledge a secret. Housemaids stumbling upon the skeletal remains of a human being next to the wine-racked bottles of Merlot in the basement would never speak of them. The odd visitor claiming to have seen a person disappear into the soft dirt out behind the building just after midnight on Halloween is always met with incredulity and swift dismissal.

Obfuscation and denial, the coin of the realm.

The original hotel manager had thought that there might be a killer in the area, even going so far as to employ a gumshoe or two over the years to suss out the source of the emergent problem. Yet each one failed to ascertain who might be filling up the basement with bones. And with every passing year, there would be more down there.

However, someone must have quickly realized that, in lieu of a thrill killer, what they had was an unfortunate problem of the supernatural variety turning the space beneath the hotel into a bone bathroom. After decades, stacks and stacks of yellow-white bones have built up. And today, the towering, teetering piles of human refuse—predominantly those of the skeletal variety—fill the ossuary.

And just to allay your concerns, or answer the obvious, it isn't the staff doing it.

Some of the staff—the few that might be inclined to, possess the memory thereof, or lack the sense of self-preservation to speak of such things—would probably tell you that the legend is as follows:

As long as the hotel gets its yearly sacrifice, all is well. Sure, the bones might be starting to reach the ceiling, but what can be done? If anyone from law enforcement ever goes there to verify its grim contents, there would surely be a lot of questions surrounding the accumulation of human remains beneath the Redstone Inn.

But that's a big *if*, and who's bothering to ask the right questions anymore?

Nobody, that's who. Time either heals all wounds, or it hides them. Only history decides which is which.

Obfuscation and mortal fear, the coin of the realm.

So if you ever feel an inclination, a nagging, or mayhaps that small voice in the back corridors of your psyche beckoning you to spend a spell at the beautiful Redstone Inn, make damn sure that that same voice isn't asking you to do it on Halloween.

Make sure to cover your bases, my friend. You don't want to end up being psychically chewed up, turned inside out, drained of your blood, then unceremoniously defecated as a pile of unwanted, unrecognizable bones into the dusty basement grotto of some century-old hotel in the backwoods of Colorado.

You should go trick or treating.

You should have a few brews, chew a few caps, maybe a couple tokes, or a line or two—whatever your bag is—and go to a costume party.

Meet a masked stranger and make out under the blacklights.

Go to a bar in a sexy cat outfit, then stop by your friend's mystery dinner party afterward.

Dress as your favorite Marvel superhero might and secure a designated driver.

Hang out with your friends and watch *The Rocky Horror Picture Show.*

If you're really intrepid, you could tune into KDNK Radio in Carbondale to see what kind of groovy stuff the DJs are piping through the radio waves during the witching hour before All Hallows' Eve.

Do anything—*anything*—but visit the Redstone Inn. Anything but that.

In fact, avoid Redstone like the plague.

The soiling of the past gives root to the terrors of the now. And it happens during the witching hour. It happens in the lead up to the time when, long ago—right about one hundred and thirty years by this telling—the greed of the industrial upper class trampled the sovereignty of the native population, leaving specters in its wake. Hungry specters that demand a yearly tribute of the flesh.

It's happening right now, in fact. Right at this very moment. Somebody, some hapless dullard or some Instagram-famous dipstick, heard the siren call of the inn and made a plan to stay there for the evening.

Right now, this very Halloween, that same siren call is marching them out the back door, to that spot of ground between the lodgepole pines. Next to the closed pool, where the ground is especially soft. Where they often have weddings in the summer. Where there's no big boulders to get in the way of the descent.

And once that hapless sap reaches that soft spot of land, they will be drawn down into the earthen tomb where the sins still spoil the soil. They're about to be digested by the malice of past indiscretions.

With a mouthful of moist soil, no one can hear you scream.

Right now, you live here because someone once lost their property for you. Right now, you eat because someone else is starving. Right now, you are safe and snug as a bug because you don't have to pay the price.

Up in Redstone, somebody is paying the price for you. Somebody's being swallowed by the earth, spiritually absorbed, somehow digested and swiftly shat out into a goddamn wine cellar.

You're safe because the Redstone Inn is digesting somebody for dinner, using their essence for menial structural repairs and crapping them out into its basement.

I'm dying if I'm lying here, boys and ghouls. Not dying like whoever's currently being shat—nay—rather being positively sprayed into the subterranean wine cellar is, of course, but I suspect you get my meaning just the same.

Be wary, folks. This is a dangerous hour. The witching hour. The same hour when, one hundred and thirty years ago, so many died for the land you now occupy. So if you get the sudden desire to visit the Redstone Inn on Halloween, I'd run the other way.

If I heard the call, I'd run for the literal hills. But that's just me.

Happy Halloween, Carbondale! And the sweetest of sweet dreams to all.

POTATOES

Hot bolts of sunshine blasted the lush, green, and freshly watered fields lying at the top of the wide open pasture that most folks in the town of Carbondale, Colorado referred to as White Hill.

John Neezblahnuk had never really cared much for the rusty old name given to the picture-perfect place his family had called home for generations, and for any number of reasons.

First of all, it had long been his family's farm and homestead land—since the mid-1800s, as a matter of fact—and the name only derived from a meager part of a much larger swath of acreage, for it was the ivory-hued escarpments which elevated and separated the farm from the town proper that lent the area its colorized moniker.

Second, the slopes around said fields weren't actually white, but more a chalky yellow mixed with scattered brown rocks and dotted with dry, brittle shrubs.

And third, perhaps most importantly, it really wasn't a hill at all. It was clearly a plateau which had sat comfortably overlooking the township for well over a hundred years.

Along the eastern ridge lay St. Mary's of the Crown Church, and across the fields from there along the western edge of the property lay the publicly available Hillcrest cemetery. From his family's land, located at the town's southern end, the area also afforded one of the best views from which to look at the beautiful, often snow-capped peaks of nearby Mt. Sopris—the slopes of which lay just ten miles further south.

Standing nearly seven feet tall, with dusty blond hair, a stubbly face, a chiseled jaw, and a large, rugged frame, he'd been the literal big man on campus in his scholastic heyday. Back then—the Roaring Nineties, specifically—when he tossed around the pigskin for the Roaring Fork Rams, he'd played a key role in the triumphs of his high school's middling, albeit not completely inept football team. They'd made it to the district playoffs twice, but had never succeeded in nabbing a state championship title while he was doing his part as a forward tackle for them.

Some nights, after his day's work was done and he'd finished up with the big family supper at the main ranch house, he'd set out alone to catch a local game. Just to keep the old nostalgia flowing.

Always astride his beautiful brown and white Shagya Arabian horse, Bessie, riding her down from the ranch along the winding dirt track of White Hill Road, he'd come around the fields and take up a nice vantage point in the newly asphalted parking lot behind St. Mary's of the Crown Church that lay just on the edge of his family's property. From there, he could secure a clear view of his old stomping grounds, the football field behind what used to be Roaring Fork High School, but which was now Roaring Fork Middle School. (The new high school had been finished some years back.) A place where the town's athletic successes were communally shared, and their defeats collectively lamented. And, luckily for John, this was still where the Rams played their home games.

As dusk fell, and often under the cool veil of moonlight, he'd sit atop Bessie and crack a few cold ones. Peering through a pair of leather-strapped binoculars, he'd watch the field fill up with the home and away teams, the coaches, the students, and the old-timers to see if the Rams could still pull out the win when it mattered.

And usually, they could. Much as it pained him to admit it, they were better than the Rams of the nineties ever had been. Still had a solid defensive line, *and* even had a top-shelf QB holding it all together.

However, here in the days of the now, his head was often filled less with the victories of yore and instead was more than a little preoccupied with an emergent problem that had been cropping to the top for the last few years.

See, while his brothers and father handled the riding lessons, cattle breeding, and ranch rustling that had put their family's name on the proverbial map, he'd always been the one in the family with the natural green thumb. His father, Jacob, prided himself on spotting that sorta skill early on. And spot it in John, he surely had. So when the time had come to do his part for the family business, it fell upon his broad shoulders to oversee the large fields of potatoes that his family had used to make up a large part of their fortune for over a century. And he'd enjoyed it ever since. He was a natural, and every year the ranch's coffers were equally filled up by the spoils of his agricultural contribution.

But then, the bugs had shown up.

As a prideful kind of man, just like his father (pride being part and parcel with the Neezblahnuk bloodline), he hadn't wanted anyone to worry too much about the rapid and growing influx of crop-chomping insects. He had thus set himself about fixing the problem as best he could on his own. Sure, his family knew that the potato beetles were posing a nascent nuisance. But the scope and depth of said troubles were something he alone knew, and had thus far kept to himself.

Furthermore, once he starkly realized that, despite his best efforts, more drastic measures were needed to rectify his emergent agricultural woes, it was he alone who phoned up the chemical distribution folks and asked that they send someone out to get to the bottom of things. And as quickly as possible. That way he'd be able to report back good news to the family, minus all the needless worry and interpersonal drama—to say nothing of doubts about his own occupational capabilities—that such trivialities might unduly cause among his kin.

So it was that on a nice day in April with only sparse clouds overhead and a cool northwesterly breeze to soothe the senses, someone finally showed up.

John was surveying the fields with his leather-strapped binoculars when he caught sight of a telltale dust cloud, signaling a vehicle fast approaching as it passed by the church on White Hill Road. Clicking at Bessie, she took hoof forthwith, bringing him to around the south side of the pastures and over to where the vehicle had stopped just shy of the cattle guard that delineated their property from that of the town's.

As the visitor pulled into the front parking lot before St. Mary's of the Crown, he saw that it was a brand spanking new, damn near straight off the lot wagon paying him a visit to ease his troubles. Well, not exactly a wagon, per se, but more specifically a jet black 2024 RAM Pro Master 2500 Cargo Van. To John, it looked like the sort of thing your modern electrician or plumber might cruise around in when working on the houses of the rich and famous further up the valley, in and around Aspen or Snowmass—but for the big white *PERMATOX INDUSTRIES* logo emblazoned along each side.

John tugged the reins, nudged Bessie to a stop just a few yards away from the lot, and placed his yellow-gloved hands on the horn of the saddle.

A young, clean-shaven, oily-haired man in a well-tailored navy suit with grey pinstripes stepped out of the vehicle and began to stride confidently up to where John comfortably sat upon his trusty steed. His eyes were beset by dark, reflective aviator sunglasses. As the man in the suit neared the lifelong potato farmer, he gave a courteous wave and affected a plastic-mannequin smile.

John, despite not quite liking the frozen falseness of the expression the man bore, put up his gloved right hand to tip the brim of his black Stetson hat and nodded at the dapper fellow. "You the fella they sent from the chemical distribution place?"

The business-class dude standing before him shook his head, sniffed hard while squeezing his nose, then cleared his throat before he said, "We prefer to be seen as a manufacturer of industrial goods that enrich the lives of the many, while aiding the common man in achieving success in his business of choice."

"That's a right fancy mouthful, fella. But I hope you don't think I'm the type that needs to be smoothed over and silver-tongued. So long as you can help me fix this problem we've been having, I'll count myself a happy man. That said, I'm damn glad you came, all the same."

"No trouble. Beautiful place you have up here."

John's eyes did a job of scanning the fields behind him. "We like to think so."

The man in the suit held out his hand, and John turned back toward him, leaning over to meet his shake. "My name is Daniel Matranga, and as you know, I am a representative from Permatox Industries."

"That you are. Name's John Neezblahnuk. How do you do?"

"I'm good, thank you."

John glanced at, then nudged his head in the direction of the van the man had arrived in. "If you don't mind me sayin', Permatox is sort of an ominous name for a company that's supposed to be helping out the working folk, ain't it?"

Dan pulled out a small portable Samsung tablet from his right pants pocket and tapped a few times on the small screen. "I didn't come up with the name. I just play the game."

"And what game is that?"

"The one where we take care of any troubles our customers might have, so you and yours can keep on making money with the crops, free of any future concerns."

"Fair enough. That's a square deal right there. Much obliged."

"Good." The man stared down, tapped on the tablet for a few moments, then returned his gaze to John and Bessie. "As I understand it, you've been having some problems with our Double Trouble Pesticide?"

"Well, yeah, you could say that. More like a small hiccup in production, really. The taters ain't coming out as big as they

Patrick Quinn Kitson

have in years previous. And iffin' our spuds don't come big and plentiful by mid-June, we won't be making the kinda money it takes to keep the lights running 'round here, if you catch my meaning."

"Completely understood, and precisely why I'm here. How long have you been applying our product?"

"Well, we've been having a year over year increase of those pesky little potato beetles coming in."

Mr. Matranga tapped the info into the tablet. "I see. And you've been applying it to all of your crops?"

"The only thing we harvest up here is those potatoes over yonder, but to answer your question, yeah. It's been used on every field we got. We were happy it was both good for killing bugs, but also as an antibacterial agent. Seemed like a damn good combo."

"And what is the exact nature of the infestation you've been using it for?"

"Well, historically we've only ever had to beat back your average garden-variety aphids, and they generally don't require anything that we can't or couldn't handle ourselves. But with the warmer weather rolling over the ridges these last couple years, we've seen a big boom in them beetle buggers and lost a good, well...right around ten percent of our crop last year as a result. And as we like to say around these parts, them ain't no small potatoes."

The man sniffed again and nodded as his digits raced across the tablet's touch screen. "Very clever—funny and quite apropos. These are potato beetles you're speaking of?"

"Right you are, and damn pesky is what they are. When we saw what the early indicators of the weather would be this year, we knew that the number of lost spuds would only grow, iffin' those beetles came back. And *whoo boy*, did they ever."

"Can you roughly estimate what the increase in potato beetles you saw at the outset of the season was? Compared to last year, that is."

John sat back against his saddle to give his lower back some welcome relief. "I can be even more specific than just estimating. When we surveyed the soil a few months back, we figured that we had at least twice as many of the immature ones kicking around the fields. That was around late January. We, or rather I, counted near twice as many as the year previous. And we damn sure can't afford to be losing no twenty percent of the yield this season, I'm tellin' ya. Ten was bad enough, but twenty..." John sat back in the saddle and whistled through his teeth. "I don't mind sayin' that twenty would be devastating for our bottom line, I'm sure you can imagine."

"Indeed I can. A loss such as that would set any farm back more than is reasonable or fiscally tolerable."

"Glad we agree on that."

The man in the navy suit sniffed hard and rubbed his nose, then started to enter the information into the program open on the tablet.

When he said nothing more, John continued, "Anywho, we figured that we'd give your product a try, and damn if we weren't pleased as punch at the early results. Our fields seemed to have been completely vacated of those ugly little bastards by March—right when we started to plant this year's crop. Timing worked out perfectly. And at first, everything seemed to be moving in the right direction. But then, we started to take a peek at the product around late April, and it seems like the spuds are smaller than they should've been by then. Frankly, we know from experience that they weren't growing as large or as fast as we would normally like to see."

"Understood. And let me first allay your concerns by telling you that, while rare, this is not unheard of."

"No?" John sat forward on his saddle, interest piqued.

"No, sir. Naturally, we've seen a few cases of what you're reporting cropping up after using our patented Double Trouble Pesticide."

John's eyes narrowed as he scratched his stubbly chin with his free hand. "So this is a thing you've been seeing with other folks?"

"Correct."

"I don't wanna tell anyone about their business, but shouldn't y'all pull the stuff off the shelves until you know if it's having an adverse effect on people's livelihoods?"

"We're assessing the situation."

"What do you mean you're *assessing the situation*?"

The young man with the dark sunglasses straightened his lapel and shot out his sleeve cuffs. Adjusting one of his cufflinks, he sniffed.

"And why do you keep sniffing like that?"

Dan Matranga wiped at his nose and took another good, long sniffle, then countered, "I'm not sniffing, am I?"

John tilted back his black Stetson and shot the man a curious look. "Yeah, you sure as heck-fire do keep sniffing, city boy."

"I don't believe I am sniffing, Mr. Neezblahnuk. Also, I'm not exactly a boy."

"Okay, alright. Suppose you ain't. But I do think there's a little bit of sniffing going on there." John placed both gloved hands on the home of his saddle and studied the man. Then, as playfully as he could put it, John soft-queried the man. "You, uh—you been getting a little nutty with that white powder or something?"

"Nutty?"

"Yeah man, nutty. Kooky, loopy, twisted, tangled, jacked, shifted, what have you? You know…*nutty.*"

"Nutty how?"

"Nutty how?" John repeated with a snicker. "You know how nutty, buddy. Like you been clearing your sinuses with some of Señor Escobar's chief international export."

Dan stared up at John, shook his head, and frowned. "I'm lost."

John cracked a big-toothed smile. "Well maybe that's because of the cocaine. Maybe that's why you're lost."

Dan lowered the tablet and shot John a cold, unamused stare that surprised him a bit. "Look, sir. I came here today with a purpose. Unless I'm mistaken, you're a man with a serious problem and I'm here to help you out with it. Let's try to keep it professional, okay? Besides, you're not a member of law enforcement, are you?"

John chucked out loud at this. "No, sir, I am not a member of law enforcement. What kind of question is—"

"Well then, by your own admission, you don't need to worry about what I do with my nasal cavities, nor do you need to continue barking up that particular tree. Can we agree on that?"

"Whatever you say, bud. Your funeral if you're a tootin' and toolin' about with the devil dust. But you're right, a man's life is his own to keep. Ain't my brain to toss down the ol' crapper, and I sure ain't no Johnny Law. If you're fixin' to help me mend up this here issue in a jiffy, I won't do much else but thank you kindly."

"I appreciate that. And just for your edification, I don't mix work with pleasure." The rep for Permatox Inc. then promptly sniffed once again.

John briefly studied the other man's eyes. After years of working in the cattle 'n' crop business, as well as chatting with many of his fellow townsfolk, John had realized that he possessed a secondary sense which most of his friends and family simply did not. He knew not of where it came from, but could rely on it just the same as he could his trusty steed, Bessie. It was, in fact, that rare and indefinable ability to spot some ol' bullshit of the verbal variety whenever it drop-plopped out of somebody's lying mouth. And as far as he could figure, this Wall-Street-looking bucko's jaw was dropping dung down in large, stinkin' heaps. Still, he knew he shouldn't point to the pile and hold his nose, so to speak, and thus decided to back off it.

John loosened his look and offered a friendly grin. "Well, of course you don't. My mistake, and I apologize for assuming anything."

"No apology necessary, Mr. Neezblahnuk. No offense taken. I think I know what can help with this issue."

"Yeah?"

"Yes, sir. As I've said, we have seen a few rare cases where the agricultural output of a farm such as yours has been slightly slowed as an unfortunate byproduct of applying Double Trouble Pesticide to specific root vegetables, such as your potato crop here. Rest assured, while we attempt to investigate the cause of this aberration, we have already developed, tested, and adopted a solution that has shown an efficacy of over ninety-nine percent in our trials. To be blunt, we've got a fix for it."

John let out an exhausted sigh of relief. This was exactly what he'd been waiting for the man in the van to lay down for him since he'd first arrived. Really, since reaching out by phone to Permatox and telling them of his troubles. *Here comes the cure,* he thought to himself.

"Whoo! That there's some great news! This thing had me about as worried as a choir boy on a Cub Scout camping trip, I don't mind saying."

"Worry no longer. We got you covered. We have been able to isolate a proprietary chemical in the last year which can immediately nullify the effect of Double Trouble's..." Mr.

Ferris sniffed yet again, then finished, "…aberration. Should help you get back on schedule and make it smooth sailing on into your harvest."

"What is it?"

"Follow me."

Mr. Matranga hurried over toward the vehicle parked in front of the church overlooking the football field of John's well-spent youth. John clicked his mouth to get Bessie moving toward the back of the man's van. Once he was just a few feet away, he hopped off the saddle and tossed the reins over the pommel. Bessie stayed exactly where she'd stopped.

Opening the back door, Dan leaned in and bent over to pull something from the back.

John's excitement at solving the potato problem got the best of him and he couldn't help but ask the door-obscured man, "What's it got in it?"

Unseen, Dan answered, "I'm sure I don't know."

"Then how can you be so sure it's safe? I mean, the other stuff was supposed to be and—" Before he could finish, the man in the navy suit shut the door with one hand, while using the other to put a big four-gallon jug into the rancher's hands. John saw that the name of this novel chemical solution was printed on the side of the large, opaque vessel containing a greenish liquid. In all caps, solid block lettering against the image of a sundowning horizon, it read, *HERBAL WEST.*

"As I said before, the exact makeup of the compound is proprietary, and as such, were I even privy to that sort of information—which I most assuredly am not—I am legally prevented from discussing what the base elements are that make up said chemical composition. Suffice it to say, it is non-toxic, won't hurt any livestock or wildlife that might accidentally graze upon or ingest it, and it is quite effective at its stated purpose."

"Can you at least tell a fella what that stated purpose might be?"

"Certainly. Its functional purpose is to mitigate the slowed or stymied development of agricultural products that have been adversely affected by our patented Double Trouble product line."

"Sounds like a slippery slope of chemical fixes you got us farm-folks sliding down though, don't it?"

Dan smiled, convincingly this time, and whistled breezily. "I reckon so, but it's what we have on tap for what ails ya, pard'ner. And do the trick, it certainly shall."

This last comment surprised John, as it was said with a distinct playfulness and warmth that has been wholly absent from their conversation up to that point. *Maybe,* he thought, *just maybe this guy ain't so bad and stuck up after all. Maybe he's just having a rough day.*

"Well, if it's as good as Grandpa's homemade cough syrup, then it should do just fine for my gurgling gut," John volleyed back with a wink.

Mr. Matranga smiled, then crossed in front of John to head back toward the front of the vehicle. He swiftly opened the passenger door, set the handheld tablet down, and reached between the console and driver's seat to pull out a clipboard.

From the top clip of the board, he slipped out a single black business card and turned to hand it to John.

The son with the green thumb set down the container and took the card in hand, immediately noticing how cold and utilitarian it appeared. No logo, and utterly devoid of any of the normal visual flair or information you'd see on a card of its like. In gunmetal grey over a rectangle of obsidian, and all-caps lettering, it simply read, *Daniel Matranga, Permatox Industries.* Then just below that, a phone number.

"Mr. Neezblahnuk, it's been a pleasure. Directions for dilution and application are on the side of the container, and it should handle up to two hundred and fifty acres. If you need more of this product, or have any more issues, please contact me directly at this number. For future expediency, do not reach out to the home office, nor our distribution center. Just give me a ring and I'll personally handle any questions or concerns you might have."

"Thank you."

The man in the grey suit nodded, closed the passenger door and moved toward the front of the van.

John held up a single finger and asked the departing man, "But, just for my own peace of mind, I really shouldn't have any more questions or concerns though—should I?"

Dan paused for a few seconds, as if considering this question carefully, then, continuing to walk around the front of the black van toward the driver's side door, he called over his shoulder, "Doubtful. Near impossible. But I'm most definitely your first call, should any other developments arise. Your *first call*, just to be clear. Have a good day."

As John took a few small steps back toward his waiting Arabian, he watched the van back out of the dirt lot and come to a stop, then spied the man from Permatox Industries yank a small, powder-filled vial from his pocket. Dan Matranga held it up to his right nostril, pushed the index finger of his other hand against his left nostril and sniffed hard at the container. His eyes blinked rapidly as his face contorted. Then, as he shifted into gear, he turned his head toward John, gave him an emotionless wink of acknowledgement through the passenger side window, and sped off, kicking up a dust cloud as he departed.

John waved away the brown haze, slipped the odd business card into his front shirt pocket, and walked over to where Bessie stood, wildly disinterested in the brief encounter between the two men. He patted her mane and muzzle softly. "Creepy guy, that'n? Don't cha think?"

Bessie whinnied lightly, but said nothing. For how could she?

She's a horse.

————··◁◇▷··————

Several weeks later, everything seemed back on track. The crops sized up in a matter of days, resuming their natural growth pattern, while the bugs remained out sight, and therefore, out of John's now contented mind.

On a particularly starless night, when the moonshine off the fields was much lower than it normally would've been, he was riding Bessie to watch his Roaring Fork Rams take on the Glenwood Springs Demons when he was struck by an odd sight along the way. Despite the failing light, he thought he could see the slightest of greenish glows coming from the ground around where the potatoes were planted. However, given the oddness of the sight itself—combined with the fact that he'd been slowly sipping on a 750 of Johnny Walker Blue for a few hours—he wasn't sure that he should fully trust everything his eyes were seeing.

The Rams went on to beat the Demons deftly, and by the end of the game, any glow he thought he'd seen earlier had disappeared from the fields.

The next evening, he came back, and much to his relief, there was nothing like the eerie glimmer of the night previous to be seen. Just his spuds, doing what they did until the harvest came the following month. He thought himself silly, and quickly chalked it up to a simple trick of the light. Though how such a disquieting sight might've been achieved escaped him entirely.

But that wasn't the only thing that stuck in his craw following the visit from Permatox Industries.

In the days following, he noticed an increasing buzzing sound emanating from the fields carrying his family's signature breed of potatoes. A small symphony of humming at first, like you'd hear a mess of crickets make during their mating season, began to increase a little each day. By the third sundown, the sound had swelled into a high-pitched chorus of buggy mania.

Curiously though, on the fourth day, when he set about checking the fields for the potato beetles he was worried had come back with vengeance, he found nothing of the sort. The sound had completely ceased, and he couldn't find any trace of the beetles. Nor that of any other bugs that one would commonly see in a shovelful of dirt, for that matter. All he found was the odd, torn apart carapace or crushed exoskeleton of a creepy critter peppering the mineral rich soil.

But taking himself a closer look, he noticed a strange thing, indeed. It was as if those dead bug bodies he'd found had been ripped up by some unknown attacker, and left discarded. Generally, if something got to a bug, there was little trace left, as the assailant was usually predatory and would consume the body of the bug whole. Birds and small creatures would slurp up critters by the beak full, but they sure didn't leave anything afterwards. Yet this, tearing a bug up without swallowing it, was a horse of a different color. Certainly nothing he'd ever seen—and he'd seen quite a bit in his ten years as the de facto head of the spud harvest.

Still, despite these odd occurrences, the potatoes continued to grow on schedule, and by the time the harvest neared, they were actually a bit larger than usual. He supposed that Daniel Matranga's mystery solution played a role. When he tested a few in the small lab he'd set up in one of the hay barns, they seemed absent any odd genetic markers or cause for concern. Just a bit bigger. All that meant for the family was more money.

The spud harvest came and proceeded as smoothly as ever.

His family's particular breed of tater (a slight cross variant on the more well known "Red McClure" of state-wide notoriety) was a key ingredient in the many dishes served up at the annual Potato Days Celebration in Carbondale. A three-day agricultural festival that was in its 116th year, the run-up to eponymous parade, as well as the ensuing days of starchy revelry, saw the town's spirits as high as any year previous.

Each year, the Neezblahnuk family farm always set aside one large shipment of spuds for use by the residents of the town during said festivities. Said denizens would use them to make all matter of tasty tuber treats, including but not limited to: pulled pork and potato pie, potato stew, potato slaw, crispy kettle chips, bacon bit potato cakes, fresh salted french fries, garlic and rosemary mashed potatoes, tapioca-tinged far far, marinated croquettes, gnocchi pasta, fried fritter rolls, potatoes au gratin, to say nothing of beer-battered baked potato bonanzas.

People often spent the weeks following the event losing the weight they put on during it. Local gym memberships surged and grocery sales took a small, but noticeable hit as many took to fasting in a vainglorious attempt to stabilize their respective body fat indexes. Then after a month or so, the gym's would empty and the stores would get back to pre-parade levels. The local economy was all the better for it.

Two days before the festivities were set to commence, and while loading a large truck bed affixed with custom wood paneling, which created high sides to provide more space for the Potato Days spuds, John caught sight of yet another odd thing. Several black crows, standing in a row on the top wire of the fence outlying the southern side of his field between the church and Hillcrest Cemetery, were cawing loudly at something which had transfixed all their collective attention.

John paused his potato tossing and pulled off his yellow gloves. He stuffed them into his back pocket as he approached the fence line. Noting his motion behind them, the ten or so fan-tailed fowl began to take flight, but before the final straggler could depart, a small furry creature leapt up and grabbed into the bird. Tumbling about like a shoot fighter taking down an opponent, it dragged the unlucky crow onto the ground while the bird screeched and yowled.

At first glance, he thought it might be a fox or particularly nimble raccoon that had initiated the attack. But as he closed in on the wire fencing surrounding his field, he saw that it was a rather grotesque, overly large rodent tearing the bird to pieces with its claws. Feathers and blood shot up in a flurried frenzy of animalian violence, and he nearly stumbled backward at the wretched sight.

Horrified, he rushed to where his truck was parked twenty feet away and pulled out a three-foot-long potato fork from the bed. Hastily returning to where the attack was happening, he heard the bird go silent, instead replaced by a guttural snarling coming from the quadrupedal oddity on the ground.

Patrick Quinn Kitson

Stepping forward and looking down, his eyes beheld a giant rat—its limbs emaciated and oddly misshapen, its bloodied maw contorted, and its fur-patched husk of a body riddled with jagged holes that oozed out glowing greenish puss. The same sort of dull green he'd seen in the fields a couple months prior.

Slamming the tines of the fork down, he pierced through the ugly bastard in one fell swoop. Its mutated body went rigid from the impact, but did not stop squirming and grunting out air in wispy tufts. Surprised, John withdrew the fork and stabbed down again, this time landing along the animal's skull and neck.

It immediately went limp.

John whistled between his teeth. After a long moment of nervously waiting for it to move again, he cautiously raised it up and studied the creature on the end of his potato fork. As he looked at it under the bright midday sun, glowing green fluid seeped from its injuries and dropped down onto the dry ground. The thing looked already dead, as though it had been killed weeks ago—its eyes the same milky white that you'd see in roadkill after a few days. And yet, he'd just seen it bearing down on the unfortunate crow.

Disgusted and confused, he shook the farm tool until the carcass slid off the end of the piercing tines. It plopped onto the ground next to the largely decimated and ripped up bird. Then, as if on cue, the corpse of the crow began to wriggle and its broken wings extended. It could not right itself, but flopped around on the grassy field floor, seeking purchase with his damaged physical frame. The thing's beak opened and let out a guttural wretch, similar to the one he'd heard from the seemingly long-dead rodent.

He stared in complete disbelief as it rolled to one side, revealing a gash where its internal organs had slid out and lay in a pink pile. John damn well knew this thing should be dead as a doornail, and was surprised when he reflexively slammed the fork down a third time, crushing the bird's skull in one well-timed strike.

It ceased all motion and lay as dead as he had thought it was before it began to flutter about.

John let go of the wooden handle and took a few furtive steps back, wondering what could be happening. Wondering if whatever he had just seen was related to all the half-devoured insect carcasses he'd been seeing. Wondering if the man in the suit from Permatox has given him a whole new thing to worry about in the days before the annual Potato Days celebration.

Wondering what in the formula for Herbal West might account for bringing seemingly dead things back to life.

Then, as the sun shone down on his hayseed hair, his eyes slowly moved over to the tombstones and markers of nearby Hillcrest Cemetery, along the western side of his potato fields.

And he had a feeling that whatever the trouble, it might not yet be over.

FLICKER

For fifty four years (as of 2025), the annual Mountain Fair in Carbondale, Colorado has served as a colorful, cross-cultural, sometimes chemically fueled vortex of cacophonic camaraderie. Swirling with local creativity and artful expression, exploding with the effervescent energy of youth unbound, and booming with bustling booths of bewitchingly Bohemian bacchanalia, it's the defining event of the year for the town's dancing denizens.

Dispensing with reckless abandon the trappings of the daily drudge that too-often consume and control the lives of its attendees, the fair offers something for everyone. Sizzling meats flavor the air while liquid libations flow freely amid the pulse of musical revelry. Contests and costumes and continuous commotion. Wood splitting, artisanal pottery, tie-dyed anything, children in glitter-specked face paints, flowing dresses, stylishly curated cowboy hats, flashing lights, and crunchy popcorn with sweet and sour lemonade to wash it down.

Folk, bluegrass, rock 'n' roll, country, and a fair dollop of experimental music provide the soundtrack for a weekend filled with endless star-dotted nights and three utterly glory-filled days. All of it with an ever-present tapestry of happy human faces representing all walks and talks of life.

This is to say nothing of the hidden gems and shadow events within the larger festival. The backyard afterparties. The horseshoe hangouts with Grey Goose and sticky-icky Bubba Kush in hand. The barbecues, bar-binges, and beer-battered bashes. Or maybe even an offering or two for the truly adventurous. Something like the moonlit, butt-naked bike ride on Friday night. That particular one sees a hundred-plus of Bonedale's most daring and intrepid revelers stripping down to their birthday suits, hopping on their favorite glow-light adorned bikes, and making a nude sojourn through the heart of the town while giving all onlookers and passers-by a sight they won't soon forget. Star-dappled, naked flesh upon which the eyes desire to feast.

Naturally, the cops do nothing to stop it. Nudity, unofficially allowed for this brief moment during the year in Carbondale, Colorado, only causes the town's police to smile and wave as they pass by—eternally bemused by the spirit of the unclothed youth. For who are they to complain?

You really must see it for yourself.

Still, as with all things, the Mountain Fair remains eternally in cultural flux. Times are always changing, and so with those times, the face of the yearly party. Nowadays, local folks would be pained, possibly even remiss, to admit that for a great many of its attendees in the seventies and eighties, the fair served as little more than a three-day-long excuse to get utterly wasted on any and all drugs one could reasonably procure for said event. Sheets of acid, handfuls of barbiturates, bullets full of uncut Colombian snow, pinner-joints twisted up with Paonia Purple, and gallons upon gallons of homemade alcoholic offerings were the coin of the realm for many in the event's heyday.

This undercurrent of orgiastic chemical consumption often left the growing event with two problematic by-products. The first, a smattering of well-meaning folks getting drug-lost in the swarming crowds and oft falling into unfortunate bad trips that required a safe haven for one to compose oneself and get back into the psychic swing of things.

And the second, the children of those harder partiers getting separated from their parents and needing a place to hang out until their caretakers came around to finding them. Hence, the Lost People's Booth was breathed into existence by the event's organizers. To help the druggies cool off, and to help kids reunite with their parental custodians.

The unlikely combination made for quite the sight. Hopped up hippies, tripping their balls off yet gleefully playing with the same toys and trinkets that the lost kids used to distract themselves until their moms and dads came a-calling. Multi-colored drinks and fresh fruit to keep everyone's blood sugar stable while they waited for their collective salvation.

It may sound strange, but the tripped-out attendees and freaked-out adolescents made for oddly complimentary company. Parents would arrive, and the joy the children expressed at reuniting with their family would provide emotionally uplifting scenes that often broke the bad-trip set out of their bush-brained, drug-fueled mental stupor.

The fair is like that though; magic moments that only a few might bear witness to, but mean so much to those who do.

I know of the booth because it was my father who was a key figure in the setup and maintenance of it for nearly a decade. And with him, I volunteered many years to help with the day-to-day operations thereof.

And it's where this story really begins.

The fair. The fair! Oh yay, the fair. So many faces, so many stories, and so many fading memories. Still, amid the cloud of constant communalism, there were those in the populace who made names for themselves. These fabled folks may have been small fish in a small-town pond by any other measure, yet nonetheless attained legendary status within the annals of local lore. Some known for their guidance with keeping the ever-growing fair tied to its hippie dippy roots, others known for their continual contribution to the festival's ever-beating heart that continuously grows from season to season.

One such man still walks within the rows of familiar faces to this day. A golden god amongst the mere mortals. A deified Dionysus of the hometown festival. If you've been to the fair, you've likely seen him before. He wears no shirt, but always has on a pair of dark blue jeans and open-toed sandals. His skin is deeply tanned. His hair, a long, flowing brown mane that shimmers in the summer sun. And upon his face, a thick yet well-kept walrus mustache that seems straight out of another time. Tucked under that 'stache, an ear-to-ear smile that warms the soul and offers a reminder that the best times may yet indeed lay ahead.

I came to know him as Shirtless Terry. A local legend, to be sure.

When I first saw him, he appeared as any other of the latter-day hippies, cruising the crowds during the annual fair. A friend of my father's, we would sometimes travel up to his forest-dwelling house throughout the year. A tree-hugged cabin somewhere up in the woods surrounding the town proper, though I know not precisely where, as at that age, spatial reasoning and relation were still somewhat of an esoteric construct. It was where my dad and he would crack a few brews and turn on the Hendrix while I ran around his backyard which bled into the surrounding forest. My father would smoke cigarettes, and Shirtless Terry would smoke joints. And I would find oddly shaped sticks that became protective relics imbued with untold power with which to fight off the various beasts that flooded my imagination while I ran through the needle-dropping trees.

Years later, my father, Ed, confided that Terry was, by all accounts, the veritable psychedelic Pablo Escobar of his day. While mythic writer of global renown, Hunter S. Thompson, historically held the undisputed title of de facto valley drug user firmly within his trigger-happy grasp, the crown of de facto valley drug peddler in those days rested comfortably upon Shirtless Terry's head of long brown hair.

When the annual Mountain Fair rolled around, he would occasionally swing by the booth as he made his rounds.

Still mysterious to me was the means by which he transported his wares, as he was only ever wearing the aforementioned blue jeans and sandals. So he must've had some stashed nearby from which he filled his many customers' orders.

Apparently there was no drug too exotic or rare to procure from the man with the walrus mustache.

Though absent any understanding of what my ears were taking in at the time, I'd overheard his sales pitch to prospective clients on a number of occasions throughout the years. My child-mind recalling the notes, but wholly-absent any intellectual context. These pitches usually happened while I was cleaning up squishy pillows or pouring Solo cups of lemonade for the misplaced children to drink while they awaited their parents' not-always-so-swift returns.

Years later, I understood that he was about as popular as one man can be in the microcosmic subculture of the Roaring Fork Valley. As such, people were always happy to make his acquaintance and even happier once he'd hooked them up with some of his signature wares. Yet it seemed that he was largely locally famous for one special party favor that the residents of Carbondale so readily craved, and only he could provide them.

Peyote.

Petōtl to the Nahuatl peoples of southern Mexico, *Hukuri* to the Huichol peoples of Jalisco and Durango, and *Patecatl* to the Mesoamerican Aztecs of Tenochtitlan. And ol' Shirtless Terry had that good shit, apparently.

He certainly didn't mince words about the quality of his goods when making solicitous spiels to his many customers. Usually it went something like this:

"These buttons right here are special, I'm telling you that. These buttons I brandish today are, quite simply, the purest way to pull at the brittle strings connecting all living things and tethering our otherwise free-flowing energy into a semi-grounded state. That polymorphic prism through which we view our own fleeting existence." All said with that signature grin of his.

Followed most commonly by a glance of suspicion mixed with excitement from the maybe-buyer, as they would then inquire, "Well, that's all well and good, but what are they exactly?"

"A tripped-out, toe-tapping tapestry of Technicolor transcendence."

"So, it's a drug?"

"Okay, yeah, sure—it's a drug. *Lophophora Williamsii* specifically."

"Buttons… You do mean Peyote, right?"

"If forced into the most banal of layman's terms, then yes, indeed. That is what we are speaking of."

"Are they safe?"

"Is anything in this life?"

"I mean, I won't have a freak out or anything if I try them, will I?"

And Terry would again offer up his starshine smile, proceeding to swiftly allay their concerns. "Well, I can't assure you that they won't demolish your preconceived notions of reality and your place within the universe, but I've yet to have anyone go to the hospital, if that's what you're asking."

"That's what I'm asking."

"Yes, they're safe."

"Sounds groovy. I'll take enough for ten people."

A clandestine deal was then quickly struck. The purchaser of said potables off to mind-bend through the fair while the man with the plan tended to other customers.

Rumor even had it that Shirtless Terry would endeavor to bake some sort of peyote pie for his most loyal of customers—though one could not begin to speculate upon its composition, other than to say it was a pie, and it had peyote in it.

This was his most cherished and sought after offering to the vibe of the party, what most would call peyote, though the active chemical is in fact mescaline. Several other cacti subspecies possess notable concentrations of said psychoactive chemical, but none as high as that of the famed peyote cacti.

In the late nineties, my dad gifted me copies of both *The Doors of Perception* by Aldous Huxley, as well as *The Teachings of Don Juan* by Carlos Castaneda. I never asked him why he provided me with them, though it's safe to assume that some part of him had a longing to impart some wisdom onto me via the two most well-known books dealing with philosophical drug usage by two of the most well-known psychonauts. It was upon reading said tomes of psychotropic knowledge that I finally understood the power and importance of the wares which Terry was so readily hocking to the hordes of Valley drug users.

For years, everything was busy, and blissful, and beautiful. Mountain Fairs came, and Mountain Fairs went. Then the fateful summer of 1991 rolled around, and everything changed.

That's the year that the travelers begin to come through the veil, so to speak. And it was the last year of the Lost People's booth. Such days one can recall as though they were yesterday.

The booth itself was, in point of fact, hardly that. Instead of a fabric envelope encasing a simple tabletop supporting artists potables and a register, it was an octagonal structure made up from dozens of wooden beams connected by circular star bracings. Wrapped tightly over this spherical construct lay what most would describe as a multicolored tarpaulin, giving the whole thing the apropos flavor of a small hippie commune dwelling. A Technicolor tent made of, by, and for the love generation—not entirely dissimilar from those cheeky parachutes kids of the eighties and nineties used to play with in Phys. Ed.

I was doing my usual thing in those bygone and much storied days, hanging out in the booth with my parents and their friends while doling out fruit and juices to the trippers and toddlers awaiting their respective salvations. My parents were—as was the case with so many others of that time and paternal mindset—somewhat lax about the way in which they conducted their fair assignments. As such, I would sometimes find myself sitting around and keeping an eye on the booth by myself for handfuls of time. Not for too long, but occasionally they'd go get some beers, and unless someone was with me, I'd be there—just eight years old, holding down the fort.

Early on the second day of the 1991 fair, the first traveler appeared before me.

So many things like this are somewhat hard to form into a cohesive account of what actually happened. Memory is often dabbled and disrupted with the passage of time. But I do know this: One minute I was there alone, then the next, an almost imperceptible shift in the focus of the air around mixed with high pitched buzzing sound and *BOOM*, I was alone no longer.

A man—short, rugged, grey-haired, and dirty with tie-dyed regalia and a frightened look upon his bearded face—was standing over by the fruit basket. Startled and mayhaps a bit spooked, his eyes cast about in a fuzzed-out search for mental tethering. He scanned the surroundings—the throw pillows, the rainbow tarpaulin—then landed his gaze upon me.

I was, as he, mostly confused by the moment. So I struck up the first line of our parlay. Taking a step toward him and holding my palms up in a sign of friendliness, I asked, "Where did you come from?"

His glazed-over look locked into the here and now, then took a full accounting of me before he softly spoke, "I-I, uh… I was in front of the stage. I remember…being there, and I could see the music rolling out in waves toward me. I thought I was finally reaching some heretofore undiscovered peak of spiritual enlightenment, but then there was this awesome flash of light. Albeit a terribly brief one. So brief. So dashing. Like a flicker. I was there, and now…I'm here."

"Sounds fun."

His eyes resumed casting about the fair and attendees with a cocked eyebrow. He closed the distance between us and asked, "Why does everything look so strange? What…what is all of this?"

"It's the Mountain Fair. You must have gotten lost in the crowd and ended up here. Luckily, that's what the booth is for."

"For what?"

I pointed up at the hand-painted wooden sign hung loosely from one of the support beams above our heads. "This is the Lost People's Booth."

Dazed and glazed, he wonderingly gazed up at the sign and echoed, "The Lost People's Booth?"

"Yep."

"What year is this?"

"It's 1991."

"No, it isn't."

"Yes, it is."

"It can't be."

"Well, unless I'm mistaken…"

"Wait. Are you— Isn't it 1978?"

"Nope. Hasn't been for, well…" A small pause while I did the math in my head. "Thirteen years, I guess."

And when that rugged man looked into my unlying child's eyes, he knew that my words, combined with the difference in clothing and culture surrounding him on all sides, might just not be chock full of horse pucky. He knew that I meant what I said.

Suddenly, a flash of fear mixed with wonder crossed his stubble-strewn face. "It can't be 1991. It's 1978."

"Yes it can, and no it isn't."

"How in the jumped up Jehoshaphat is that even possible?"

I shrugged. "Probably because you just got a bit confused. Do you want some fruit?"

At this, he finally chuckled. "Fruit?"

"Yeah. Fruit. We got some apples and some oranges and more than a few grapes in the bowl over there. We also have some grape punch and I think a few granola bars left."

"You're serious, aren't you?"

"As serious as I'm allowed to be with a grown-up who thinks they've time-travelled over to the kiddie booth by the pool."

"This is really 1991?"

"Yes. Do you want me to grab you an orange?"

He shook his head, rubbed his eyes, then sighed loudly. "Uh, yeah. Sure, I could use some Vitamin C."

"Okay." I stepped past him, walked over to the small foldable table on one side of the dome structure, and snatched the fruit of choice from our big wooden bowl. Yet when I turned back to hand it to the man with the stubble and out-of-time clothing, he was gone.

Just as suddenly he had arrived, he was gone without a trace.

Yet he was only the first of many. Over the course of those three strange days in 1991, no less than eight other travelers showed up to visit the booth. Sometimes they would arrive when others were around, and a few more when I was alone. And the conversations usually went much as it did with the first gentleman.

The second person to flicker in was just an hour or two later. A shapely, dare I even say buxom woman in her forties wearing a flower-patterned dress, with long blonde hair tied up in a ponytail that hung down to below her knees.

My father's friend's daughter—a loud hoot of an older teenage girl named Rhody Donahue—had joined me and taken the lead on keeping the kids corralled with distracting toys and huge body pillows to lounge on.

I was mixing more grape juice from concentrate when I felt the same shift in the air nearby, only to turn around and see the arriving woman twirling on her toes, her wispy white and turquoise-hued dress spinning like a top. Her arms were out and her fingers were tickling the air around her. As she came to a stop, her eyes met mine and she gave me a severe look of fright.

Rhody passively noticed her arrival as well, but assumed that she had just appeared by way of wandering over from the center of the fair.

The woman stood silent for a good ten seconds before she narrowed her eyes and whispered at us, "Who are you guys?"

Rhody scoffed playfully. "We work here. It's our humble charge to keep the place running while the adults are away. Also we dole out the juice and distractions."

"Distractions? Juice? I don't get it. What just happened?"

I allowed Rhody to continue the convo without interjecting. "What do you mean?" she asked.

The woman shuddered and her eyes rolled in her head. "I was dancing under the moon with my ladies, but now it's day. It was night, now it's day. How did that happen?"

" I dunno. Did you take something?"

"That's a strange thing to ask, isn't it?"

"Maybe, maybe not. Some people end up here purely as a result of heavy drug intake, others are just bored and wander-y. Are you feeling okay? Would you like something to drink?"

Patrick Quinn Kitson

Ignoring Rhody's line of inquiry, the traveler rambled on, "And, I mean, you guys are sorta strange. Your clothes are funny. Funny *odd* more than funny *ha ha*. They just look strange."

"Well, you know what they say…people are strange when you're a stranger."

The woman's hands came together in a loud clap. "Hah! That's good! I love that song. Great jam, that one. Morrison was such a poet, wasn't he? I mean— But wait a second…does that mean I'm the stranger here?"

"Not anymore. Not now that you have arrived. My name is Rhody and this mute little pipsqueak is Patrick." She nudged me in the shoulder with hers like the big sister she sorta-kinda was to me.

I smiled and nudged her back, hoping she could make more sense of the sitch than I had thus far.

The woman, as so many of them were prone to doing, rubbed at her head. "Oh. That's…well, that's strange, 'cause I just don't know how I got here. You guys are real though, right? You look real. Strange, but real. Because I must confess that I just might have taken in some bodaciously strong party favors and I'm still not entirely believing this is real. But you are real, aren't ya?"

"Real as the sun that shines down upon your face." Rhody offered a kindly smile, which the woman met with her own.

My older compatriot took the initiative and trotted over to the fruit bowl to snatch up some grapes. But as she did, the hum-buzz and air shift occurred, and I spied the woman in the dress evaporate before my eyes. I was shocked that no one else nearby seemed to notice.

Turning around, Rhody saw she was gone and frowned. "Shoot. I guess I must have freaked her out."

"I don't think it was you. She disappeared into the past, I think."

"Hah! Right, Pat. Right. That's what happened. Sure." She sauntered over and patted my shaggy-haired head patronizingly. Her eyes narrowed. "You weren't munching on mushroom caps while I was away getting that pizza slice from Peppino's earlier, were you?"

And at my tender age, I was genuinely confused by this question. "I hate mushrooms. They taste totally gross. What would mushrooms have to do with it, anyway?"

"Never mind. You'll know when you're older and much, much wiser."

This turned out to be a comically prescient thing for her to have randomly tossed out there, as by the late nineties, I had taken to buying up a few ounces of Liberty Caps from a hippie friend named Kevin, and did my own rounds of selling hallucinogenics to the revelers at the local fair.

But that's a whole other story, right there.

There were a few others who showed up over the next twenty-four hours. All just as confused, and all just as existentially fleeting.

I wasn't alone when the last traveler arrived and departed in a matter of minutes. This was in the late afternoon of the final day.

As I recall, the final flicker was a tall, dark-haired, and likewise bearded man named Russell Ellis. He wore parachute pants and a tight white Doobie Brothers T-shirt. Most of them came and went before I could get their name, but I did catch his. And this one also stuck out on account of the fact that his was a name I vaguely recognized, as well as the fact that he seemed to take the whole thing in stride more than the average, I dunno...chrono-visitor, let's say.

The only other person present with me during that final visitation was a young girl who had shown up a few minutes prior and who was busy playing with some of the Lincoln Logs we had in a bin next to the pillow pile.

As the air trembled, buzzed, and blurred for the briefest of moments, the man came jumping into the booth from thin air. The young girl looked up, somewhat startled by his airborne arrival. She had seen him appear from nothing as well.

As he deftly landed on both feet, he immediately rose up and addressed me. "Yo! What was that? Where is everyone? I thought the crowd would catch me for sure!"

"The crowd?" I asked.

"Yeah, man. The crowd. The crowd in the, uh, audience. I thought I was gonna surf the crowd. Cuz, you know man, I was on the stage."

"The stage?"

"Yeah." His eyes did a rapid scan of the area. "The stage on the other side of the park, over there. At least I think I was. No, I was. Me and my lady were on the stage. I know we were. And I was tripping my mind off. Riding the wave, and riding it hard. I was riding the flow of the energy piping from those double stack Marshall speakers. And the music was so groovy, man. So good and so pure that I was up on the stage, feeling out the vibes and having a jazzy ol' time. That's when I told Michelle to hold my beer while I stage dove. She was laughing. We both were. And I dived, or I guess I dove off. But then…"
He trailed off, rubbing his face and eyes, as if to scrub away the reality in which he now found himself. His hands waved in front of his face and went wide.

"You were with the band?" I chuckled softly whilst nibbling on a Ritz cracker.

"No way! I couldn't have played an instrument in this condition! I could barely keep my legs under me. I was all tripped out and mind-slushy. Still am, honestly."

Having figured out the basic essence of what was occurring by that point, I flatly replied, "You came here from several years ago. When you took off, it was 1978, but you landed in 1991. The year is 1991. I don't think you'll be here very long, but I promise you, it's true. Would you like an orange?"

"Whoa, whoa! Dial it back, little buddy. That's some hectic hoopla you're laying down right there, bud!" A trace of recognition crossed his wild, wandering eyes. "Don't I know you?"

"You probably know my parents." Because back then, everyone knew my parents. Everyone knew everyone, really. Small towns and all that.

"What's your name?"

"My name is Patrick. What's yours?"

"Russell. Russell Ellis. Are you serious about the stuff you're spoutin'?"

"Totally. And it's okay, you'll be back in your own year soon enough, if past is prologue. And to that end, if you do happen to see my parents when you get back, try not to do anything to stop them from having me."

I had recently seen *Back to the Future* and seemingly taken its underlying messages as both instructive, as well as quite literal.

"Dude, you are blowing my mind." He looked around and, as so many did before him, asked the obvious question. "Why does everything look so different? Everyone's dressed differently. And what are those cars over there? They look so odd."

I followed his pointing finger toward the nearby parked cars that surrounded Sopris Park on all sides.

"They're just normal cars and trucks. But new ones. Those are nineties cars."

"For real?"

I patted my sternum, then made an X sign on my chest. "Cross my heart and hope to die."

He waved his hands in front of his eyes for a moment, then closed them as his face grew more serious. "Okay then, future boy, if this is really 1991, then who's the president?"

"The new one is a guy named George Bush."

"George Bush? That's—" He slapped one knee and giggled loudly. "Damn, dude. Hot diggity damn. That's just…way too damn trippy. And I'm not sure I can handle this sorta mind-warpy weirdness. I might need to sit down for a second. Who are your parents?"

But before I could respond, the flicker took hold again. As a flash of sunlight passed by, the outline of his body evaporated before my eyes. Well, our eyes. For when I looked over at the six year old sitting a few feet away, I could tell that she had seen it all as well.

The kid with me, incidentally another daughter of my parents' friends, and one who I would eventually attend school with named Lexi Crawford, looked up at me with wide, curious eyes and asked, "Did you see that man disappear?"

"Yes. Yes I did."

And in a surprisingly mature assessment of the situation, she said matter of factly, "Well now there's something you don't see every day."

I couldn't help but smile. "You got that right."

"Wow. Weird." She stacked another cross section onto the little Lincoln logs cabin she'd been working on. "When do you think my mom will be back?"

"Karen is around here somewhere, no doubt. She'll be by soon, I promise."

And Lexi seemed to swiftly dismiss and discard the oddness of the moment as she shot the fruit bowl a cursory glance. "Can I have an orange?"

"Sure you can." And with that, I finally got to get somebody an orange.

Her mom came over a few minutes later to carry her off to the fair proper.

After that, I never again saw the travelers. It seemed to have been a supernatural splash in the pan that ended randomly, and without further incident.

Still, one thing stuck with me and began turning around in my mind in the years that followed. Much like the hot meats hanging from the spits of the various food vendors that the fair employed.

All the travelers seemed to have blinked into our current time from the year 1978. That much I knew, but could not understand why. That is, until many years later when I asked my dad if there was anything unique about that particular year.

He first said he could think of anything too important, aside from it being the year that Dire Straits released "Sultans of Swing" from their eponymous first album. Pressed more, he acknowledged that—*oh yeah*—it was the same year that blessed the world with John Carpenter's "Halloween" as well as Cheech and Chong's "Up In Smoke"(Pops was never short on random bits of pop culture esoterica). But after another moment of crinkle-browed recollection, he finally landed on the one local thing relating to the fair that he could recall, snapping his fingers as it came back to him.

"Well, not that this is neither here nor there, but, that was the year of the Sandoz Purple."

Curiosity piqued, I asked, "What is Sandoz Purple?"

"What *was* Sandoz Purple, you mean."

"Okay, yeah. That."

Smiling at the wistful memories of yore, he recalled that, "It is—or was—a now-extinct form of LSD that was developed by Sandoz Pharmaceuticals in the 1950s. The very same acid that the CIA employed during those sketchy MK Ultra tests on troops they conducted in the sixties. All the early trip-troopers took it. Jerry Garcia, Tom Wolfe, Albert Hoffman, Tim Leary, to say nothing of Ken Kelsey and his Merry Band of Pranksters. That Jimmy Hendricks song, "Purple Haze" is about Sandoz Purple, actually. The Grateful Dead used to keep boxes of it on the tour bus for easy access, and the story goes that the guy who designed their skull logo was supposedly on Sandoz Purple when he drew forth his inspiration for it. Course, once the government took to its performative disliking of the drug and scheduled it back in 1965, Sandoz Pharmaceuticals stopped production entirely."

"Okay. But if they stopped making it in 1965, what does it have to do with Carbondale in 1978?"

"Because several people knew that the ban was coming down the pipe and stockpiled cases of it. It was purchased in these little lab-sealed ampules that could be frozen for many years without significant degradation of the chemical. However, by the late seventies, even those lurking in the freezers of the former hippie guilds were rapidly losing potency, so those who still had it were set on cleaning out their respective reserves thereof. All hands on deck was the bygone ethos of that particular year. We were going through the very last of the very best acid to ever grace the neocortex of the common man."

"It was the best acid ever?"

His eyes closed and shudder ran up his back as he recalled wistfully, "Oh yes, it was, son. Yes indeed."

"So you did some for yourself?"

"Damn straight I did. Quite a bit, truth be told. Tell ya, 1969 was quite a blur because of that bygone blend. It was the legit shit, yes sir. No doubt about it. Beyond any reasonable comparison with the bathtub-grade stuff that soon followed. Me and the other weirdos in town used to drive up Thompson Creek to camp overnight, and when we did, we rocked out to Credence and dropped ol' Sandoz like it was going out of style."

"It was really that good?"

"Oh *yeah*. It was the tip-top of the crop. Not a thing ever came close to it."

"So, okay, but you still haven't told me—why 1978? Why do you call it the year of the Sandoz Purple?"

"Because one local guy had several vials left and had made it a point to offload the last of it during that fateful summer of '78."

And before he could confirm it, I suspected I knew the dude who had done so. "Shirtless Terry was the guy with the good shit, wasn't he, Pops?" I asked.

"Of course it was Terry. Shit, who else? Most of us hadn't seen Sandoz for years, and when Terry arrived at the fair that year, he made shockwaves with the news that he was still holding over a thousand doses." Then, after a moment of silence, as if to wrap up the story up into a neat little bow, he mused that, "People would mix and match drugs like crazy back then, you know. It was a different time. I vaguely remember that some of the folks who took it that year got so blitzed out that they claimed to have travelled ahead in time some years to a future version of the fair, if you can believe it."

"I can. Believe it, I mean."

And I could. I could easily believe it, because that was the proverbial nail gettin' hit straight upon its psychedelic head in my book. The dots seemed to finally connect.

In hindsight, I lack sufficient empirical evidence to make a determination one way or the other about this forthcoming conclusion, certainly not enough to say for sure that this was the case. But still, it seems likely (and remains my ardent belief) that the combination of the usual peyote buttons Terry was slinging in conjunction with the mythical Sandoz he had been peddling that particular year was responsible for making a, uh, *condition* of sorts, by which people were somehow able to... Well, I guess I'll just say it: travel into the future, then back again.

Just like Marty McFly.

And I know how that sounds. Believe me, I get the silliness it endears to speak of such seemingly ludicrous things.

Which is precisely why I never told anyone, not even my father, about the travelers. Until this moment right here.

Who knows why these things happen? And when they do, what do they mean? I'm still not sure if there's any kinda moral or point to glean from its telling, even now. Other than to remind those who might read this of those rare, magic moments that few ever bear witness to. Those sacred artifacts of knowledge that only one person ever learns. I was the only one who knew about what happened, until today. Whatever the purpose, it's out on the table now, for better or worse. And I'm glad.

I've never met a ghost, never seen a UFO, never stumbled upon a cryptid, never found God, and never had an out-of-body experience or any other such supernatural shenanigans, to speak of. But I did see those festival fellows fade in and out of our time-fabric a few times, by golly. I *did* see that shit, up close and personally, in fact. And I'm happy I did. Because it made me a believer in the absence of things hoped for, and the evidence of things not seen. Maybe our brief time together made some difference in the future, or maybe it had no effect at all.

Today, if you seek out the foundational fair's fortune-filled festivities, you might catch sight of ol' Shirtless Terry striding about in the hustle and bustle of the crowd. He doesn't sling mind-benders like he used to, but he does have a weekly Hold-'em game down at The Black Nugget on Tuesday nights. If you see him, say hello and be sure to thank him for the lost memories.

Over at the fair, you're sure to encounter all the usual revelry in full swing. All the fixtures that make it the pure and beautiful thing it always has been. But one thing that you won't see any more is the Lost People's Booth. Now, some old-timers will tell you that the booth had served its purpose, and that its retirement was ultimately reflective of changing attitudes about both parental supervision and the tolerance of wild drug usage among the proletariat. Still others would have you believe that its absence from the last twenty years of festivities was the result of a maturation of the population. Or mayhaps a mixture of both.

Perhaps it's just like anything else. Gone without much reason.

So now the booth, too, is lost to time. Flickering out and away from our collective memories, just as the snow melts from the rugged peaks surrounding the town proper. Trickling between the cracks of our community and coalescing into the rivers of our forgotten histories.

The booth may be gone, but the vibrant spirit of the Mountain Fair moves ahead, unabated.

Every year in July, that's where you'll find me, at the same park where my grandfather used to sell homemade fishing rods back in the early seventies. Where my father dutifully set up and co-managed the Lost People's Booth in the latter half of the eighties. And where I now sell my speculative version of the town's histories to the raucous revelers and ravenous readers of every stripe.

That special place where the heart and soul of Carbondale burns as bright as a thousand distant stars, exploding cosmic life into the collective consciousness until it too flickers into the vast, veiled time fog of our universe.

RELATIVISM

An eldritch moon of dark blue hue cast a spectral volley of light down upon the slowly approaching ridges of Mt. Sopris, perforating the dark veil of night as the two men's eyes stared through the cockpit glass of the small helicopter.

Silently cutting its way through the wisps of cloud hanging lazily above the sleepy town of Carbondale, Colorado, the blades above the aircraft spun just as any others would. However, they produced noticeably less sound than Daniel Kelley had been accustomed to during similar flights he had taken with his childhood friend, Sean, over the years. As such, he adjusted his headset, turned his gaze toward the other man, and at a near shout, exclaimed, "I can't believe how quiet this thing is!"

At the controls sat a mid-thirties man in a sporty grey Dolce & Gabbana winter fleece. He had short brown hair, stylish wireframe glasses, and a chiseled jawline. Sean Smith kept his hand firmly fixed on the haptic control yoke set dead center in front of the wide-screened display console, visibly wincing as he shot Daniel a pained look and replied, "Yep! It sure is. So you needn't shout in my friggin' ear, dude! I'm reading you very loud and very clear. One of the many amenities offered by this particular model of air transport." He tapped his own headset with his free hand.

Dan shifted in the posh white leather seat, ran a hand through his short black (salt and pepper by most standards) hair, and sheepishly lowered his volume by a factor of, well, a lot. "Sorry, man. I didn't— I wasn't meaning to yell. I'm just used to a lot more noise. Like, way more. This thing is unbelievably quiet for what it is."

The significantly wealthier man at the controls nodded. "Oh yeah. Tends to be a smoother ride when you're on the bleeding edge of innovation, as you can tell. This purrin' puppy is a bit like the Tesla of the skyways, if you'll forgive the regrettable comparison."

"I can see that. Why *regrettable*?"

Sean offered his signature wry smile and replied, "'Cause those fuckin' things crash more often than you'd like to know."

"I don't want to know, you're right. From what I hear, they can explode too. What type of bird did you say this was?"

"It's an HX50. The latest technological offering from a new company you've probably never heard of. But a good company, nonetheless. I even own a little stock in them now. This baby is one of the first hundred that came off the line in the last year, as a matter of fact."

"Bleeding edge safety measures as well then, I'm assuming?"

Sean's grin widened even further. "Ah, well actually, *technically* it's not quite legal to fly just yet. 'Least not until it passes muster with the National Avionics Safety Board and the FAA. But I don't think we're gonna get pulled over between here and the peak of Sopris, if that's what you're worried about."

"That's not what I'm worried about, now that you mention it."

"What then?"

"I just want to know that this whirlybird is safe, especially if it hasn't yet gone through the rigors of testing that the FAA deems—"

"Hey," Sean interjected, smiling at his friend of over thirty years. "Come on, man! Would I ever do anything to put you in harm's way?"

Daniel scrunched his nose and frowned. "Sure you would. You *have*. Several times in fact, as I recall."

Snort-scoffing, Sean pushed the frame of his designer glasses back up the bridge of his nose and asked, "Like when?"

Dan shrugged and sighed. "Uh, like when you were playing around with that .44 millimeter handgun in the living room of my old place in El Jebel—"

"Knew you'd bring that one up."

Dan continued, "And accidentally put a round into the fiberglass countertop in the kitchen."

"Well, okay—yeah, sure. That was not my best hour, I'll admit that. Handguns and SKYY vodka are not a match made in heaven, that much is true. But you just said it yourself, that one was an accident."

"I can name others."

"Don't. No need to rehash old shit. But surely you must admit that I haven't yet, nor would I ever *intentionally* put you in any mortal danger. Never that. And I'm a little hurt you'd even think otherwise. Besides, this thing has been rigorously tested, and re-tested, and then tested some more by the manufacturer. Otherwise we wouldn't be flying it right now. She's as rugged and sturdy as a, uh, I dunno…Bavarian milkmaid."

"A milkmaid?"

"That's right. A Bavarian one."

"Bavarian milkmaids are rugged and sturdy, are they?"

"Based entirely upon what I gather via the travel docs I've seen and my limited experience with German pornography—quite. All those butch European women are."

"So, Bavarian women are the same as German women in your mind?"

"They're the same thing, I think, yeah."

"Isn't Bavaria a state in Germany?"

Sean shook his head in dismissal. "Whatever. I think you catch my drift, Dan. But seriously, for how much I paid, it damn well better be of the higher order where durability is concerned. And if you're still plagued by worry-wart trepidation. Do you see that small red lever by your seat's right side?"

Daniel looked down to where the reclining handle would normally be on an automobile and spotted the aforementioned metal pull-handle. "The one that says 'seat ejection release'?"

"One and the same. Three guesses what that little bad boy does."

"Shoots me outta the top of this chopper like I'm James Bond in *GoldenEye*?"

"Precisely."

Dan smiled and clapped his hand on his friend's shoulder. "Well that's a little terrifying. But good enough for me."

Developed by Hill Helicopters and selling itself as the forefront of the next generation of air travel, the small yet sleek aircraft was indeed at the forefront of modern civilian avionics. Sporting a price tag of right around $700,000, it wasn't exactly affordable for the average flight enthusiast. But then, Sean was hardly that. He'd had his pilot's license for about ten years and a multi-million dollar net worth to boot for much longer. Hailing from one of the richest bloodlines in the Roaring Fork Valley, he was regularly impressing Daniel with his latest "toys."

Sean nudged Daniel with his shoulder and mused, "You like the look of her, though?"

Dan cast a casual glance around the cockpit of the helicopter with its futuristic control panels and opulent interior design. "Very sleek. Very smooth."

"Too smooth. Like the inside of a woman's thigh."

Daniel finished his visual survey of the craft's interior and chuckled. "If I'm being honest though, it sorta looks like something a super villain might take off in after threatening the hero at the outset of the third act in some cheesy Marvel film."

Sean's smile did not waver. "You're half right. However, in this rarefied instance, we might actually be the heroes setting out to foil the nefarious plans of some sinister ne'er-do-wells."

"How's that?"

"All in good time, my friend. All in good time. How's the wifey?"

"Rebecca? She's good. Overworked. And she has her hands full with the kids this weekend, but she's good. Just started up at some new gym, so she's been in extra high spirits as of late. Endorphins and all that. Gettin' laid more than usual this month."

"Nothing wrong with that. The kids?"

"Good. Expensive. Yours?"

"Same."

"Yeah."

"Yeah."

The air closer to the 12,965-foot peak of Mt. Sopris opened up into clear sky, with the fast approaching ridges luminously outlined by moonlight. Sean pulled the control yoke down toward his lap, climbing the small, wildly expensive aircraft up to where a small plateau near the top waited. Cresting the first major ridge, the rocks and sparse snow blanketing the mountainside gave way to a break in the tree line.

Slowing in approach, Dan spied a small grassy meadow with a spot of orange flicking on the otherwise open landscape. Getting closer, the two men made out that it was a campfire.

Sean hummed, musing, "Looks like we aren't gonna be entirely alone when we reach our destination."

"Looks so."

Slowing to a hover over the meadow, Sean pushed the yoke forward and initiated their brief descent. The few trees nearby whipped and bowed in the whirling winds, while a circular concavity formed in the grasses below. A few seconds later, the dual landing skids touched down gently onto the soft green of the meadow's earthen floor.

As the rotors slowed and the engine's whir began to slow down to a whisper, the surrounding landscape stopped moving and the two looked out at the man sitting by the fire. He'd been holding a black, silver-studded cowboy hat against his head to keep it from flying away as the chopper approached. Now he stood up just a dozen or so yards from where they had just landed. He had on a black leather jacket and faded, torn blue jeans of the nineties callback variety. Curly blonde hair that peeked out from under the stylish Stetson and a forced look on his face.

Daniel thought that he'd seen and/or met this dude before. Some local metalhead/outdoors-y type that he might've run into at some random senior party or one of the many local punk shows. Maybe the X-Games? Who knew. Once you'd lived in the Roaring Fork Valley for more than a decade or two, you basically knew everyone worth knowing.

"Think I know that cat," Dan said, pulling off his headset.

Sean nodded as he pulled his PNR cans off as well. "I'm sure I do. We went to school together. Niklas…something is his name. He was pretty cool back in the day. We used to run with some of the same kids and got a high a few times together. Now though, he's more than a little bit of a tool."

As the two men opened their respective ergonomically wide carbon fiber doors and stepped out into the brisk air, Niklas stopped several yards shy and hailed them. "You nearly put out my fire with that dumbass maneuver! What if you had landed on me?"

"Perchance to dream. But we didn't, 'cause I'm not an idiot. Is that you Nik?"

"Sure is. Sean, right?"

Sean nodded. "Yep. And my co-pilot here is not in fact Jesus, but rather my affable cohort Daniel Kelley. He may not be the lord, but he does a serviceable job, in a pinch."

Daniel offered up a weak smile and waved. "I think we've met before."

Unimpressed would be an apt descriptor of the expression on the man wearing the silver-stud spiked Stetson hat. "Right, whatever. The fuck are you two looney tunes coming up here for this late at night? Just flaunting some of that old generational Valley wealth to us meager mortals?"

"Look, Nik. Nik...Nik Proton, or Pillsman, or whatever the heck your last name is," Sean began, eliciting a cocked grin from the black jacketed man sitting next to the small fire. "Why don't you do us all a favor and bite off a nice heapin' helpin' of *shut the fuck up*?"

The curly-haired fellow chuckled and turned away from them, poking at the smoldering fire with a long stick. Then he walked over to grab another log from a small stack nearby. As he tossed it atop the dwindling embers, he offered up an ear-to-ear grin. "Still the consummate dickhead, I see. And I was here first, before you two vacuous interlopers arrived. Did you two cucks come up here to jerk each other off or what? Little homo-hammed moonlight rendezvous? 'Cause if that's it, I can go find another place for my fire. Iffin' you queer-mos wanna be alone."

Stretching his arms above his head and yawning for effect, Sean glared at the grumpy fire-fondler. "No dice, Niklas. Ya see, unlike you, I have little to no desire to dirty up my palms with the dicks of my fellow Valley denizen."

Niklas chuckled again as he pulled a cigarette from behind his ear and leaned into the fire to light it up. Touching the end of the Vantage cig to the nearest ember, he drew it up to his lips. Sucking in a lung full of nicotine, then exhaling, he surveyed the other two men. "An inspired retort, to be sure. Didn't realize you were so fucking clever."

"You likely wouldn't, it's true. But here's another idea, just a little suggestion if you're amenable: Why don't you go fucking die?"

"That's harsh. But, again, I was here first, ya' silver spoon slurping gonad goblin."

"An unfortunate and wholly undeniable fact, I'll admit. Still, we do have much bigger fish to fry. So just shuddup and back off, will ya?"

Dan took a tentative step forward. "Guys. Guys. That's plenty. Save that shit for the YouTube comment section. Sean, It's pretty friggin' cold up here. Did we just come to score a quick view, then jam, or what?"

"Kinda. But not really. As I alluded to earlier, we have a much loftier purpose for our moonlit sojourn on this particular evening."

"Okay, well what is it?" Dan asked, stretching his arms above his head.

From several feet away, Nik snickered. "Yeah, do tell. Not that I didn't come up here to the middle of nowhere to have my nocturnal peace utterly shattered by—"

Sean waved his hand dismissively in the direction of the third man, cutting him off. "Now, Nik, if you keep talking like a bitch, you're gonna get smacked like one."

Niklas shot the two men a fierce look as he cracked his knuckles. "You can fucking try it, knuckle-cuck."

Daniel took another step forward to position his body between the two alpha males, hoping he wouldn't actually have to stop a physical altercation.

Sean read the disdain for the brewing conflict on his friend's face, and his features softened. Shooting Nik a hard look, Sean shook his head at the man in the black cowboy hat. "No time for such distractions, I'm afraid. We've got much more pressing matters to attend to. The very future of mankind is at stake."

Daniel and Nik both waited for more, but Sean just stood there, bathed in the clear moonlight.

Finally, Dan went ahead and bit down on the verbal hook Sean was dangling. "What are you talking about?"

Sean's face opened up to a wide grin. "An experimental launch of some high-altitude munitions. Really just a few small test flights."

"Like drones?"

"No. Not drones. Something else. Something with a higher altitude threshold."

Without knowing what on Earth he was talking about, Dan tapped one foot and pressed his friend further. "Okay, so how does this pertain to the future of mankind?"

"Help me with these cases, then I'll tell you what we're doing with them." Sean walked over to the now silent HX50 and pulled open a small storage compartment hatch on the helicopter's side, located between the cockpit and the rail section. Upon lifting the latch, the inside light revealed six rectangular, gunmetal grey containers standing about three feet tall and a foot or more in diameter.

Walking up to join him and get a clearer look, Dan asked the obvious. "What's all this, Sean?"

Sean wrapped his hands around the closet case and pulled it free from the compartment. "A means to an end."

"To what end, prey tell?"

"To the end of several threats posed by man toward his fellow man. A pre-emptive strike against the enemies of man."

"In English?"

"They're…well, you'll see for yourself soon enough. But in the interest of expediency and full disclosure, they're rockets."

"Rockets?" Nik and Daniel both asked in near-perfect synchronicity.

"Rockets," Sean confirmed while pulling another case free and setting it on the ground next to the chopper. Dan grabbed the next one and hauled it out of the small compartment. After a moment, they had emptied the storage area and Sean closed it up. He patted his palm upon the shut hatch, then started to drag two of the cases by their silver handles away from the craft.

"And what sorta rockets are we setting off tonight?" Daniel shivered as a small gust kicked up, rubbing the sleeves of his green Lands' End sweater. "'Cause really, I don't relish the idea of drawing a bunch of attention to ourselves, and then having to explain to whoever might show up—"

Sean paused and looked over his shoulder, cutting off Daniel mid-worry. "Nobody's gonna show up. Trust me, man.

This is something you'll be able to tell your kiddos about one day."

Dan scowled. "How's that?"

"I am—or, rather *we* are—about to save the world, my friend."

"Sean, if you're doing something crazier than usual, then I honestly don't want any part of it. I don't know what you brought me up here for, but if it's some nutty shit then I think you can count me out."

"Well, it's not that. Quite the opposite, actually. Still I did come prepared just in case you felt that way. Do me a favor and don't take this personally, okay?" Sean set down the cases, and as he approached Daniel, he pulled a small black object from his pocket while clicking the switch on the side.

Daniel barely registered the flickering flash of electricity between the two small metal contacts on the Taser's business end before Sean buried it in his rib cage. Sensing a white-hot jolt that immediately sent him crashing to the ground, Dan cried out as he landed hard, shaking and holding his side. Groaning and coughing, he rolled over on the cold dirt, struggling to put his words together. "F-f-fucking sh-sh-shit, man! Wha— What did you do that for?"

"'Cause I shan't be delayed nor denied. Got a timetable to stick to, good buddy. My true aim is to save us all from the genocidal tendencies of other bad actors, I promise. But I apologize if that hurt." A brief pause, then, "You'll be okay. I'm sure you'll be okay. Are you okay?"

"N-n-no. N-n-not really, d-d-dickhead!" Dan managed to choke-stutter out between labored breaths.

"You'll be fine."

Niklas finally chimed, taking a few steps toward the other men. "What did you do to him?"

"Chill out, Nik. And stay right where you are. You don't want any piece of this shit." Sean pointed the still-sparking twin tips at the moderately terrified man by the fire, zapping the contacts again, then winked.

Niklas stopped dead in his tracks—frozen, wide-eyed, and doubting nothing about the warning he'd just be issued.

Nodding his head in the relative direction of his felled friend, Sean assured him. "Don't worry; he'll come out of this unscathed. I just need to finish what I'm doing here and we'll be out of your hair in a few minutes."

Niklas raised his palms in a tacit show of acquiescence. "I'm not gonna do shit."

"Damn straight you won't." Sean zapped the contacts once more, then promptly flicked the switch on the Taser's side as he returned it to his jacket pocket. "Smart boy. And who said you didn't have any brains rattling around in that thick Nickelback-lookin' skull of yours, eh?"

Nik calmly replied, "I think you did, once or twice."

Forehead scrunching, Sean quizzically asked, "Really? When?"

"Back in school. When we were at CRMS. 'Least that's what I was told by a few of our classmates. Frankly, it doesn't matter now; I'm not gonna do anything but sit here and hope this doesn't get any weirder." With that, Nik stepped back a few yards and plopped down on the smooth rock near his campfire.

"Good. And I apologize if I ever said anything like that. I was a selfish dick hole back in high school. So, if I did that, my bad. I apologize in arrears. Either way, thank you for your cooperation." Sean leaned down and helped Daniel move into a leaning position against a small nearby tree stump.

Daniel leaned his weight against it and continued to hold his side whilst intermittently groaning. "For the final time, why the fuck are we here, Sean?"

"Rich bitches with their greedy fingers on too many kill switches."

"How does that relate to a case full of rockets?"

"*Cases.* Not singular. I have several rockets in tow. And it's because forces bigger than you and I are, this very moment, conspiring to ruin the world for future generations to come. I come packing the cure for what will soon ail us all."

"Stop speaking in goddamn abstracts! Explain! Please!"

Sean walked back over to the two cases and dragged them to a spot about fifteen yards away from both small aircraft and the fire where Niklas watched. Coming back toward the craft, he started to pull another couple cases behind him and asked, "Do you know what dark forest theory is?" He placed the cases by the other then set off to grab the remaining two.

Dan winced and held his side. "Sure."

After remaining silent for a few moments while he dropped the last two cases by the others, Sean stood straight and addressed his friend directly. "What is it then?"

Propping himself up a little more, Daniel took in a few deep breaths, steadying his words. "It's the idea that aliens we might meet would be hostile and that we shouldn't seek to contact them. Or something like that."

"Couldn't have said it more succinctly myself. A plus on the ol' science quiz. Neil DeGrasse Tyson would be proud. How about the Kessler Effect?"

Daniel propped himself up on one knee and replied, "No, I don't know what that is."

"Me neither," Niklas chimed in from his seat by the fire, curiosity now clearly piqued.

Sean knelt down and flicked up the locking mechanisms one after another, then removed them from the silver-sided cases. As he did, each one flipped over a rectangular panel with a miniature LED screen, lights, buttons, and knobs of varying size. Sean began to fiddle with the control panel on the side of the first large case. After a few taps on the touch-screen, the crate let out a small hydraulic hiss. Two flat metal panels on the top opened up and revealed one of the fabled rockets. It was about a half foot in diameter, white with a red nose cone, and with fins that looked capable of movement on three sides.

As Daniel and Niklas gazed at the rocket, Sean said, "It's the idea that eventually low Earth orbit satellites—like those employed by that dipstick Nazi butt-fucker, Elon Musk—will eventually number so many that the probability of collision will effectively drop to zero. This would cause a complete collapse of our telecom networks by creating a cascade of space debris that would effectively set global technologies back a century or more. The bigger issue comes if he's able to help anyone arm space before that happens. Then we're off to the fucking races, lemme tell ya."

"So?"

"So, lastly, do you know much about a hubris-laden dumbfuck named Sam Altman?"

Niklas spoke up again. "The OpenAI guy? That who you're talking about?"

Sean smiled and pointed both index fingers toward the man by the fire. "Right you are, metal man! One and the same! The AI guy. Dude is basically our very own Miles Dyson. And operating with the same breezy, reckless abandon."

"Miles Dyson?" Daniel asked, now regaining some of his composure.

"Yeah. Miles Dyson. From *Terminator 2*? I know you know that! And just like that numbskull, Sam is well aware of the danger his technology potentially poses, yet continues his hell-bound handiwork, unabated."

"Sean, I can clearly see that you're not—"

Sean held up his hand to quiet his friend. Dan fell into silence. Moving from case to case, Sean tapped on the screens and flicked a few switches, several lights on each beginning to glow in slow pulses. "I'm hoping to take out all three of those troublesome birds with one rocket-propelled stone, if you'll forgive the strained metaphor."

"How?"

"By expediting the process a bit. You see, the development of AI is an all-encompassing threat to every man, woman, and child on this planet Earth. One which simply cannot be allowed to continue. That mixed with the current climate of economic uncertainty, the ever present threat of nuclear war, and the Kessler Effect that ol' Muskie seems dead-set on triggering, makes the whole of humanity proper rife for an oncoming apocalypse. Worse still is the aforementioned danger we all face if he's allowed to arm space, which according to some of the sources I've been receiving intel from, could be truly cataclysmic."

Niklas finished his cigarette and tossed it into the fire. "How does that relate to the dark forest theory?"

Sean smiled. "Well, if the Chinese and US get into a space-based arms war, then the detonation of untold numbers of nuclear devices could provide enough for any lookie-loo space civilization to become aware of us, provided they haven't already. AI proliferation is of equal concern in this regard. Self-replicating machines being but the mere tip of this theoretical iceberg."

Dan wheezed from the dull pain in his side. "Pretty fanciful stuff you're peddling there, Sean. And sorta risky in its own right."

Sean shrugged. "Well, yeah. But it's all relative, you know?"

"No, I don't."

"Sorry to hear that."

"You're not worried about this coming back on you somehow?"

"Nah." Sean waived away the notion with a dismissive wrist flick. "I've taken some serious precautions in the lead up to tonight's launch. I shan't be deterred. And if all goes well, I shan't be detected."

"Stop saying shan't."

Sean's lip curled into a snicker. "I shan't."

Dan winced at the still-throbbing pain in his ribs. "Okay. Meticulous planning aside, to the casual observer it would appear as though you've gone completely 'round the proverbial bend, my friend. There are plenty of obstacles getting in the way of all three of those possible—"

"Look, it doesn't matter what I think. Or you, for that matter. Or even ol' Niklas over there. Smarter men than all three of us have made it clear that the dangers posed by such follies of man are dire and urgent, indeed."

Dan finally managed enough strength to shake off the pain and rise up to a standing position. Sean cast him a suspicious glance and Dan waved at the air to imply he wasn't going to try and stop him. "Yeah?"

"Yeah. And Lord knows that the dipstick tinpot dictator we currently got taking up space in the Oval Office damn sure ain't gonna do anything to quell the misdeeds of his fellow man. He's too busy consolidating power, destroying democracy, and swallowing Putin's dick for breakfast. So I figure it might just be my time to step up to the proverbial plate."

Daniel brought his right hand up to his face and rubbed it with closed eyes. "Oh fuck! Are you—are you fucking serious? This is…what, some sort of bullshit over-reaction to the election? Surely you must be fucking kidding me!"

"No. I'm quite serious. And don't call me Shirley. It's not a reaction to that per se. Still, did it have some effect on my decision? I'd be lying if I said this wasn't already in the works long before that, though I must concede that the election did *not* help matters any. If nobody else seems bothered by the ramifications of their choices in this day and age, then why should I?" Sean continued to move from case to case, arming the rockets with the tap-tap-tapping of each respective LED screen controls.

"That's your dumbfuck rationale for kick-starting a mini apocalypse of your own?"

"It won't do that. As a matter of fact, and as I've clearly explained to you, I suspect it will deter several of the other so-called mini apocalypses to come."

"That doesn't really make it any better."

"Sure it does. Look, we're all living through the supervillain origin stories of a cadre of sociopathic tech-bros. Lex Luther runs Amazon, Werner Von Braun owns SpaceX, Tesla, as well as Twitter, and Wilson Fisk is the fat bastard holding the presidency—and by extension the very future of our democracy—by its throat."

Niklas lit up another cigarette and laughed loud enough for both of the other men to shoot him a look. "Sean ain't wrong about that part, Danny Boy."

Dan shot Nik a severe look. "Don't call me Danny, Nikky."

Nik put up his hands in surrender and smiled. "Whatever. Just saying."

Finishing up his round robin of rocket arming, Sean stood and glanced at his leather-banded Nomos Glashütte wristwatch. Then his bespectacled eyes gazed skyward. Stepping back from the silver cases with their glow-pulsing diodes, he walked over to within just a few feet of Daniel and stopped. "Best thing for all parties concerned." He then proceeded to pull out his smartphone and tap away at the screen with his thumbs. "How's your side?"

Daniel's fingers rubbed his ribs. "Fucking terrible. And it'll be hard to explain to Rebecca. Got any ideas?"

"Tell her you and I were breaking up a fight outside of the Black Nugget and in the ensuing confusion, some Bonedale cop accidentally hit you with a Taser."

"That doesn't sound much like something I, nor the police force of our small town, would do, and will likely just lead to more questions."

"You'll think of something." Sean ceased typing on his touch screen, exhaled loudly, and muttered, "I'd do some sorta dramatic countdown, but truth be told, I don't wanna give anyone any time to get clever."

His thumb swept from left to right on the small screen and the nearby rockets began to beep and whir. Puffs of pressurized air blew out of exhaust ports near the bottom of each stainless steel container. Without any significant delay, they began to whizz-fire from their launchpads, and as quickly as they'd left, they disappeared from sight. All three men watched in awe as they vanished into the thin air above Mt. Sopris.

Lowering his gaze back to Sean, Daniel asked, "So that's it then?"

Sean clicked the button on the side of his phone and the screen went dark. "That's it. Easy as peach pie from the Tiny Pine Bistro on Main Street."

Niklas scrunched his brow and asked, "Tiny Pine has a peach pie?"

Sean nodded. "Sure do. At least they did a few weeks ago. Shit was utterly delish."

Niklas grinned in response. "I'll have to check that out."

"You should. *De-lish!*"

Daniel's sigh drew both of their eyes to him. "I really wish I had asked this before you sent those bad boys into the stratosphere, but what about the unsuspecting folks onboard the ISS?"

"Ah yes, the International Space Station. Quite the quandary that would be, wouldn't it? But for the fact that I saw that little hiccup coming down the pipe and have it covered. Rest assured, they'll be fine. I have the explosives on the rockets set to execute the detonation sequences in three weeks exactly. The onboard CPUs are encrypted, and therefore aren't able to communicate with nor be bypassed by any of the high-end electronics that NASA might employ in any possible, futile, and ultimately doomed attempt to gain control of them. In what can only be described as a truly fortuitous turn, the current crew of the ISS is going to be leaving the station in the next two weeks. They won't be replaced for another two weeks after that. I've timed it to line up with the first time in decades, really, that the station has been temporarily unmanned."

"You don't think Nik over here is gonna wanna turn us in?"

Niklas cleared his throat and spoke calmly, "Actually, I gotta say, I think this whole thing is pretty goddamn boss. And well planned, I must say."

"Really?" Dan asked, only half-believing him.

Niklas gave a nod, then tipped his black hat bill in their direction. "Really. If I myself possessed the inspiration, money, and means to execute such a plan without getting caught, I just might go ahead and do it of my own volition."

Dan rolled his eyes. "It's going to send us back to the stone age in many ways. You realize that, right, Sean?"

Sean shrugged and slipped his phone into his pocket. "Sure. But fuck it. Better than any alternative I could come up with."

"Any part of this could be short-sighted on your part, you know."

"It's all relative, Dan. Just as I said before. It's all relative."

"Holy shit! Stop saying that!"

Sean's hands clapped together, slightly startling his friend. "Water under the galactic bridge. Let's get you home. I'm sure Rebecca will want to know you had a great time visiting, but could use the reinforcement where the kids are concerned."

"The kids? The *kids?* Do you have any idea what kind of bullshit this might have set up for our children?"

"Of course I do! I did this for them. One day we'll be gone from this fucking world, but our kids will have to deal with the consequences of our decisions. I'm happy with mine. Tonight, I spared the world a worse fate."

"I think that, at best, you probably just hit the snooze button."

"It's the best I can do, absent superhuman abilities like those chucklenuts in the comic book movies do. But such is the sad line we tow. I'm a mere mortal. And Daniel, I know that this— I mean, I'll understand if you don't, you know…" Sean trailed off for a moment, and looking into his oldest friend's eyes, Daniel beheld the sorrow the following words carried for his friend. "While I hope you'll keep this to yourself, I'll completely understand if you don't want to see me much anymore."

Daniel scratched his head, rubbed his side, and sighed yet again. "Oh, shut the fuck up, Sean. Just don't. This is hardly the craziest thing I've ever seen you pull."

"Really?"

"Actually, no. This kooky shit takes the proverbial cake. You've well and truly lost your fucking mind. But no, to be clear, I won't drop a dime on you. Unless, of course, the feds come-a-knocking on my door. Then I'm gonna have to prioritize my family and rat you out like I'm Sammy the Bull."

"So you'll still come over for Christmas?"

"Yeah, sure I will. Me and the fam. If you're not arrested and executed for crimes against humanity between now and then."

Sean's lips cradled the faintest of smiles as he slowly turned his attention toward the man by the nearby campfire. "We cool, Nik?"

Niklas stretched his arms above his head and yawned. "Sure, man. We're cool. Cool as a cucumber in a bowl of hot sauce. You could even say I've gained a new level of respect for you two dweebs this evening." He flicked his finished smoke into the fire. "And who knows? You might have just saved us humans from the technological terrors which have misguided our lives for the last hundred years or so. I hate our dystopian now. I hate Starlink and Siri and all this government surveillance bullshit. Shit, I left my smartphone at home for this weekend trip. Besides, if I were to tell anyone that you guys flew up here in a high-tech, spy-film chopper and shot off a bunch of rockets to stave off multiple oncoming apocalypses set in motion by a bunch of tech billionaires, you really think anyone would believe me?"

Sean's grin stood ear to ear. "I suspect not. Unless this was a *James Bond* film, which it ain't."

Dan audibly scoffed. "Says the man who's acting like a misguided Bond villain over here."

Niklas strode over to the two men. Once he was within a few feet, he assured them, "Well, you don't need to worry about me. In fact, I have kids of my own, and if it's okay—"

"You have kids?" Sean asked. Nik nodded. "Congrats, dude! That's great. You and Shauna still have a thing?"

"If by 'thing' you mean, *is she my wife*, then yes."

"Well, that's great. Good for you."

Dan shot Nik a look of tacit defeat but nonetheless asked, "You don't think this was a bit reactionary?"

Niklas shrugged. "It's all relative, right?" He smiled broadly at Sean.

Sean, in turn, pushed his glasses up his nose and held out his closed fist for a friendly nudge. "My man!" The two men shared a knowing bump.

Daniel shook his head. "This is crazy. I still can't believe you tased me, bro."

Sean laughed and put his hand on his lifelong buddy's shoulder. "One day, you'll realize this was a good idea. One of my many."

"Right," Dan mumbled as the three men stared up at the silver-hued moon hanging above their heads. "Guess we'll see soon enough."

Unknown to the three men atop Mt. Sopris—unknown, in fact, to nearly any of the Earthbound humans clinging feebly to the spinning rock placed third out from the nearest star upon which they all stood—the government of North Korea had successfully spent the last decade prior to that fateful night's events developing a sophisticated space-based ballistic missile system capable of covert concealment within the confines of a larger reconnaissance satellite.

The space arm of the DPRK—The National Aerospace Technology Administration (NATA), formerly the National Aerospace Development Administration (NADA)—had launched just ten satellites since its inception in 2013, and of those ten, only three had been successful. The seven others had either failed to achieve orbit or had simply blown up during their respective launches.

The most recent of these was the Malligyong-1. Launched on November 21st, 2023, and achieving a sun-synchronous low Earth orbit soon thereafter, the supposed goal for this satellite was little more than military recon and surveillance. However, despite other international space agencies knowing of the launch and its resultant orbiting pattern, the general consensus was that Malligyong-1 was precisely what it purported to be.

Unknown to them, it was actually carrying a small nuclear payload.

A single nuclear-tipped air-to-ground vehicle weighing just seventy pounds, and placed discreetly within the primary capsule, had been developed using covert intelligence procured by domestic spies embedded within the US nuclear weapons agency. Loosely based on America's W54 nuclear warhead (itself weighing a mere fifty-one pounds) it was built using ultra lightweight material for the housing and plutonium-

239 as its fissile material. The detonation yield was capable of a blast comparable to 1000 metric tons of TNT, or 4.184 gigajoules of energy.

This possibility could—and arguably *should*—have been ascertained by any number of the other space administrations on Earth, given that remote monitoring of the satellite by those agencies had never detected any ground communication between the satellite and the DPRK to validate its stated surveillance purposes. Yet, given the North Korean space program's international reputation for being as woefully behind in their space capabilities as their nuclear arms technology, it was always assumed to be a badly functioning telescope that the DPRK was too embarrassed to admit had failed in its intended goal.

When the six rockets fired that night from Mt. Sopris launched into space and quickly entered into congruent, geosynchronous orbits at lower altitudes, one of them failed to reach its intended goal. Instead, it improbably (impossibly?) ended its journey by slamming into the side of Malligyong-1 as it passed by, immediately detonating the North Korean spacecraft's nuclear payload.

This extremely unlikely outcome would, in itself, not have been too great of a problem, but for the fact that the Americans had covertly placed a cobalt-based nuclear warhead (the first of its kind) on the International Space Station just a year earlier. Unknown to the astronauts onboard, and intended to safely test the sheer destructive power of such a weapon via future space detonation, the cobalt bomb developed by

Lockheed Martin was one of the first casualties of the space debris storm caused by the explosion on the Malligyong-1.

As a torrent of tiny metallic shrapnel traveling at thousands of miles per hour perforated the International Space Station, the cobalt bomb (codenamed Reaper-8) detonated spectacularly, killing all three astronauts on board and immediately triggering the long-speculated Kessler Effect—thus initiating a catastrophic chain reaction, destroying nearly all satellites in low Earth orbit in a matter of days.

Even more dire than the webwork of destructive debris or the nuclear fallout that began to pepper Earth's atmosphere with immense radiation, was the resulting yield which created a distinct isotopic chemical signature that could be detected as far away as several light years.

And it was this very signature which led to the ΔΔ-66 class heavy cruiser starship of the star-faring Güüß-Næçœ race, which had been making its way past the outer reaches of our solar system on a recon directive, to take immediate notice of it.

The revelation that the self-warring creatures on Earth—who had long been monitored by no less than three different civilizations ranking above type-II on the Kardashev scale—had harnessed such energy called for an immediate intervention by the Güüß-Næçœ ship. Adjusting its path for possible interception of the nearby star system, it sent a light-wave signal to its planet, notifying its homeworld of the discovery. The collective AI consciousness which had dictated

Patrick Quinn Kitson

the will and fate of the Güüß-Næçœ for more than 11,000 solar years, replied in swift fashion.

Put simply into Earth terms, the well-armed Güüß-Næçœ ship was called upon to destroy the fledgling civilization, forthwith.

Correcting course, It took only .5 solar years for the ΔΔ-66 class heavy cruiser, with its planet-imploding, dark-matter payload, to reach its galactic destination, a safe distance away from Earth (just beyond the gravitational reach of nearby Jupiter). Once in position, the Güüß-Næçœ vessel fired its munitions and vaporized the small blue planet in a matter of nano-seconds. It then communicated to its controlling intelligence that the Earth (designation 0101001111010101-x) should be wiped from the vast databases of the Güüß-Næçœ civilization so that knowledge of it was extinguished forever.

And so it was. As though it never existed.

Because we didn't, and because we don't.

HARVEST

This very moment, I'm running for my damn life.

I can't stop, or I suspect that I might die as well. And I don't want to die. At least, I don't think I do.

No...I definitely don't wanna do that.

Things are a little crazy right now, you see, so please do forgive me. I'm trying to keep it all together, but it's been a rough trip thus far.

I'm scampering like a spazzed-out Looney Tune down Cattle Creek Road while the last slivers of light disappear from the horizon. And I'm hoping somebody, *anybody*, picks me up. Because I can't go back to the insanity from which I just narrowly escaped.

I don't do well with the sight of blood.

And now, after what I just saw, I know I'm not into being around a mob of religious zealots ripping flesh asunder with farm implements, either. So that's undeniably a factor.

And so I'm running, and screaming, and crying, and currently tripping my goddamn balls off on mushrooms ("albino penis envy" or *psilocybe cubensis*, if you're curious about the specific strain), as I head back toward the salvation of civilization.

Hopefully I'm headed the right way. I can't yet see the lights of the town beyond the crests of the high canyon walls and I'm relying on a tenuous trust in my perception of gravity to guide me down the rocky slope of the road, since I can barely see in this damn twilight. My clothes are dirty and my short brown hair is dripping with sweat.

How did this happen? How has my friend's weekend birthday bash to end all birthday bashes mutated into a crimson field of slaughter? I'll tell 'ya how. It's 'cause my homegirl Jenny tempted fate. Rolled the dice and came up snake eyes.

That's how.

Let's rewind the tape to earlier this afternoon. Friday May 7th, 1999, to be specific.

Me and my cadre, baking atop the hot asphalt parking lot of Roaring Fork High like so many fortuneless beached jellyfish. All of us stylishly detached and tragically hip, as we simply can't help but be, and out of the blue, my good friend Jenny drops the news. She says that her parents are leaving for the next week, and with that one statement, we were off to the races.

This is outside, between classes, and at first I'm as jazzed as anybody in my groovy little social group. Anytime one of us has a parent-free abode to take advantage of, we are all quite grateful. Rapid acquisition of drugs and booze have become an easy thing by now, so *location location location* is the name of the game.

Jenny and the rest of the loosely assembled raver/goth/stoner/slacker amalgam we've formed all agreed that we must take advantage of this newfound liberty and test its tenuous bonds straight away. I expressed trepidation, but was met with the usual adolescent ribbings because, per usual, no one ever listens to this guy. They should, but they never do.

Que cera, cera.

And as they roughly formulate the planned debauchery ahead, I'm thinking, *This is starting to sound a whole lot like the lead line in tomorrow's newspaper.*

I could see the headline:

"Local knucklefuck kids do dumb, get caught."

I'm thinking this could be a big stupid mess. And boy, was I not-even-a-little-wrong. But each time I winced at the next shitty turn in the unfolding plan, no one seemed as bothered as I. Jen, as well as the rest of our gregarious and impulsive constituency of ne'er-do-wells, seemed dead set on the risky enterprise.

Casually trying my hand at being the patronly voice of reason, I say to Jenny, I say, "Jenny, this could easily get out of control, ya know."

Then—*get this*—she says to me, she says, "That's sorta the point of a party, ain't it, Pat?"

And what could I say, really? She had one unassailable point right there. Unlike myself, apparently Jenny—just like Kevin Bacon—knew what fucking time it was.

You gotta cut footloose.

The plan was simple: split up and drop a carpet-bombing campaign of invitations across the whole of the parking lot to any and all who would lend an ear. And the beats were easy: Jenny's house up Cattle Creek Road, bring drugs/booze, invite anyone you want.

Bada bing, bada boom. In less than ten minutes, everyone in all four grades knew where the happening gathering was to occur tonight.

And like Hunter Thompson heading for Vegas, the rest of my day was spent in the vainglorious pursuit of appropriate clothing for the affair, as well as acquisition of the proper party favors to enhance the event. Shrooms and herbs are the easiest things to get on short notice. Then a backpack filled with the essentials: water, suckers, Snapple Elements, flashing lights, Red Bull, Vicks VapoRub (in case anybody had any E), and two fresh packs of Camel Light Menthols.

Oh, and the handheld strobes to enhance visuals—you gotta have those.

Situated roughly eight miles up Cattle Creek Road from where it intersects with Highway 82, the place Jenny and her parents call home is a couple of buildings corralled at the end of a large, unfinished turnaround driveway that, absent completion, is really just a big dirt lot, maybe a hundred yards in diameter.

It was once owned by a few flower child baby boomers who, among other hippie-era nods, fashioned a nice rustic barn just a stone's throw from the main house. Presumably to have drum banging sessions and smoke outs in. Said barn is replete with a massive hand-carved oak and naturally rainbow-striped peace sign no less than fifteen feet in diameter hanging above the double doors along the building's front.

In fact, not that it's neither here nor there, but it was due to the aesthetic of this particular structure that, in 1988, the location scouts for a sixties-nostalgia buddy comedy starring Kiefer Sutherland and Dennis Hopper came a calling. Titled *Flashback* and largely shot in and around the Roaring Fork Valley, they used the house and barn as the stand-in for a fictional hippie commune.

Yeah, Jenny's house was used in a Kiefer Sutherland film, so there's some random Valley esoterica.

And in a fun little turn for my own internal biographic, Jenny's house was incidentally the first place I ever smoked pot. But that was years ago on her thirteenth birthday—

And *holy Goddamn hell*, do I digress. Where the heck was I?

Oh yeah, so it's early in the afternoon when everyone starts to pull to the party location and fill up the dirt lot in front of Casa de Jenny. And while the goal was admittedly to get as many attendees as possible to be part of Jennifer's birthday debauchery, the magnitude of it was soon overwhelming, if not more than a little worrying. Soon, pickups, station wagons, Acuras, Toyotas, lowriders, topless Jeeps, and even a few motorcycles filled the area.

Generally, these types of affairs run on an always implied, always assumed *bring your own brews and drugs* edict. But one way Jenny ensured maximum capacity was to assure all prospective attendees that plenty of beer would be on hand. Most of Roaring Fork High, from freshman to seniors, came for the anticipated revelry. And not only did essentially everyone in the school who was of the disposition to party show up, so did all kinds of creepy, too-old-for-this-sorta-thing, invited by God-knows-who knucklefuckers.

With people of all shapes and sizes pouring into the confines of Jenny's big, but not nearly big enough, homestead, the flood tide was not to be withstood, but rather embraced. The house's cup was running over with the usual evocative party trappings—thumping beats, hip hop, rock, country, rowdy cheers, chants, high fives, keg stands, metal sneak-a-toke hits, cigarettes, swigs from various brown bottles, and people doing cartwheels across the green backyard grass while others tossed tiny white balls into red Solo cups.

The shrooms were kickin' like a desert mule in heat by the time the whole keg fiasco unfolded.

Now, what's that, you ask? Well, have a pew and allow me to elucidate.

When kids of a certain age and disposition find themselves in a way to imbibe libations of the alcoholic variety in the formative pursuit of mischief and mad hattery, we often require quantity over quality to meet our intoxicated ends.

More beats better when you're young and looking to get all twisted up. Everybody knows that.

So what's the easy solution when you get together a whole mess of young folks hoping to pack down a whole mess of booze?

Kegs, baby. Kegs all day.

And how many did we (*not me*) bring to such a grand occasion?

Three. Only three.

This was the initial problem. Someone, in their vastly under-prepared quasi-wisdom, saw fit to procure a mere three kegs—two filled with Bud Light, the last one brimming with Fat Tire—for the massive soiree-to-be. But three was never gonna cut it for the half-anticipated numbers that ultimately showed up. Six *might've* done, but not three. Especially since there was an effort to allow cliques to take over the various kegs.

And this brings me to another relevant bit of backdrop for this unfolding situation that I'd do well to mention before going further: The ever present, oft-simmering and utterly fake-as-fuck racial tension that still exists in the minds of some adolescents here in Carbondale of the late nineties.

Like, I see it, and it's fucking stupid—for realzies, okay?

So, dig this: Whites and Mexicans in Carbondale—both obviously primarily saddling up with their own racial precepts because it's an easy common denominator and nobody wants to face the world alone—have invented this pseudo-Cold War of would-be gang proportions.

In one corner, you've got a bunch of JNCO Jeans-wearing dipshit wanna-G, white boy nut-scratchers in souped-up pickups acting like they're all hard because they buy expensive weed and listen to Biggie in the shiny new F-150 that mommy and daddy freshly picked from the fortune tree in the backyard.

And in the other corner you have these admittedly much harder, yet ultimately still laughably fucking harmless and thinly-'stachioed, cunty little SUR13-imposter gangster cucks, mobbin' past the Main Street Art Center in their dippy lowriders like it's fucking East Compton or something. Like they don't live in a big ass house with massive TV screens and remote-controlled garage doors. Bumping Delinquent Habits (which, as one Hispanic friend has explained to my "simple white boy ass," real Sureños do not bump in their loc'd-out whips) down Second Street like a train of trite twats.

Both sides, fraudulent as *fuuuuuuck*.

In a tiny little town like Bonedale where everybody's making good money, nobody is truly oppressed. Shit's all good most days, and the single most dangerous aspect of walking the rough and tumble streets is the heightened risk of stepping in some rando pile of horse shit (yeah, totally a thing with the cattle drives 'round these parts).

I don't know what the actual fuck is driving the quasi-racial tension. One suspects just blind, aimless boredom fueled by our MTV-imprinted fantasies of being waved into an imagined East Coast/West Coast proxy war.

Still, deluded though it is, it has boiled over here and there, throughout the years. A big melee at Two Rivers Park, or a couple of fists thrown behind the bleachers during a darkened homecoming dance in the gym. And yet, a lot—if not most—of the outright violence has been quelled by tenuous armistices, largely borne from a mutual need for drug acquisition. The Mexicans have cheaper weed and they can get that all-important Valley favorite: cocaine. The white boys have pricey pot and can score exotic hallucinogenics like LSD and E, which are both still a bit of a novelty to the masses here, I'll admit.

I'm a raver, so I'll candy flip because it's a fuckin' Tuesday, ya know?

One hopes that in the future (say, in the year 2025 or something), any racial bigotry or imagined creations thereof will not be a thing for the classes of Roaring Fork High School in the new millennium.

They'll be above that petty bullshit, I'm confident.

For now, it's a thing—a dumb thing, and it's only worth mentioning because it's what arguably served as part of the catalyst for the aforementioned keg-fiasco.

The first Bud Light keg was initially placed on the back porch in an effort to divert some attendees toward the large backyard for their revelry—specifically a hubristic contingent of slovenly jock douchebags. Sadly, it was pretty much drained dry before we entered the party's second hour of jubilee.

The second keg of Bud was routed downstairs in the blacklight-illuminated basement grotto where, probably on account of there being a pool table down there, it had been taken over by our Latino classmates and their constituency of well-dressed, stone-faced homies.

The much-coveted Fat Tire keg was first hidden in a back room behind a locked door adjacent to the living room. However, an intrepid partygoer wielding what one must assume was either a well-formed hairpin or amateur lockpicking kit had made short work of that barrier and the third keg was soon absconded with into the darkness of the thumping basement as well.

With the festivities in full swing, half the party was thus trying to score a fresh Solo cup of beer or find someone to take shots with.

And me? I was relatively unaware of this whole unfolding problem.

Why?

Well, because cruising through Jenny's crib on caps is like walking around inside of that Beatles cartoon, *Yellow Submarine.*

That is, until Jenny randomly appeared before me.

I was attempting to cross the threshold to the front porch, adjusting my pitch and angle to account for turbulence and avoid all the drunken passersby when Jenny snagged me by both wings (my outstretched arms, really), stopping me mid-flight.

"You gotta help me hide the remaining keg, Pat!" she pleaded, sorta freaking me out a bit. Her cheeks were full of swirling spirals of skin, and despite the floor beneath us rolling around in waves, she seemed unaffected by the motion.

I winced and pulled my arms back, asking, "Why do I have to do it?"

"Because I don't know where anyone else is and they're destroying my parents' house, Patrick! They're breaking shit and somebody kicked a hole into the wall in the bathroom! The fucking bathroom, Pat! This shit is completely out of control!"

I grinned. "Well that's sorta the point, isn't it, Jenny?"

"Patrick!" she cried aloud. And you know I'm a complete sucker for cringy-ass whining of the female-in-distress variety, so I immediately cracked.

"Okay, okay! But what do you want from *me*, Jenny? What do you want *me* to do? I'm tripping my goddamn balls off!" I said, rubbing my face just to make sure it was still connected.

(It was—thank you, Jesus!)

Jenny swatted her forehead and wailed, "Just...just, just, just go get the keg from downstairs and bring it up here!. Yeah! Or, I mean, bring it up to my room and I'll go find Matt and we'll lock the room once it's in there! And then everyone will eventually leave."

I laughed, cause to me, she speak-a-da'-dumb. "That shit ain't gonna work. I'm totally, you know, woo-who and shit, and even I don't think that's the right play. Why would that work?" Asking a surprisingly valid question given my tripped-out state. Yay for me.

"Because it will. It *will*. Just—Look, if we hide the cheese, the mice will just have to go and find someplace else to party and destroy shit! Now go get it! Please!"

"This is a bad idea, Jenny." (Yet another valid quip from this shroomin' dude over here. I was on a roll.)

"Just go and bring it up there and I'll meet you upstairs. Ready?"

"No," I said flatly.

"Great. Let's go!" She scurried off into the Technicolor blur of the partying multitudes and I'm lost in the glare of the tracers she leaves behind. Peaking like a motherfucker—what's happening to this guy.

And so I turned and crossed the landing to the stairwell which leads from her kitchen area to the downstairs.

I rigidly marched directly down into the blacklight abyss. As I stepped onto the concrete floor, my ears filled with thick bass and my eyes watered from the din of dense chronic smoke. I waved my hands in the air to clear my vision, but it had no effect. Sauntering aimlessly into the misty breach, I passed by lots of partially obscured classmates. Fortuitously, my feet swiftly arrived at the keg. It was situated next to the wall not too far from the bottom of the stairs, *thank God*.

And flanking the little metal ball on all sides was a cadre of vato-loco-mofos that would peel me like a goddamn grape if I did anything to raise their hackles. So what does this little gringo go right on ahead and do?

Exactly that.

I raised up their damn hackles by walking up like some automaton, kneeling by the Fat Tire keg, and wrapping my arms around it. Then I hoisted it up like I was giving it the Heimlich maneuver, but instead, I just fucking flee.

The immuno-response from the system of partygoers around me was swift and all encompassing. Several stood up, pointing, and began to batter my brain with questions I was simply in no condition to answer. Others began to follow the keg. My mission was not to be deterred.

Rushing past people in a kaleidoscope of faces, I felt often not empty Solo cups and crumpled cans hitting my head, while the room started to shout for me to be stopped at all costs before I made off with their alcoholic totem.

But the thing is—and I'm not sure if it was some sorta Mario-level fungus power granted by the shrooms that was giving my muscles extra *oomph*, or if the keg baby I held so tightly in my arms was just largely empty—I scurried up the stairs with speed that surprised even me. A flurry of mad grasps swiped at my head as I ascended the two flights of stairs between the basement and the second floor. It felt like the scene from *Labyrinth* with the hands in the dark well snatching at Jennifer Connolly's hair.

Unfortunately for me, once I reached the summit, the beer-less multitudes milling about the first floor noticed me being all-but-chased by the basement dwellers and joined in on the pursuit.

Trailing a train of the hella hostile, I rushed down the hallway and pitched my body through Jenny's door. She and her dude were there with a few of our other friends. (Can't recall who—maybe Tami, maybe Amy, maybe Crystal, but I'm barely making out faces by now.) I dropped the keg while Matt tried to throw a blanket over it, as though this was gonna work to quell the advancing horde of beer mongers.

It did not.

Bursting in the same door I just had was a thick stream of ravenously beer-hungry underagers, clamoring for the keg which was not particularly well hidden beneath the blanket which they were already pulling at.

And this kid, some freckly red-headed dude wearing a white wife-beater and JNCO jeans, started to yell some shit at Matt and Jenny about being team players and hospitable hosts, and I felt like I was in a hallucinatory episode of *Divorce Court* with all the damn shouting. Words becoming muddied and weird.

It wasn't more than five seconds before these two would-be big men on campus came to the questionable conclusion that, much like the *Highlander*, there can be only one, and started to brawl.

A bad boy batter brawl.

Inside a bedroom that is barely suited to have more than a handful of occupants, we now had this unfolding chaos of a fistfight erupting before us. People streamed in to join the impromptu melee.

Jenny's got this crazy hanging chair which is affixed to the ceiling support beams, and she was utilizing it as a swatting implement to beat at the red-headed kid. Meanwhile, her man Matt was just a storm of flying fists, like in a kung fu movie. And like some Irish pikey with a bone to pick, the red-headed licorice whip was holding his own by landing blow after blow into Matt's rib cage.

Eventually, Matt and this kid—I think his name is Jack, my buddy Ryan's brother—were pulled apart while others immediately supplanted their positions amid the ensuing chaos and resumed the indiscriminate pummeling.

It was all too much, and I didn't want to wait to see who emerged the victor. I'm thinking, *Where's the fucking exit, man? I gotsta get the hell outta this hellish hellscape of hellish hell.*

And so I did.

Nearly tumbling through the open door as I scrambled past reinforcements for both sides of the quarrel currently afoot, I squeezed past body after body and booked it down the hall, shooting to the bottom of the stairs.

Back on the main level, I jetted past the landing and through the front door. Emerging into the crisp, cool night air, I was suddenly awash in relief, and the paranoia completely subsided.

Sometimes it just takes a small change of scenery to wildly alter the course of your drug experience.

Stepping out onto the porch where a good thirty people had gathered to smoke or hang out, I reached into my pocket to grab myself a smoke. Lighting it up, I noticed my sometimes chum—a goatee and faux-hawk-rocking tall drink of pharmaceutical intake named Calvin—standing by the mailbox with several other partygoers. He was smoking a bowl and staring up at the windows to Jenny's room. I approached, and he handed me the glass pipe.

As I took a toke, he asked me the obvious question: "What's going on up there?"

In the moment, I found it difficult to fully summarize the terrifying Thunderdome I had just barely escaped from without receiving any obvious bodily injury, so in lieu of a coherent or relevant reply, I mumbled something about the moon making everyone nuts that even I didn't really track.

Understanding all too well that I must be on some hallucinogenic, he smiled, nodded, and accepted that as a reasonable response to his query. "Cool," he said with a dopey fuck grin.

And for a few minutes, everything seemed better, chiller, more manageable. I had my peak visuals going, and the fight upstairs seemed to have subsided.

Then—

The attention of Calvin, as well as several of the people around us, diverted from the party and toward a parade of lights rolling up the long, dusty road that runs past Jenny's place and further on up Cattle Creek. This, in turn, naturally drew my attention.

By the pricking of my thumbs...it's the Church of the Dusk Harvest.

That's what they call themselves. A flamboyantly titled, albeit sheltered and secretive society of agrarian sycophants/religious zealots of unknown deity that live just outside of Carbondale, somewhere o'er hill and dale. Nobody knows exactly where their homestead lies, but you see them in town from time to time. Truth be told, I'd always made them for your average run-of-the-mill Amish/Mennonite wannabes.

But I was wrong. Deadly wrong.

Which happens sometimes—me being wrong. I mean, not *often*, but sometimes. I want that to be clear up front.

Surprising everyone standing outside of Jenny's house, me included, they pulled those Hallmark TV movie carriages they drive around to a slow approach on the asphalt. And, even more interestingly, actually turned down the winding driveway toward the sprawling and already overfilled parking lot area in front of Jenny's place. Slowly leading the procession of dark chariots were gorgeous black stallions, manes softly reflecting the light that each carriage's single swinging oil lamp afforded. Bridled in black leather straps, they'd be all but invisible in the darkness without the glow of the lanterns.

Winding between the parked cars, they made a line to form a sort-of barrier between the house and most of the vehicles in the parking area. Shrouded drivers pulled at taught reins, bringing the black boxes to a full stop.

Despite the silence of the night and the soft murmur that the sight of the unholy parade had drawn from the previously boisterous crowd (which had largely fallen silent), the music still pumped loudly from inside the house. Ricky Martin's "La

Vida Loca," of all things, was flowing into the air when the first one made his grand entrance onto the scene of the soon-to-be slaughter.

Yeah, you read that right. Slaughter.

One of their kindred (this is apparently what they call one another—the *kindred*), a taller man with pale cheeks and bloodshot eyes, stepped out of the closest carriage. Standing maybe one hundred yards away, he was wearing a priest's four-point biretta and sporting a sparse beard of white that ran down nearly all the way to the brass toe buckles set upon his anachronistic, handmade shoes.

The handful of us watching this bizarre sight saw that the line of carriages must've been ten or fifteen strong. Twenty, maybe? I dunno, I'm fucking tripping, so just…please stay with me here.

What could've been as few as fifty, but to me (at a hallucinatory glance) appeared as hundreds of dark-clothed cultists, flowed from the open doors of their carriages. All with small black caps, most with wire-rimmed, old-timey glasses, and each with a long, dense beard. All men. It was impossible to count the scores amid the rapidly disarming sprawl, to say nothing of the thin zig zags that the lanterns on each carriage were creating before my eyes.

Then, the real bullshit jumped off.

They pulled out scythes, pitchforks, and axes. Chaff cutters. Spades. Trowels, and large pairs of gardening shears. Goddamn *shears!* Can you imagine? Some brandished sharpened shovels and spike poles, and one even had what sure looked like a hammer with a spike on top. Sparkling, shimmering, tracer-rippling metal implements of all types, cutting through the night air.

They flowed like angry bees from the open-door carriages, and slithered like serpents between the cars, trucks, and jeeps—all at a slow but steady pace.

Then, without pause, they began to swing at nearby partygoers.

In response, chaos erupted. People scrambled away from the porch, some darting inside in the hope of finding shelter; others darting into the dark, closely chased by the weapon-brandishing lunatics.

One madwoman with a pitchfork and a long blonde ponytail wrapped in black lace brought the tongs into the ground with a thump. Her target was obscured by a car, but I prayed that it wasn't somebody's head. Otherwise that person was...just so totally not alive anymore.

By this point, the weapon-wielding loons were storming toward the house. As they did so, the music player faded out Ricky and began to blast out the playful opening chords of Len's "Steal My Sunshine."

Amid the cobwebbed clutter of my mind, a horrifying thought dawned: *They'll kill us all if we don't run. I need to go, go, buffalo!*

Feet don't fail me now. Amid the screaming and clamoring and weapon brandishing and partiers fighting for their lives, I jetted.

Darting between the house and cars parked in front, I didn't stop, and I didn't look back. No way was I giving those creepy, churchy, culty rat-bastards the chance to get anywhere near me. I cut across the south lawn, wrapping around the house and bypassing the car-filled dirt lot.

"The fuck are you going, buddy?" an unaware partygoer hollered as I passed, but I paid them no mind. I just kept running. Behind me, a swirling blur of shouting and screaming and God knows what wickedness—and I was *not* staying to see what happened.

Not what I signed up for. *Nuh-uh.*

So, that's how I've found myself running down Cattle Creek Road away from the scythe and sickle-swinging sect members presumably slaughtering my schoolmates and friends.

Will any of them still be alive after this? The thought fills me with dread. And what if they finish up there then set their demon-nags upon my heels? Why, I'd just have to go for their goddamn eyes. With my thumbs.

Heavenly salvation arrives in the form of light beams from an oncoming car. I wave my arms frantically, yelling for the car to stop. It does, slowing to a pebble-crackling crawl, and a sigh of relief gusts out of me.

The moment is made more comforting still when the window rolls down and it is two of my closest friends, Cholla and Colette, in a Chollas gray '88 Volkswagen Jetta. I clamp my hands onto the passenger side door and swallow to clear my chalky mouth.

Staring out at me with humorous pity, they ask what's wrong and why I'm down here instead of up at the party.

I try to tell them, but it doesn't go smoothly. I shake my palms and shriek, "Cholla, Colette; thank fuck it's you! We are turning around and we are *leaving!* They have pitchforks! Seriously big pitchforks! Creepy, farming fuckers. Like that painting—the painting! You know…" They look at me blankly. "Uh, the one with that wrinkly old couple… *American Gothic!* That's the one, that's the one! They had forks like that—big fucking forks! And goddamn gardening shears! Can you imagine?"

Collette, seated in the driver's seat, shoots a giggle-infused look to Cholla. Then they both look at me like I'm just hallucinating. Which is fair, 'cause I am, but I'm also speaking the truth.

Cholla, clearly hoping to calm me a bit, pats the top of my hand.

I frown. "I'm not just hallucinating."

"Uh, okay. Well, let's just go back up to the party and see if we—"

"No, we gotta leave! We can't go back! We gotta roll. They're gonna kill us! Everybody is dead up there. Everybody! We gotta get the cops."

"Pat, dude, are you tripping?" Cholla asks, eyes wide.

"Well, yeah. Of course I am—too much albino penis envy. *Lotsa* penis envy. But that's not why I'm making this up.

Or…no, I mean I'm *not* making it up. Damn it! Fucking shrooms make it hard to talk, Jesus. We gotta go! *We gotta go!*"

"Hey, hey!" A voice echoes off the narrow valley walls from further up the canyon.

Whoever it is, they aren't on the road, exactly. They're down the slope from Jenny's place by a good bit. Maybe one hundred yards away from us.

But not knowing who the fuck it is, I yank open the door to the backseat and dive in head-first. Then, yanking the door shut, I roll onto the floorboards and cover my head with my hands, as if that's going to stop the long tongs of a pitchfork. "Oh fuck, oh fuck! That's them! We gotta go! Oh shit, we're gonna die," I hiss.

Both of my homegirls in the front seat think it's a joke, laughing accordingly. But it is *no joke*. They know nothing of the kegs or the carriages or the cultists or the backdrop of Caucasian vs. Chicano Cold War contempt! Fools, I say! *Fools!*

And now—footsteps outside.

Oh, Jesus, who in the hell is this coming forth from the harrowing unknown to kill us? Have they a pitchfork of my imminent demise firmly in their grasp? I can't bear to watch!

Cholla leans her blonde, makeup-less, vegan head out of the window and calls into the dusty cloud just up the road from us. "Hey, who's that out there?"

"It's me! Just me. Jack Wolfe. Are you guys heading back up to the party? Can I score a ride with you?"

My stomach is in knots. What if it's one of them just pretending to be Jack Wolfe? And wasn't Jack just up at the party? Wasn't there a fisticuffs? Wasn't he part of said fisticuffs? He was wailing on Matt's beefy ribs, as I recall.

What the hell is happening? Why would we go back there? Who the fuck wants to get impaled by madmen with machetes and pitchforks? Only a chain of fools would do that. And why doesn't Jack sense the danger I am? Did he not see the—

Cholla and Colette wave him over to the "Midget Mobile" (this is literally what Cholla calls her unreliable Jetta—long story, nevermind).

Jack strides up to the driver's side and Colette rolls down her window. She brushes her long brown hair from her face as she asks, "Is the party normal?"

He wrinkles his nose, but smiles. "I don't know about normal. Aside from a drag out that just occurred, it's been pretty cool, I guess. Why?"

"What are you wandering in the woods for, Jack? You take the phrase, 'huntin' beaver' just a bit too literally?"

Both of my friends laugh out loud, but I don't think it's funny. Not funny at all. Upon the upholstered floor, I merely twitch with fear.

Jack lowers his head slightly, peering down at his shoes as he sheepishly confesses, "Ah, no. No, I just—uh, I got asked to take a twenty minute walk by my brother because I was getting a bit handsy about the keg. And like I said, I got into it with that one dude. Jenny's meathead boyfriend. Whatever, dudes a prick. So I ducked out the back to take a stretch and a leak. I was smoking and pissing in the woods over there and was about to head back up in a couple minutes when I saw

Patrick run past. Then he was screaming like a bitch on the road, flagging you down. I'm friends with his sister and thought he might be having a freak out." He leans in enough to see me on the floorboards in the back and laughs at me. "You okay back there, dude?"

"No, I'm not. I'm fucking not! Because those fuckers at the house have weapons and are killing everybody!"

Jack scoffs. "No they don't, and no they aren't. And who are *they?* The guys in the basement had weapons? So what, man? Those *vatos* always have weapons."

I shake my head, not that anyone can see me. "You had to have seen them! Bunch of culty thugs."

"Who?" he asks.

I think he's just being difficult, but I keep indulging it in the hope that it delays our return to the murder house. My tongue rolls around nervously in my closed mouth because, uh, *mushrooms.* Still, I manage to cough out, "A bunch of horse-drawn buggies showed up after the fight for the fate of the keg kicked off! And—and I saw everyone starting to get hit with farm implements and so I ran, and we should go get help! Before they rend our flesh in twain!"

"In twain?" Jack raises his gaze from my shuddering form in the back seat to Cholla and Collete. He chuckles and quietly asks them, "Is he fucking serious?"

Cholla shakes her head. "Serious? Patrick? Rarely. Essentially never, actually. Though you gotta remember, he's loopy and tripping pretty hard, so…" She shrugs. "Still, it *is* getting a little old, Pat. Little too looney, even for you."

"Lies!" I hiss back.

Jack chuckles and crosses his arms while shooting a glance back up in the direction of Jenny's casa. "I guess I must have missed all that bullshit. So—wait, you mean to tell me that you think everyone is back there getting murdered, and you're just running away like a bitch?"

"Yes!" I cry from my floorboard hidey hole.

"No." Cholla leans over the console to answer Jack. "We just ran into this crazy bastard headed to town on our way up to the party. There probably isn't anything happening up there. Ignore Pat."

And just then, in a rare sign from God that I am right way more than people ever wanna freely admit, what sure sounds like several gunshots ring into the night air. All three of my cohort turn their heads toward this puzzling new addition to the scenario.

Jack scrunches his brow (I'm assuming, since I can't see fuck all from where I'm hiding). "Actually, that does sound like some shit is going down. We should get back there, right now. Let's go!" Jack pulls open the rear driver's side door and drops himself into the seat in one smooth motion, while I scramble up and into the other side of said backseat to avoid being crushed. The door shuts behind him as he slaps the seat back with his palm. "Let's roll, baby!"

Cholla shifts the VW into gear and mutters, "Not your baby."

Ignoring her, Jack claps his hands together, as if he is actually reveling in this harrowing fucking tilt-a-whirl. "Was that a gunshot?" he asks, eyes wide and enthralled. "That sounded like a fucking gat."

"*Like a gat?*" I start to laugh uncomfortably. "What, like in *Dick Tracy* or something?" I notice a tiny spot of blood on his wife beater and point my finger at it. "You got a little blood there."

Jack cocks an eyebrow my way. "Matt punched my nose and it got on my shirt. Who's Dick Tracy?"

Collette's face is suddenly serious. "That actually did sound like a gun. Wait, Pat, is there—was there a shooter up there? Is this like a Columbine thing?"

Justifiably nervous glances all around, minds on the events of a couple weeks ago.

And now I'm shouting again. "That's what I've been saying, damn it! You heard it—gunfire! See? See? What did I fucking say? There's a big fight with big forks and we are fucking fucked if we don't go get somebody or something to help us escape them! *Let's escape!*"

"Shh! Pat, you're barely making sense. Just do everyone a favor and shut up for once in your—" Cholla cuts herself off, exasperated.

"I'm serious. This is gonna be bad." I say this as we round the winding road and spy a glimpse of some of the backyard area.

Jack leans in between the seats, shoving me aside in the process, and says, "It…does look like some unwelcome guests crashed the party alright, but it doesn't look like they're doing very well."

"What do you mean?" I ask, looking through the foggy glass toward the light of the house and barn, seeing nada.

"Take a look. It looks like some Amish dudes and..." Jack trails off.

Coming around the bend to the drive, we see that not only has the chaos died down, but the battle has taken a hard turn away from the assailants' favor.

Upended black cloth carriages now lay strewn around the dusty parking lot, tethered to broken frames. Fleeing horses dart past the windows as we approach. They whinny and drag bridles behind them, kicking up dust.

Near the house, which is still bumping out music (at this moment the appropriately manic "The Rockafeller Skank" by Fatboy Slim), there is a blurry flurry of activity. While several screams and a mad frenzy of shouts fill the air, so does the song's chorus.

Right about now, the funk soul brother. Check it out now, the funk soul brother...

However, it doesn't seem as though our friends are being made mincemeat of. On the contrary, more than a few of the cultists that I saw attacking before are now subdued and on the ground in front of a positively ferocious mob of teenagers. Others scattered about are likewise ground-prone, being beaten and tied up. It's suddenly all feeling a bit too much like *Lord of the Flies*. But what it isn't, is a scene of my classmates dying.

No.

Rather, they've actually turned the aforementioned tide just as readily as the wave had come crashing onto the metaphorical shore—or something.

Parking and rapidly jumping out of the vehicle, we see that the meat of the battle, brief though it surely must've been, is essentially all but over. Cholla, Collette, and Jack stride toward a shouting group who have subdued four of the cultists onto their knees. The group is led by our other friend Alise, who has a blood flecked wooden baseball bat slung over her shoulder.

I follow behind the other three anxiously, snake a fresh Camel Light Menthol from my pack, then light it up to calm my nerves as we draw closer.

I cannot understand what I am seeing. There are dead people in black robes, but it doesn't seem like they managed to do anything much to any of the people who came to party. Several bodies, unmoving, have been impaled, sliced, bludgeoned, and bashed with their own wicked tools of death. This one dead fucker I pass has two bullet holes in his chest.

Who the actual fuck thought to bring a gun to this scintillating soiree?

All around, people are standing up still-breathing cultists and slapping their cheeks. Glasses are being torn from bloodied faces, but it really seems like there are nil losses on our side out front. One hopes the same is true for those in the rest of the house.

Lots of chest beating and rousing cheers bounce about within the wall of sound that surrounds us. It sounds like

Friday night football with our stompin' Rams at home, not like whatever these cracker-jacks from up in the hills had planned for our motley lot.

"Is that dude bleeding from his face?" Cholla asks as we approach the settling melee. Amid the chaotic din and kneeling on the ground by the other three is some bookish Mennonite-looking cat in black coveralls. He appears to be bleeding from his pasty, freckled face, and though his wrists and fists are bound before him, he's holding a red-stained towel against his chin.

People are randomly tossing things at him, including empty shooters and sticks. And that feels...sorta appropriate, if I'm being honest. Fuck this dude.

Somebody shouts, "Tore that bitch's beard clean off!"

A roar of collective agreement from those around us. More chest beating. Whistles and the happy slapping of nearby surfaces by bludgeoning objects in Cro-Magnon approval.

"You tore off his beard?" I ask, dazed and confused, yet somewhat amused. Loud noises and bright lights are everywhere, in all directions. I can barely tell anyone apart through the trapezoidal haze.

I don't know how everybody else is focusing with all of these goddamn technicolor distractions.

"Hell yeah, we did!" This is my buddy Calvin speaking as he makes his way over to us between the flood of people. He's got blood on his bare chest. And, yeah, it's there because he ain't got no shirt on. Plus he's holding a bloody knife in one hand like he's Michael Myers or something. "Well, *I* did.

Easier done than you'd think. Just gave it a yank and *POP!* Tore his fucking shit off his dumb fucking chin! Then I stabbed this other dude to death who was gonna try and kill Jade over there."

He points at a crying girl sitting on the ground, and I recognize the friend of my sister, Jade Castellano. She is dressed in see-through pants and a shirt, with her bra and underwear on full display as result. And I'm wondering why she's clothed in such wildly provocative clothing amid all this chaos. She should cover up.

But then I remember that I was thinking about torn beards.

"What the hell?" I ask my buddy, giving him an incredulous look, puffing wildly at my menthol smoke.

Calvin pumps his fist, then explains that, "I know, man. I know. I *killed a dude.* But this crazy bastard came at us with a friggin' scythe!"

"It was a sickle, dude," some rando guy standing nearby corrects him.

Calvin's blasts back, "Who gives a fuck? Hezekiah here is just damn lucky we didn't bury it in his Day-Glo dome after that happy crappy!" Calvin turns to face the row of four men on their knees. Then I notice a row of a few muscular sportos that are milling about behind the four.

Over the heads of several people and standing atop a small bench in the front yard, there's this one short little punk wearing punker shit. (You know, rocking leather and a buzz cut.) He says, "He's not wrong, though. Tore his beard right off. Shit was funny."

"Seriously?" Colette asks.

The kid innocently waves his hands and assures us, "Yeah, but don't worry, we got him that towel. He probably won't bleed out. I don't think he'll bleed out."

"I'm going to bleed out." This from the muffled mouth of the kneeling man in coveralls.

Calvin hollers, "Oh, you should just shut up, you crazy bastard! Someone's likely to beat your brains out like they did to your boy back there!"

Then the same creepy cultist mofo hoarfs out, "Who's dead? What now becomes of the harvest?"

"Harvest?" Cholla cries, seemingly emboldened by the sheer insanity of the moment and startling us all. "What? Did you—do you assholes mean this is like a ritualistic slaughter or somethin'?"

Mumbling through a dripping red rag, this kneeling cat confirms that, "It is exactly that, yes. Oh, yeay, upon *His* decree did we come forth to spill the blood of the innocent. To bathe our flesh for the coming crusade." He coughs and clears his throat. "That was the plan, anyway." Shifting the bloody rag under his chin, he finishes, "We shall mend the Earth following the harvest."

"You loopy-brained crackpots thought you'd find innocent blood to spill *here*?" Alise spins around as she pumps her gore-smeared baseball bat in the air. The surrounding masses cheer at the medieval sight. "We're all drugged up, drunk as fuck, and there ain't a single angel among us, you Amish turd!"

The crowd cheers and hoots loudly as a crumpled-up can of Pabst Blue Ribbon flies from someone's hand. It hits the farthest left cultist in the face, soaking and covering his bruised mouth with sudsy booze.

"We are not Amish!" the beer-drizzled man protests. "We are the kindred who plow through the—"

"Shut the fuck up." Calvin swats his hand through the air. Two more crumpled cans soar past, but miss their mark and hit the ground between us and the four mental patients/religious zealots.

I'm puffing on my cigarette like a dope fiend sucking on a lightbulb when my chemically addled brain tells me to randomly jump in and ask, "Harvest? What harvest? Who's harvesting?"

Enter this rando from stage left; some big brawny bastard with a gold and blue Rams jersey who strides through the crowd and points a red-stained fingertip at the four Dusk Harvest dipshits. "You thought you were gonna come here and spill blood? You guys should've trained more, 'cause that was fucking pathetic!"

Cheers and bottles clinking from the onlookers.

Before the bleeding dude can expound further, some heretofore hidden member of the Church of the Dusk Harvest—a short little pipsqueak in a dark robe with blood-frenzied eyes—comes flying out from his concealment behind one of the nearby cars. He raises a fistful of shiny metal blade above his head and makes like he's gonna stab one of us.

Reacting faster than I can currently fathom, Jack deftly snatches a half empty bottle of Mad Dog 20/20 from the hood of a compact car next to him and cracks it over the little bastard's skull. Glass shatters, orange liquor sprays out, and a forehead is cut wide open and gushes with blood as the dude in the robe hits the ground with a satisfying thud. People cheer.

Jack tosses the broken shard of bottle neck over his shoulder and shrugs at us, grinning widely. He nods at the four zealots on the ground. "You were saying?"

Colette takes one step to the front of our impromptu inquisition panel and randomly demands her own answers. "Who even orders you to do this? Do you have some de facto evil priest who commands all of you to do this shit, or is this just some wacky interpretation of the King James? What's the score here, Ezekiel?"

The one in the middle she appears to be speaking to (the beardless wonder) blurts out, "My good name is not Ezekiel! For he is Ezekiel, o'er yonder! My brother is lying prone and taken of his Earthly life where you struck him down. You have felled him, so you have! You've felled my fourth favorite brother, Ezekiel! And now—oh yeay—he is felled!" He points a fingertip over to another man who is wearing the same anachronistic clothing—a white button up shirt and black suspenders—lying dead on the ground, a pitchfork sticking out it of his skull and a growing film of spit accumulating on his face from everyone hocking loogies on his dead corpse.

That's really nasty, right there. And unseemly, and I think we're all better than that, you know? But, you know…whatever.

"Yeah, that's… Yeah, he's definitely, uh, felled. But it really doesn't matter, now. So who are you, bloody boy?"

"I am Jacob and these are my other brothers who are not yet felled. Their names are as follows—"

"Stop!" Calvin shouts, and the four go quiet. "That's a great story. But you zealots always miss the fact that your hibbidy-who is all null and void when you use it to justify your own disgusting ends."

Just as Calvin is laying into these creepy buggers, Jenny comes tearing ass from around the house with a large metal stick in her hands. "What the ever-loving shit is happening? What have you all done to my parents' house?"

Calvin holds up his hand to calm her and explains, "Some culty nutbags came to kill everyone here, failed spectacularly, got mostly merc'd, and now we're poking them in the nug bone for the haps, ya dig?"

The only person who actually lives here screams back, "No! No I don't *dig*, Calvin! I don't dig *any of this!* Look at all this blood on my lawn!"

I have just about had enough of Jenny's *Chicken Little* routine, so I say, "Dude, Jenny, shut your shit all the way down! Breathe and take a goddamn chill pill. This shit could've been so much worse."

"How, Patrick? How in the fucking shit-smeared kangaroo cockup could this have been any worse?"

Alise ignores the sideline convo we're having, points her Louisville Slugger of doom at the kneeling cultists, and presses the dude with the bloody rag a bit more. "Why did you assholes just do this? Or…fail to do this, rather?

"It is our divine charge to do so. We must rescue the soil from the perpetuation of corruption. For only sixty harvests remain—"

In an unsettling little cue, the other cult members within earshot affect a somber tone as they all repeat his words in spooky unison. "Sixty harvests remain."

The music from the house suddenly switches to The Prodigy's "Smack my Bitch Up."

"Wait, what? You guys are creepy as shit, by the way. But, what do you mean 'sixty harvests remain'?" Cholla demands.

Again the voices call out in unison, "Sixty harvests remain."

Cans start to fly toward the heads of the cultists who spoke. Foamy beer fully coats their hair and beards and they all bear the helpless look of college pledges being mercilessly hazed.

They should be so lucky.

"Stop with that harmony of horror horseshit! Just answer the question," Calvin deadpans at them.

Calmly, Jacob—the bleeding face one—Jacob, says, "Earth science tells us that, within sixty years, the world will lose all plantable topsoil, upon which ninety-five percent of the planet's food depends. That's only sixty more harvests."

The echo of the statement carries from the mouths of the others, and this time the "Sixty more harvests" is cut short by a cacophony of booing from the crowd around us.

More beer cans. More chest bumping. More laughter.

"Uh, so you guys believe in science?" I blurt out.

Jacob scoff-snorts. "But of course we do. We aren't Amish, for Christ's sake."

Calvin takes a toke off a joint that has randomly appeared in his left hand, and studies them. "So you're...what, then? You're just like a bunch of demented eco-terrorists or sumthin'? That's why you came and wrecked the party? Are you fucking serious? That's all this is about? 'Cause you think the world is gonna end and your hyped up bullshit is gonna stop that?"

The swollen crowd bellows and giggles at this statement.

"Ain't shit stalling out the future, buddy. We *are* the future," Jack Wolfe quips to further laughter. He smiles widely at the reaction, soaking in the fleeting moment that he has any role in the scene.

Jacob raises his head defiantly, withdrawing the rag so his words are clearer. "The world cannot survive with the wicked spreading as they do. As you do. *All* of you. You are all the wretched demon-seed of a generation who failed you and led you from the one true God!"

Alise smirks at this. "Which one?"

Jacob's eyes swell with anger. "If you have to ask, then it's only too clear that—"

Alise then waves her hand dismissively. "Yeah, okay; whatever dude. Just shut it. No one cares. No more bullshit. No more demonic eco terrorist sermon. Save it for the piggies."

"Has someone called the police?" I shout, immediately realizing I didn't need to yell and sheepishly recoiling as if that will somehow retract it.

"Yeah, yeah, someone called. I think Nathan or Tami might've. They were both headed inside to—" Jenny catches her words as she notices a dead body on the ground not too far from where she earlier parked her red Mitsubishi Eclipse. "Is that a dead body?" She points a finger at the corpse on the grass, and the sea of people part so we can see the guy clearly. "Is—is that a dead person on my parents' front lawn?"

This big, stocky, letter jacket-clad jockosaurus rex in the Rams jersey takes a step toward the body and kicks it in the ribs, eliciting not even a wheeze from it. "Yeah. He's dead. A bunch are. Super dead. The fuck have *you* been?"

Jenny's face sinks as she closes her eyes and murmurs, "I was inside trying to clean up the guest bathroom and heard screaming. How the hell am I going to explain a corpse to my parents?"

Calvin takes a big swing of a tequila bottle that is randomly handed to him and winks at me. "There's more than one, actually." He holds up his hand for me to slap, and I go ahead and high five him, because why not?

"Okay, *corpses*. How do I explain corpses to my parents?"

Before she can pontificate further, there is a loud crash from inside the house and she turns to rush back inside. Me and a few others follow her instinctively through the front screen door.

Just inside the mudroom, a fresh body has dropped to the floor. He must have been one of the last Harvest mofos to meet his end. His head is twisted around like someone snapped it. I didn't think this was a thing that happens in real life, but apparently it is.

Stepping over him, we hear what sure sounds like the Roaring Fork Ram cheer bouncing off the walls of the house. It sounds crazy, like some unholy chorus, but more jovial.

Crossing through the foyer into the rest of Jenny's abode, I hear shouting from downstairs, and it sounds like a wave of bodies are rapidly rushing up from the basement where the keg had once lain.

Amid a flood tide of fleeing Chicano gangster-types in black low-rider sunglasses, our charming Latina pal, Tina, comes flying out the door to the basement. There is a splash of blood across her face, but she seems otherwise unharmed. Brown hair tied back, with a form-fitting black dress on. Always fashionably dressed, this one.

"Hey!" she shouts in an unsuitably bubbly fashion. "Is everything okay up here?"

People scurry past in droves while Jenny runs to Tina and starts to check her over, asking, "Holy fuck! Is this your blood? Are you bleeding? Did you get stabbed by one of those fuckers?"

"No, no. Not for a lack of trying, though. I'm good."

"Did they come down there?"

"Oh, yeah. A bunch of 'em came downstairs, but they didn't make it far. They're all dead."

"What?" Jenny screams, horrified and looking like Carrie at this point, with the blood on her face and the whole nine. "Who got killed now? Tell me there aren't more corpses in my parents' basement!"

"Uh, can't help ya there, chica. They're fucking dead, alright. *Muy muerto.* It makes sense, though. I mean, what do you think? That these hooded clowns came rolling down into a backlit basement where thugs 'n' locs are catching brews and rolling blunts and just start trying to off fools like it's GTA or something? Most of these homies were carrying at least a blade or two. I saw one kid with a gun. They filled one of those nutty faggots full of holes! I even managed to kick one square in his fucking balls before he got beaten to a bloody pulp. Damn, girl. We just stopped a massacre."

Jenny eyeballs Tina and gives a half smile, clearly resigned to the crazy story we'll have to tell the police when they come to collect what is left of The Church of Dusk Harvest. "You know, you're right!"

"Course I'm right!" Tina holds up her hand, and Jenny high fives her.

"They broke into my house, right? We have witnesses, and even if my parents want to kill me and never again leave me the house alone again, at least we didn't lose anybody. Wait—is everyone okay in the basement?"

"Not those eight or so dead *putos* in the black robes. But yeah, everybody who matters is good. I think Johnny might be puking, but that's 'cause he mixed Cuervo shots with some—"

I jump in. "Ladies, ladies; let's go! We should make our way back out front to see if everyone really is okay. Plus we might wanna tell everyone not to kill those nut bags—just in case the cops wanna question them or something."

Tina and Jenny nod, hug each other, then follow me back outside. I've got the tail end of my smoke in hand, and as we head toward the front door, I take another drag.

Jenny scowls at me. "You can't smoke in my parents' house, Pat!"

"Shut up, Jenny," I say good naturedly.

Coming back outside to the few cultists in front and an adolescent mob scene of spectacular proportions, we hear cheers and clinking glasses. I snub out my smoke on the front stoop and we rejoin Cholla, Colette, Calvin, Jack, and Alise (who's still holding that bloody bat).

Jacob cradles his de-bearded chin and mumbles, "Well, what now?"

And we're all standing there, not knowing what to say to this asshole when we hear the distant sound of sirens. Immediately, half of the party attendees are running to their cars and find themselves working to move carriages out of the way and shoo horses. All so they can make a beeline before the police show up. It's one thing to brazenly leave the scene of a fresh crime—especially one sown with so much bloodshed—but when there has been wholesale slaughter on this scale, there are hundreds of you, and you have drugs on your persons, fleeing the scene is a much more explainable endeavor. You can always say, "I was scared I was gonna die." And *BOOM*, you're probably off the proverbial hook.

It is with this foreknowledge (and just a smattering of panic) that at least twenty cars carrying a hundred or more attendees leave before the red and blues can arrive.

Once said coppers do arrive on the scene, it's about as funny as you'd expect—factoring in the large number of dead bodies. But I think for once, the cops sorta get what happened pretty quickly and cut us a break. Shoot, you might even say that whole thing was a badge of honor for those involved.

I thought that what we had come back to was going to be forever known in the Roaring Fork Valley as the day when some whacko cult from the snow-capped hills made bloody the earth with untold scores of hapless victims. But what I'm witnessing instead is that if you fuck with a bunch of Kid Rock, Tupac, and ICP lovin' wannabe tough guy white boys swinging metal baseball bats, to say nothing of tangling with a basement full of knife-wielding Mexican badasses, then you're gonna get your neck broke or your cheek sliced up—if not worse.

This is the whole thing about us Gen X'ers: We may be self-deprecating goofs (who think we possess some of the most progressive ideas the world has ever seen, as well as some of the most suicidal recording artists), but we also know how to fuck a motherfucker up and do not give much in the way of shits. They came to kill us, but instead got it back in droves. They brought their beliefs and got nothing good in return.

However, I don't think it was just their kooky beliefs which led to their ill-fated and rapid downfall. Beliefs don't kill people, as far as I can tell.

You wanna know what can kill ya deader-than-shit though? A goddamn scythe, that's what! Ever seen one of them big sonofabitches when it's razor sharp and being swung hard by a loon in a black robe? Thing'll take yer fucking head off, bruh. Forget about it.

And the moral of this story is…always do drugs and carry weapons?

Eh, who cares?

The End.

PITCHBLENDE

Deep within the labyrinthine network of interconnected chambers and winding tunnels in the subterra of Mount Sopris, Alex Thompson found himself wincing in the dim light provided by the handheld flashlight he'd been carrying for the last several hours. Certain that the batteries were rapidly losing their energy, he pulled off his yellow hardhat and turned the headlamp on.

A piercing bolt of white halogen light shot into his face, causing his eyelids to reflectively close. With one gloved hand, he rubbed his mop of dirty brown hair—slicked and sticky from hours of sweat—and slid the hat back on. Slowly cracking open his eyes, his vision adjusted to the increased light filling the cavern.

Allowing himself a moment for the white blur in his field of sight to dissipate, he could finally make out the open, subterranean passage that lay before him. Peering into the darkness of the narrow mineshaft, he noted that the ceiling was high enough that he could stand up straight, but low enough for him to reach out and touch if he so desired.

Not that any such desire was present.

Sure, he'd watched the obligatory training video on modern ceiling supports and how much safer the hydraulic lift chocks that held up the mine's roof were compared to the wooden supports most people thought of when they conjured the image of deep-mountain mining. Still, tempting fate was not something he'd signed up for with this gig.

As a matter of fact, this was not a gig he'd wanted to sign up for at all.

Removing it from his belt, the radio handset in his hand crackled lightly as he turned the transmit switch back on. Bouncing its signal through a series of comm relays placed intermittently throughout the winding tunnels of the Sopris Mine, it provided the sole communication tether to the chamber just off the mine's entrance which served as the supervisors office of sorts. The same area where his co-worker was currently watching his progress from its comparatively safe confines.

Alex hacked some dusty phlegm and spat on the floor before he hit the push-to-talk (PTT) button on the radio's side.

"Shit, now that's a vast improvement right there. I couldn't see half as much with that little hand torch. Think these batteries are on their last legs. You still gettin' me loud and clear?"

From the handset speaker, he heard the gravelly voice of Marcus Doma, the company man watching from a laptop in the supervisor's office/chamber. "Very loud, very clear."

"Good. Groovy. So, and I'm just asking here, but aren't we supposed to have someone with us at all times when we're this far in? I'm not complaining, but I thought I saw something about that on one of the videos I had to slog through."

"Hah! Yeah, yeah; you're not wrong. Not exactly standard operating procedure. Still within the technical constructs thereof, as long as I am monitoring you from a nearby location, it falls under the broader definition of the so-called buddy system. I'm monitoring you via camera feeds and radio, and I'm close enough to come and drag your ass to the surface should you choose to pass out."

Alex looked directly at the nearest camera lens mounted on the wall about fifteen feet away and frowned. "That's comforting."

The voice from the handset chuckled. "I'm just cracking your nutsack, buddy-boy. You're doing fine. Better than fine. A few more lights to hang, then you should go to the console, kick on the Komatsu, and wait for however long it takes. Probably ten minutes or so to hit our mark. Then turn it back off, check the readout, and update the log. We only need to

Patrick Quinn Kitson

chew four feet along the track for maybe fifty yards, so yeah, about ten minutes, I'd guesstimate. Day crew will be down here tomorrow to double-verify the chock support integrity and then the real work on this area can commence. We are probably still a good fifty feet out from the vein of marble that Robert is aiming for us to reach. You're close to it now, aren't you?"

"Close to what? The drill?"

"Yeah. Though if we're still being technical here, it's a Komatsu longwall shearer, not a drill."

"You know what I mean. And yeah, I can see it about fifty yards down."

Along the western wall of the narrow shaft under the support chocks which appeared every five feet or so was a long, orange track, known as the flexible conveyor train. It looked much like a metal slatted conveyor belt and was tasked with carrying the tension-broken rock debris away from the end of the primary drilling mechanism (shearer body). At the end of said mechanism, the J7500 ranging arm that pushed against the targeted area was fitted with a large cutter drum, over three feet in diameter. Once activated, the arm would effectively guide the cutter drum—fitted with hundreds of carbide steel-tipped teeth—against the wall and the debris would drop into the conveyor track, which would move the shorn rocks away from the drill site.

Marcus' voice came through his handset again. "When you get closer I'll switch to the primary shearer cam. Number nine. I'll keep an eye out, but we've no reason to worry."

"Great," Alex mumbled.

"Not having any second thoughts, are you?"

"Course not. Why do you ask?"

"Just checking for good measure. Robert said we'd be fine for tonight, but you certainly are correct about the buddy system. We try to have two bodies within thirty yards of one another for this kind of shearing. Kinda against the rules, kinda not."

"That's great. More comforting still. But it's gotta get done, right?"

"Right. And Robert knows damn well that this isn't an ideal sitch we got going down here, so it'll possibly gain you some credit in his view."

"Hope so. But I think we both know he won't notice."

"That we do," the voice from his radio agreed.

Alex unclipped another hanging light from his belt and secured it along the electrical mining cable high up on the eastern wall of the tunnel. "Anyway, this is what I signed up for, so giddy up, I guess. Not like there's any real option."

But he knew that that wasn't really the case. For as with any harrowing and physically treacherous activity, there were always options.

In fact, he was acutely aware that he could've done something else entirely. With his arguably overqualified resume, he could have easily scored almost any retail job within a hundred miles. With his education and flawless employment history, he could've landed a gig as the day manager or night auditor for any number of the area's posh hotels. And with his exemplary work record such as it was, he could have settled for a job as a server at one of those ritzy Aspen country clubs. The pay was okay, if a bit unpredictable, and they were always hiring.

Not that he seriously considered any of these possible positions. At the age of forty, those other options felt a bit more like glorified summer jobs better suited for a college kid—not a middle-aged man with a six year degree—and therefore would've taken a good chunk from his already flagging sense of self-respect.

It wasn't that he thought such jobs were beneath him. Still though, if he was honest with himself, he did think he was suited to a better line of work than the aforementioned entry-level gigs.

So to preserve a rapidly fleeting sense of self-worth, while still bringing home the proverbial bread required to finance a small home in the hyper-inflated real estate market of modern Colorado, he'd decided to take a night survey gig at the newly reopened Sopris Mine, located ten miles south of Carbondale, along Highway 133.

It was really the full medical coverage that had sealed the deal. Turns out a master's degree in aeronautical engineering was neither the cross-market qualification, nor the money machine he'd hoped for during his college years. If you could find work in the field after graduation, the money was decent enough. But placement wasn't as assured as one might assume, and he'd been lucky to find a good job with Boeing back in Washington after a two year search.

It was a comparatively cushy desk position, which he'd had for about five years before his wife, quite suddenly, had gotten some nostalgic hair up her butt and insisted that if they were to raise a family the "right way," they would need to seriously consider moving back to her hometown of Carbondale, Colorado. This was because, as she so eloquently put it, "It's the best place on Earth. Everywhere else sucks donkey balls, and I wanna go home."

Hard enough to argue.

There had surely been some back and forth over the decision, but ultimately he knew he was going to have to accept and adapt. *Thems is the breaks of love,* as the wise man says. Compromise is often key.

And thus, he'd given up his hard-won job and its inherent financial security to bring his growing family (one baby girl, with another bun in the proverbial oven) back to the native land of his one and only—the many-splendored Roaring Fork Valley. And now, through largely chance circumstances, he had ended up nearly a mile down into the hard earth of an old marble mine. Yet again proving that time-old adage that you never know where life will lead you.

As with so many of its type, the Sopris Mine had been in a near constant state of flux for over a century. A myriad of similar mines for gold, silver, alabaster, coal, and marble dotted the foothills of the eponymous mountain. This particular shaft had been first dug out in the late 1800s, and had seen on again, off again operations in the decades since. It was long operated by the Mid-Continent Mining Company.

However, an explosion inside of a nearby mine in April of 1981, which had claimed the lives of some fifteen local miners, had spelled the end for Mid-Continent, and with it, the end of the area's mining heyday.

Since then, possession of the claim had switched hands a few times, and now it was enterprising local resident and former miner Robert Congdon who held the reins of the operation firmly in his grasp. Once he'd realized the treasure trove of marble and alabaster that this particular mine possessed, he'd been working to have the mine back on its feet and at full production by the spring of 2025.

And that meant getting investors, updating machinery, reconnoitering the existing shafts, and filing out the permits to ensure the place was turning a profit by the end of the fiscal year. It also meant convincing people that the juice was worth the squeeze on the whole endeavor. No easy task.

Alex walked some twenty feet down the shaft along the side-wall drill track and muttered into his radio, "Just keep talking to me. Keep the line alive. I'm gonna confess something to you now Marcus."

The radio in his hand crackled. "Yeah? What's that?"

Alex squeezed the radio, clicking the PTT. "This was not my first choice for occupation when I came with Rachel back to the valley."

A moment of silence followed, then his radio sputtered back alive. "You don't say," Marcus deadpanned through the handset's receiver. "Never would've guessed that. Certainly not with how you've spent most of your two weeks with us none-too-subtly implying as much."

"Have I?"

"You have. Your cup of disdain for this place runneth over, I should say."

"That's...oddly worded. And here I thought I was hiding it so well. I'm not saying this job is beneath me; I'm as good for a hard day's work as the next fella. Far be it for me to say or imply any different overtly."

"Really?"

"Really. This job may be hundreds of fathoms below the peaks of Sopris, but it isn't beneath me."

"Could've fooled everyone here. All six of us. And ya must've fooled Robert for him to have hired you on with essentially zero experience to speak of."

"That was his call. I was clear about my lack of mining chops. Though I do appreciate that he was willing to take me on without much concern for my occupational knowhow. I guess he figured that a body is a body, and as long as I could handle the confined spaces, that I was just a few weeks of training away from being employee of the month."

"Shit. That's not gonna happen. We retired the employee of the month program years ago."

"Why?"

"They kept dying on us."

Alex stopped moving and scowled. "Seriously?"

"No. We never had any employee of the month program. Just fucking with you, and verily so. Trying to keep it light, good buddy. If I had to pitch a guess, I'd say he likely hired you because he hasn't hired anyone else for months. And I further suspect that you were the first dipstick to actually see any potential in this here career opportunity."

"He really hasn't hired anyone else for months?"

"No, sir."

"Why?"

Marcus' laugh was loud, even though the radio handset. "Because most folks can't handle the gul-dern confined spaces! That's usually the big hangup. It damn sure isn't the money, because there's plenty of that to be had. But also, it can be a might bit creepy down there. Specters of dead miners lining the walls and all."

"Oh, shut the fuck up." Alex knew when he was being playfully ribbed, and smiled in spite of his cohort's grim sense of observational humor.

"Serious, man. Are you aware that some 1200 souls have given up their lives whilst digging in this big rock since the turn of the last century?"

"No, of course not, but thanks for that, really. Comforting stuff. Keep it coming."

"Can do, will do. Shit, why do you think I stay out of the far reaches of the mine? I'm a born surface man, myself. Sure, I've been down on plenty an occasion, but those handful of trips were enough for me to recognize that I ain't custom made for the ol' daily digger role. I'm no good with the dust, the debris, nor the possibility of harrowing death and the spectral remnants thereof. We leave that sorta heavy lifting to the big brass-balled bucko's we bring down. Like you."

"Nice, Marcus. Prime-cut gallows shit. Top notch. Loving it. As if I needed another reason to reconsider my career choices."

"Just trying to keep up the chatter you requested. It's damn good pay and it's safer than ever, so what have you got to stress about? Lemme tell you, back in the seventies, this place was a real death trap. Not like today, though. We have modern methods to prevent such high rates of early retirement. And besides, nobody said you had to do it."

"My wife said I have to do it. I mean, approximately. Rather, she said we need more money—sooner than later. In her haste to get us back to the valley, it must've slipped her mind to mention that the cost of living is nearly twice here what it was back in Washington. Far as I can tell, this is about as fast as good money can be made in the valley. That is, outside of real estate ventures which everyone and their damn brother seem to be knee-deep in around here."

"Got that part right. Half the valley is in real estate. The other half are stressing about it."

Alex pulled a final hook light from his waist and clicked it into place along the mine cable. It came instantly to life. Then he walked several feet over to where a large yellow box protruded from the top rail of the shearer track. Ducking under one of the lowered support chocks, he pulled open the box, revealing a newer, albeit still somewhat outdated powertrain control module. A few green and red lights, some dials and buttons. He hit the power switch and the shearer commenced to life with a low rumble. He heard the slightest of creaks from the underside of the nearest hydraulic chock and scowled.

Raising his voice to compensate for the background noise, he hit the PTT and asked Marcus, "These things are safe, aren't they?"

"Well, sure. Course they are. Those China-made Nippon Steel chocks are as sturdy as can be. Hey—here's today's trivia question for ya—do you know why they used wooden beams to hold up the roof back in the day?"

Alex shook his head. "Is this a story I don't wanna hear right now?"

Marcus chuckled. "Maybe. But I'm gonna tell you all the same. It's because the creaking of the beams would tip off miners that the roof was unstable and that they might need to clear out sooner than later."

Alex cursed under his breath, then depressed the PTT again. "Splendid. What, pray tell, do we use now to tell us if a cave-in is imminent?"

"High technology. There are these sensor arrays on the chock plates that hold up the roof and walls. If anything was shifting, we'd see it and have time for you to amscray to the mine mouth."

"And you're seeing nothing of the sort right now, right?"

"Right. Well, not that's it neither here nor there, but there was a small shift about halfway down the track a few minutes ago, but nothing sustained so I'm sure it's nothing. Happens sometimes. Don't sweat it."

"Christ."

"Seriously, man, you ain't got nothing to worry about."

"From your lips to God's ears, Marcus. I'm trusting you not to get me killed down here."

"And so I shall. That's what buddies are for. But make sure that when the cutter drum starts up, you take a wide step back. With the pressurized water spraying at it, almost all of the rock dust and debris will be deposited into the receiver tray connected to the track. But still, once in a long while you get the occasional kickback, and they can leave a mark."

"You've been hit before?"

"Hell no. Nope. But this one fella we had down here a year back got a nasty chunk straight to his right knee. Capped him good. Dude still walks with a limp."

"You're a veritable waterfall of reassuring quips, you know that, Marcus?"

"One does what one can."

Alex rubbed his gloves hands together and clicked the PTT once more. "Ready to rock and roll?"

"Like Hendrix playing the national anthem at Woodstock, good buddy."

Alex grinned at this. "You went to Woodstock?"

Marcus scoffed in return. "Do I strike you as the hippie dippie type?"

"'Spose not."

"Right you are. But you ain't gotta be a card carrying member of the love generation to dig those grooves ol' Jimmy used to fiddle out. I still drop my copy of *Are You Experienced?* onto the old turntable from time to time. Anyway, I got you live and direct on the cam, so whenever you're game, you can light the fires."

Alex replaced the radio into its belt sheath on his waist and reached into the control module, turning the rotation speed dial. Then he used a small rubber-coated joystick on the panel to guide the ranging arm to the wall and hit the button to activate the drum. Stepping back, the cutter drum began to spin and thus the shearing began. Dragging along the wall, the drum teeth made quick work of the mine wall. The chocks, while appearing solid as ever, shimmied ever so slightly from the vibration of the cutter drum and Alex glanced about nervously. He made sure he was as far back as he could manage while he watched the arm move along its track.

After about three minutes of mine mulching, the drum made a whip-cracking sound, and Alex rushed over to get a closer inspection on it. A cursory survey of the equipment revealed that the arm and cutter were still well intact and the shearer body seemed fine as well. But as it continued its forward movement, Alex saw that a two-foot-wide hole had appeared on the wall. Not knowing what that meant, and out of an overabundance of caution, he walked over to the control module and hit the kill switch. Without any delay, the cutter drum rolled to a stop and the arm automatically pulled two feet away from the wall. The engine sputtered down, the conveyor belt stopped moving, and the mine became unnervingly silent all at once.

"Everything okay down there?" he heard Marcus call from the radio on his belt.

As he cautiously moved back toward the hole in the rock, he heard a second crack-hiss of what sounded like air escaping from the freshly shorn aperture in the wall. He stopped walking and stared.

"You okay, buddy? Why'd you stop cutting?" Marcus again.

Walking over to the hole and checking the conveyor, he noted that the drum had loosed several large, circular stones that appeared different from the rest in the return track. Stepping closer, he stared down and saw that they were notably unlike the rest of the debris in the trough, seemingly cut from the hole in the wall. Pulling off one of his gloves, he reached down and picked up one of the stones. It was a bit smaller than a basketball, but spherical all the same. Aiming his headlamp at it, he was taken aback.

"What is this shit?" Alex turned over the silvery chunk of rock in his hand. It was uncharacteristically smooth, with hundreds of small bubble-like protrusions along one side of the rock that gave it the appearance of reptilian skin.

Turning it over in his hand, he noticed small veins of some greenish substance which appeared to glow.

Making sure it wasn't some trick of the light, he held the rock away from him and surveyed it, then pulled the radio from his belt and clicked the PTT. "Quick question. This doesn't look right."

"That isn't a question. What doesn't look right? Why'd you stop cutting?"

"I stopped the drumroll because it made this loud sound and then…something—some sort of bubbly rock chunks—came out onto the belt."

"Bubbly?"

"Yeah, bubbly, kinda bubbly. Well, maybe that's not— It's a smooth stone with little formations all over it."

"Okay, so what are you worried about?"

Alex turned it over in his hand again, and in the light provided by his helmet, the rock seemed to glow even more. "Uh, should it be glowing green?"

"What, like kryptonite?"

"Not exactly, but yeah, sorta."

"Uh, no. But are you sure that's what you're seeing?"

"Well, unless we struck a gas deposit and I'm full on hallucinating, that's what I'd say we have here."

"Bring it over to Camera Nine and hold it up."

Alex looked around, and just a few yards back toward the location of the control module, he saw the reflection of the lens on Camera Nine high up on the eastern wall. He marched over, holding it in front of him like some sacred totem, and raised it up for the man in the office to take a remote gander.

Marcus' voice dropped a bit when Alex next heard him come over the radio. "Shit."

Alex felt a knot rise up in his stomach. "*Shit?* Shit what? What shit?"

After a brief pause, Marcus continued, "Well, I could be wrong—if, for some reason, my years of geological experience and intuition are suddenly failing me—but it sure looks like a piece of uraninite."

"Uraninite? As in uranium? Like *uranium* uranium? As in *radioactive* uranium?"

"Yeah. Well, sorta kinda. Uraninite, which we generally call pitchblende, is a semi-rare ore that is a fairly rich source of uranium. But I don't know what the hell it's doing in this mine. I'm damn surprised you found any."

"And yet I have. Or the drill did."

"You mean the shearer?"

"You know what I mean, smartass. Is this shit dangerous?"

"Only a little, and only if you're stupid enough to play around with the stuff on your bare skin."

Alex reflexively dropped the rock onto the ground, and he heard Marcus come back on the line, laughing intermittently. "Hey now, I'm just saying it isn't good for a man to handle it for long periods of time. Rest assured you won't be growing any extra appendages in the near and foreseeable. But it shouldn't be glowing, that's for damn sure."

Furiously rubbing his now empty hand on his right pants leg, Alex murmured, "That somehow doesn't make me feel any better."

"That's a strange thing, I'll grant ya' that. Uranium yielding ore is more common to the Uravan Mineral Belt in southwestern Colorado and Utah. Though most of the deposits in that region are made up of carnotite, and located within the Jurassic-age Salt Wash Member of the Morrison Formation."

"Huh?"

"Nothing, just some old…doesn't matter."

"So this is uncommon in Sopris?"

"Pretty uncommon. Rare, even. Back in the early fifties there were more than a few uranium mines around here, on account of the renewed post-war national interest in it. But all of them were abandoned years ago."

"It came out of this hole in the wall I think."

"A hole?"

"Yes, a hole. You know, a hole? Pretty damn big one that the drum must've opened up on the wall."

"That's odd. I never would've thought that…" Marcus trailed off.

Behind him, Alex suddenly heard another sound. He reflexively hit the PTT and whispered, "What's that?"

He turned as he heard it again. Something like a cricket chirp. After a few moments, he heard several of the sounds call out, all at once. A small harmony of noise not unlike the nights he'd had on the lake at his grandfather's house in Louisiana.

Slowly walking back toward the source of it, he narrowed his eyes.

Marcus mockingly whispered back, "What's what?"

From the two-foot hole in the wall where he'd pulled the chunk out, Alex spotted a hazy green glow that began to fill the cavity and shine out into the chamber.

"What the—" Alex's eyes darted toward the concavity, and before he knew what he was doing, he darted straight over to it and peered in. As he neared the opening, his eyes saw several specks of glowing green light moving toward him.

Exercising more caution than he had with the pitchblende, he slowly backed up. Inching away, he was startled to see a small viridescent insect crawl out of the hole and come to a stop, hanging halfway out of the opening. It looked like a thick, stubby millipede, maybe four inches long, with small arms running along its sides. Arching its body up into a more upright stance, he saw that, atop its tiny head, it had a swell of tiny glowing dots for eyes, and below that two unnaturally wide pinchers on either side of its mouth.

Alex could swear that the thing was looking straight at him.

He clicked the PTT and quietly asked his buddy-system cohort, "Are you seeing this shit?"

Marcus took a moment, then replied dryly, "I see you staring at the hole. Why? Is there more? You see the marble vein we've been looking for?"

"No such luck. But there is a little insect thing that just crawled out of the hole and it's looking at me."

"Looking at you?"

"Looking straight at me. And it's glowing green, just like the rock. Lots of eyes. You can't see it?"

"Not from this angle. Plus, the resolution isn't all that great. Are you sure it's an insect?"

"You can call it a beady eyed bugger if it makes you feel better, but yeah, that's surely what I'm seeing here."

"Can you grab it and bring it over to the camera?"

Alex shuddered involuntarily. "I don't want to, and I don't think I will. What I think is that I might hustle my ass back up to the office and get away from this thing as quickly as possible."

"Wait, I can sorta…yeah, I can see some greenish color on the monitor now. Is it getting brighter?"

Indeed it was.

As the glow behind it began to pulse brighter, Alex saw the millipede thing raise itself up even more on its hindquarters and assume a position that reminded him of a snake that had been put into a defensive attack posture. The knot in his stomach now hit the base of his throat, and he had to hack-clear it just to speak again.

The insect let out another chirp, though this one was lower, more drawn out, and somehow sounded much more threatening.

"It's standing up and it's looking at me."

"Have you checked your Geiger counter in the last ten minutes?"

"Of course I have," Alex lied, knowing damn well that it had been at least thirty minutes since he had done so. Passing the radio to his free hand, he removed the yellow glove from the other with his teeth and slowly pulled the black, oblong meter from his right pocket. As if to not startle the creepy critter staring daggers at him from its hidey hole. Clicking on the meter, he held it up and watched as the four digit readout numbers rolled up until they came to rest on 9999 mSv /hr. Then the numbers went back to quad zeros and the normally greenlit screen turned neon red.

The lump had reached the back of his mouth.

"Uh, it's capping out the Geiger. If I'm right, this says it's over 10,000 microsieverts per hour. That's pretty high, isn't it?"

Marcus' voice shifted into dead serious. "Get out of there! Come back to the portal, post haste. We need to leave and call Robert right now."

"That's really high, isn't it?"

"Hell yes! Hop to—now!"

Alex lowered the handheld counter, and as he did, he saw that the insect had reared itself back. With no time to react before it launched itself the six feet between him and the opening in the wall, he helplessly watched it land on his wrist, then latch its pitchers into his flesh.

A boiling sear of white-hot pain shot up his arm and he dropped the radio on the floor. His left hand swiftly brought down the Geiger counter onto the wriggling abdomen of the attacking creature and it exploded into a blot of milky-green goo. The glowing, exsanguinated fluid splashed up his forearm, eliciting an even greater shot of agony that made him cry out. His left hand dropped the counter and he rubbed at the goo, only serving to spread the pain to his left hand.

Suddenly, he felt dizzy. As he dropped to his knees, the back of his skull beat with the sensation of his blood pumping, and he could hear it in his ears. His hands fumbled for the radio by his knees, but as he managed to snatch it, his vision blurred and his muscles locked up.

The last thing he saw was a swirl of greenish haze growing larger in his field of vision, and then his still-open eyes went black.

———⋘∞⋙———

From his place of relative safety nearly a quarter mile from the breach, at the mouth of the Sopris Mine, Marcus Doma stared at the monitor in abject horror as a deluge of small greenish creatures, seemingly numbering in the tens of thousands, coursed from the small opening on the western wall like a smooth liquid, filling the area all around Alex.

Sitting in front of the Latitude 14 laptop which served as the control center for the mine's underwhelming communication network, he could only watch as the flood tide of glowing, radioactive insects washed over his co-worker (subordinate in any other situation).

Marcus' hand came up to his mouth as the man in the yellow hard hat tumbled over and disappeared under a glowing torrent of viridescent troglophiles.

Through the radio speaker, he could hear the fear in Alex's voice. "They're on me! They're all over me! It's burning my skin! It's burning—" His words were cut short as the voice on the other end was replaced by a hiss-chirping, mixed with the dying man's gurgling.

A few seconds later, the radio went silent.

On the screen, he could see the wave of green bugs roll over the aeronautical engineer laying limply on the floor next to the conveyor track. As the crawling mass moved past him, he remained completely enshrouded by a layer of ugly green that looked to be gnawing its way through Alex and toward the cavern's hard rock bottom.

Marcus knew what he should do, but he hesitated. If he remotely overrode and manually withdrew the stabilizing lifts holding up the shaft, then cranked the RPM's and activated the drill, the roof would almost surely cave in. In doing so, he would likely stop the approaching swarm of subterranean creatures. However, he would also be effectively sealing the fate of the man in the depths—albeit a man who he was almost certain had no chance of survival at this point. And yet, if he didn't, he just might be sealing his own.

So he tapped the screen a few times, digitally pushed his way through a few warning prompts, and effectively shut down the lifts. Then he maximized the rotations, activated the drill, and watched as the chocks lowered from the ceiling.

He was surprised at how quickly his plan took effect. Combined with the pressure of the rotating drill bit running along the western wall, the shimmying of the area caused a wide crack to open in the ceiling, which rapidly let loose a deluge of rock debris and dust.

His fingers tapped at the screen, moving aside pop up window after pop up window of varying feeds from within the now dust-shrouded tunnels. Ten cameras were placed along the main shaft and into several of the other cavernous branches which usually afforded a clear view of the mine's inner workings. Now, every single one was grey and hazy, obscured by the expanding cloud of dust rushing up the main shaft and exiting the mouth of the mine.

So, he waited.

His eyes darted about the fourteen-inch screen as he switched between the feeds in the area where Alex had just been, and along the main shaft. The lights lining the walls of the mine did little to penetrate the dark miasma on each display window. Nothing to show what had happened other than the faint glow emanating from the outer edges of several of the images.

His mind was a crosswire frenzy of what to do next. Should he leave the mine and call Robert first, or should he try to radio for the emergency services? He knew he was supposed to do the latter in this sort of situation, but knew damn well that his boss would likely prefer the former.

His hesitation was his final mistake.

His neck hairs prickled as he heard the skittering of insects coming up behind him. That same menacing green glow began to fill the room.

He knew there was no time to run. No time left to abandon the mine. No time to flee out the office chamber, as his exit was now blocked by a swarm of God knows what. No time to call Robert. And no time to activate the gate (little good though it might do) at the outer entrance of the mine before the creatures were upon him.

Panicked and hoping only to warn the outside world of this unfolding catastrophe, he opened up his Gmail app and started to type out a message.

Alex and I were running the shear along the new western shaft when a small opening in the cave wall revealed a cache of pitchblende and a—

He only managed to get that far before he felt the red-hot sensation of hundreds of small mouths clamp onto the skin of his back and burrow into his flesh with muscle-freezing speed. His whole body went taught, and like a stone statue, he toppled backward onto the hard cave floor. Crushing several underneath his weight, they erupted into milky liquid and plunged him into heretofore unknown realms of pain.

The green creatures crawled into his ears and his mouth, muffling any scream that he might have wished to eject before his eyes went dark and the last few moments of his life were spent in a bottomless hole of unrelenting physical agony.

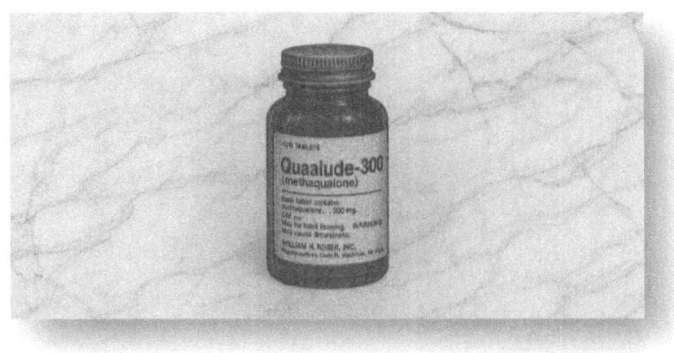

REPOSITORY

Growing up, every time I saw the green and white big rig with the giant golden ring on the side roll up in front of our modest three-bedroom house at 1866 Highway 133, on the southern outskirts of Carbondale, Colorado, my cheeks would ache sharply as my mouth began to water. With its bright green lines of neon-lit trim and an outline of dotted lights along the base of the trailer chassis, it was always a harbinger to me, albeit one of good tidings. It meant that, among other things, we were likely as not about to have a cool two liter of Coca-Cola and a large steaming pepperoni-strewn pie, courtesy of Peppino's Pizzeria, for dinner.

And that's what always happened, just like clockwork.

To my admittedly unrefined palate it may as well have been a three-star course at a French restaurant. I was, at that age, basically Kevin McCalister where that shit was concerned, especially if it was from Peppino's on Main.

The family that ran the shop back then (and still does to this day, in fact) had brought with them from New York the secret to a perfect Five Boroughs pie, as well as one heaven-sent Sicilian pizza. And it was these divine dishes which had secured their place as the premiere locale for an authentic slice in the Roaring Fork Valley. Other local establishments have long tried to measure up to the high bar set by the hometown pepperoni parlor (see also: New York Pizza, White House Pizza, Propaganda Pie, Goodfellows Pizza, and even Timbo's up in Basalt), yet have never quite reached the culinary heights graced by our own local pie parlor. At the end of the day, you either went for that top-shelf Peppino's grub, or else you were just settling.

The rig was a gleaming beast of metal and twinkling lights which, to my naive seven-year-old eyes, looked like something that might transform into an autobot at any moment. It was flanked on each side with dark green striping interspersed with thick bands of white. Set against the background color was a three-dimensional rendering of a single golden ring (what I would later come to recognize as an angelic halo) and the words, *Divine Trucking LLC.*

The two men seated in the Christmas light-lit cab of the huge eighteen wheeler were named Doug Belter and Jim Canavan, and they seemed, to me, to be much cooler than my own dad. My pops was (and I suppose still is) one helluva laid back dude, lemme just say. Maybe even sometimes to a slight fault. I say *slight* because, while he meant well, he could come off so breezy and carefree it could often read as unfeeling or disinterested. Not so much avarice as apathy. I was convinced he wasn't listening to much of what I said for the first seven years of my life.

This was hardly the case with Doug and Jim though. Nope. They always took in my endless jabbering without so much as a single complaint, and regardless of how esoteric or meandering the nature of the subject might be. I don't know why. Maybe it was the booze or the coke or the weed—or plainly the sheer boredom that made them ever-willing to entertain my long diatribes about the hidden warp pipes in *Super Mario Brothers*, the oft-spurned genius of the *Goosebumps* books, the endless depths of wisdom to be found in repeat viewings of *The Goonies*, or some other such adolescent nonsense. Whereas my father offered noticeably less in that department. In those early days, he just didn't seem to know how to talk to me, and vice versa.

One particular night in early April 1991, just before my eighth birthday (when I finally scored a much-treasured copy of *Teenage Mutant Ninja Turtles* for the OG Nintendo Home Entertainment System)—during that in-between season when the air is still frosty by midnight and the odd dusting of snow still might drop by—the two men in the big rig kicked up the dust in the driveway as the air brakes squealed and the truck came to a lurching stop. They dropped out of either side with a spring to their step that I would later come to understand was quite uncommon for long haul truckers of their ilk.

Positive vibes all the way with this duo.

Doug was tall, skinny, blonde, and always wearing a black KISS T-shirt. That night, it was a vintage Destroyer tee from 1976. Jim was much shorter, huskier, bearded, and had dark brown hair, in addition to eternally wearing a dark red flannel button-up which eternally bore the faint aroma of patchouli and ashtrays.

They opened the front door like they owned the joint and startled my mom, who was setting up metal TV trays for my sister and I—the same ones she'd had since the late seventies, I think. The kind that bore those gaudy gold-flecked floral designs straight out of a late disco-era, nuclear family dish set.

My father, gathering wood from our big winter pile out back, came in, dropped the logs by the old iron stove, and exchanged pleasantries with the men. Hugs, high fives, and knuckle bumps.

Every time Doug and Jim would roll into town in their big halo trucking rig, my mom would roll her eyes, maybe drop a few muttering complaints, but smile, nonetheless. This was because she knew what their arrival portended for her in the long run. Their impromptu visits provided her every excuse in the world to pop one of those little white pills she was so endeared to during my formative years.

In a time before they completely disappeared from all store shelves (as they had back in '84), my mom had gotten herself a couple of big honking bottles of quaaludes (I'd be lying if I said I remembered whether they were manufactured by Lemmons or Rorers, though it was surely one or the other). And she may not have said as much, but she secretly relished the opportunity to drop a lude and retire to her bedroom, where she'd kick on *Night Court* or *LA Law*, swiftly passing out for the rest of the evening under the lulling glow of a nine-inch screen.

It's worth mentioning that my mom, to the best of my understanding, wasn't a full-tilt pill popper. I know she wasn't finished with those bottles until the mid-nineties, when she finally pitched the bottles—which had been taking up shelf space in the upper hallway closet for years— into the trash.

Sadly, since their disappearance predated my own emergent interest in illicit drug use (which came about in 1996 when I'd smoked my first bowl with some buddies after school at Staircase Park, and was thus off to the psychedelic races), I had no presence of mind to steal and consume any of said pills before they evaporated into the fog of history.

She had ostensibly acted as though they were therapeutic, when in retrospect, they were at the very least semi-recreational. Most people don't know this, but "quaalude" is a portmanteau of the words "quiet" and "interlude." She liked to pretend that being around my father and his buddies while they were drinking was something she didn't enjoy, but the truth was that she just enjoyed those ludes a lot more.

And once she was out for the night, my dad would usually take me to my bedroom and wait until I dozed off, then presumably drink with his buddies until the early morning hours. Often they three would still be up once I was getting ready for school. Always saying they'd just gotten up early, always full of it in this regard—their eyes and clothes telling a different tale altogether. In retrospect, it was likely a few vials of Aspen-grade cocaine that oft-fueled their late night revelry and gave them their gusto until the following dawn.

But such late night elbow bending/dust hoovering was not in the cards this evening. No, this was an evening that would forever alter the course of my life.

Mommy dearest had happily popped into "quiet interlude" mode shortly after they'd arrived. Palming a couple ludes, she'd effectively dozed off around 7:00 p.m. But not before my dad suggested that he and the boys take a trip up Thompson Creek Road for a fire and some off-site beer swilling.

This was also something they did quite often, but on this night, it came with a caveat on her part. She'd insisted that he take me along, claiming it was so I wasn't left alone with her unconscious ass, and thus able to watch any "late night filth on MTV" I might deem worthy of my attention. After a bit of dubious verbal back and forth, my father begrudgingly relented and told me to pack up my stuff for an overnight camping trip.

Giddily, I made the whole process of getting ready a quick five minute job, and by seven thirty, we were headed straight for the western outskirts of Carbondale.

Jim and Doug didn't ride with us in my dad's day-glow orange Volkswagen bus (one of those righteously hip, 1950s-era generation T1 vans with the white widow's peak running down the front), but rather got back into their own gleaming neon-green rig and followed us.

After a quick stop by the pizzeria to end all pizzerias for the aforementioned Coca-Cola and Sicilian pepperoni pie, we made haste to the crest of Thompson Divide. Past the City Market, Crystal River Video, the 7-11 and the short-lived Benjamin Franklin outlet—driving by Colorado Rocky Mountain School (CRMS) and up the fifteen-minute ride to where the road flattened out and opened up into wide swaths of wild mountain terrain. Past the shrub-shrouded baby graves, a left turn down a dusty road and soon to a campsite not far from the Beaver Ponds, tucked away into the lodgepole pines and Aspen trees, fifty or so yards from the main dirt road.

I was surprised that Doug and Jim were able to get that huge beast of a vehicle so far out into the boonies with us, and seemingly without much trouble.

That high in the hills above Bonedale, the stars were crystal clear and I could see the white wisps of the Milky Way cradling them in its all-consuming grasp above my head.

I loved the night sky in Colorado. Still do, in fact. But back then, it was much clearer than it is these days—and don't let anyone tell you any different. The hell do they know unless they've stared at them from the same earthly vantage point for over forty years?

Once we reached the spot where they parked, Jim was quick to make a ring of rocks and spark up a campfire, while

Doug busied himself with setting up some lawn chairs and dragging out a cooler. My dad said we'd probably sleep in the van, which was cozy enough on account of the pull-out beds in the back of the bus. Then he hauled out the pizza box, the two liter of Coke, and a case of Budweiser.

We all sat around the roaring campfire while they shot the proverbial, set against the sound of the radio from the big rig pumping out music by KISS. I know my dad wasn't much of a fan, but Doug was absolutely obsessed with them, and Jim was what I would describe as tolerant. Doug was especially taken with the bass player, Gene Simmons, by all accounts. He even had the guy's face tattooed on his right arm, just above the elbow.

"He's a total badass. Helluva voice, and while his bass flows and solos aren't necessarily technically complex, they're haunting as all get out. They call him 'The Demon' because not only does he breathe fire and spit blood onstage, but his face is painted up to look like one. At least, he looks sorta like the standard version of what people *think* a demon looks like. Like a Kabuki demon. But real demons don't look anything like that, in my experience. Aside from the tongue."

"Doug…" my dad casually warned, in a tone he usually reserved for sussing out my less believable stories, leaving me inwardly curious but just shy of outwardly inquisitive.

Doug seemed to read my father's face and tone, then brushed off the subject by saying, "Never mind. Anyway, you want some Mountain Dew, buddy?"

Patrick Quinn Kitson

In my lap sat a paper plate with a still-steaming slice of Sicilian heaven, and in my hand, a Styrofoam cup brimming with Coca-Cola. I held up the bubbling blackish brew to Doug. "I'm good with this Coke and my pizza, but thank you. Besides, I don't drink Mountain Dew."

"Why's that?" Jim asked as he poked at the campfire with a long stick, kicking up swirls of embers that danced skyward.

I hesitated for a second, wanting to word it just right, but then went for broke. "I heard that the Yellow Number 5 in Mountain Dew makes your penis small. Is that true?"

Jim chuckled and my dad grinned in a thinly veiled attempt to stifle his own laughter. I swear, my pops never wanted to seem like he was enjoying anything as much as he actually was.

Doug was quick to ask, "Who told you that?"

"I dunno," I said, suddenly embarrassed at being so direct. "One of my friends, I think. Is it true?"

As if to silence the two goofs he'd come up Thompson with, Doug was fast to deflate the idea. "I wouldn't think so, no. I use magnums."

"What's a magnum?" My childish naivete, shining on through.

"Don't tell him," my dad passively suggested while polishing off the white and red can in his hand.

As the sonance of the song, "Crazy Nights" by KISS began to reverberate out from the big rig, Doug shrugged. "Your pops says I can't say. Just know that, by all evidence currently available, I'm perfectly fine on that count. Might not be as big as Gene Simmons in the love gun department, but

I'm doing alright. Got zero complaints from the ladies and I'm ready to rock it at a moment's notice. Plus, considering I've put back a liter or so of the stuff every day since I was twelve, I can only conclude that the whole Mountain Dew/small dick thing is a houseboat full of hogwash." He reached down to where a twelve ounce can of the stuff stood on the ground next to his right shoe. Then, as if to put an end to the matter, polished it off in one big chug, crumbled it in his fist, and tossed the green can into the flames of our little fire.

"Oh. Okay." I accepted his explanation without fully understanding it, or the implicit correlations with sexual innui.

After that, we watched the stars and grooved out to the music. But at that age, even lively conversation, seventies metal grooves, and the opportunity to learn formative tidbits from these world-weary adults was hardly enough for me to fight sleep for too long. By eight thirty, I was half-passing out in my chair, and my pops suggested that I go lie down in the back of the van. So, I did just that. I sauntered over to the Volkswagen, crawled in the back, lay down, and was out almost as quickly as I zipped the big, puffy, dark-red Coleman sleeping bag around me. Hours must have gone by while I lay there, snugly nestled in my cool camping crystalis.

Some unknown amount of time later, a loud noise called out, disturbing my sleep. I was only half awake, therefore had no idea what it was that had roused me from my slumber. But then, it was followed by a hollow bang. A bang that I knew all too well, because I had sometimes asked the guys if I could walk around inside the truck, and on the odd occasion they let

Patrick Quinn Kitson

me, the footfalls within the confines of the shipping container set upon a long-haul trailer made a very distinct sound.

It was the same hollow bang which my keen ears now picked up.

Straightening into a sitting position, I unzipped the maroon Coleman cocoon and fumbled around in the dark. My hands located my small black Maglite flashlight, and I quickly thumbed the bottom button. Light flooded the van.

My eyes adjusted, and when I peered out the side window to where the fire still lay, the three men I had come camping with were nowhere to be seen.

Naturally, this caused a deep, albeit brief sense of existential dread—the same that haunts the heart of any child who has become untethered from the anchoring presence of their parental figures within the vast and unknowable world around them. The same wretched feeling you got when separated from your parents in a large mall or state fair. Fear took hold, to be sure, but I quickly realized that, if anything, it was more likely that the three had disappeared around some grove of nearby bush and tree to seek out fresh kindling or dried logs for our dying fire.

I walked over to where my shoes lay on the cold linoleum-lined floor and, while tying them up, I heard that same bang. My brain finally put two and two together and told me that whatever they were doing, it must be in the storage container that was located behind our van.

Slipping on my coat, I pulled open the van's side door and stepped out into what felt like a night of bitter cold. It always feels that way when you have to leave the comfort of a warm sleeping bag for a midnight pee while camping, doesn't it?

Turning my head, I heard the bang again, but this time it was coupled with a dull whining that sounded far off. Only because it was coming from behind the big rig. I swiftly scamper-scuttled along the side of the long vehicle, and when I got about halfway toward the rear of the trailer (right next to that big golden halo), I saw that the large, bar-braced rear cargo doors were hanging open.

A hair-raising cackle-shriek from within the confines of the container immediately froze me in my tracks. Wildly terrified, though admittedly curious, I wondered for the briefest of moments if I actually wanted to see what might be waiting on the other side of those doors.

Before I could make a decision one way or the other, I heard Doug holler from inside the big metal box beside me, "Those sedatives I snagged from your wife's bottle last time we were in town must have long worn off!"

"Ya think?" I heard my father shout in response.

Another cackle. Another shriek.

Then Jim piped up, "Who gives a damn whether she's conscious or unconscious! Bitch is wild and we should make it snappy. We need to take her head and drop her into the hole before your son hears all this racket!"

Too late on that count.

My desire to proceed was briefly stymied by a distinct fear that whatever was going on back there, it was most definitely something I wasn't supposed to see. But, just as with the precocious child who sneaks a look in his parents' bedroom in the late days of December to score an early gander at the goods that surely awaited him on Christmas morning, I found that I could not stop myself from continuing my newfound quest for answers.

As I rounded the corner to look in the back of the trailer, my eyes widened at the terrifying sight they beheld.

Walking wide of the doors in what military types would refer to as a circular "cutting the pie" motion, my father failed to see me approaching from behind. He was standing on the ground before the open doors with a large duffel bag in one hand, his other resting on the edge of the metal box's opening. Within the darkened space, I could see Doug and Jim pushed up against either wall of the container, just a few feet inside. Each was holding a beer can and sipping off it like this was just another day at the office or something.

But the thing that really caught my eye was beyond them—something my young mind was hardly prepared for.

Right in the middle of the container's shadowy interior, I could make out the figure of a slender woman in a long red dress. She was young and attractive, with flowing blonde hair that came around her shoulders to rest upon two ample bosoms. A real *strutter*. Her arms were extended over her head with her hands in what appeared to be handcuffs secured to a single ring bolt in the ceiling.

Even in the limited yellow haze provided by a single dim light bulb protruding from the rear wall of the shipping container, she looked like one of those life-sized alcohol advert standup models I'd see when my pops would take me for his weekly beer run at Crystal River Liquors on Highway 133. Comely cardboard cut-outs who were always wearing something skimpy and revealing—all while holding a sweating can of beer in their hands and looking somehow surprised that they'd just been photographed.

(Personally, I was always partial to those sensuous liquor store-exclusive stand-ups of Elvira advertising Coors back in the late eighties, though that is neither here nor there.)

Before my father or his friends could register my sudden appearance, I clicked on the flashlight in my hand and the slender figure began writhing and struggling.

Lowering her eyes, she regarded me in the same vulpine way that the Big Bad Wolf had surely greeted Little Red Riding Hood. "Why hello there, boy!" she whispered in a silky, dulcimer tone that one could rightly describe as bewitching.

Hearing this voice, I was immediately reminded of the soothing stentorian vibrato the old librarian carried when she read our elementary school class a picture book during one of our monthly visits to Gordon Cooper Library.

This naturally drew the looks of all three men.

Jim's eyes rolled up, his arms lowered, and he sighed loudly. Doug dropped his head into one of his hands and shook it from left to right. "Oh, great."

My dad didn't hesitate to start in on me, as if I was somehow at fault for whatever was happening. "Oh my God, son! What in the hell are you doing back here? This is not something you need to see! You need to go back to the van, right now! You hear me?"

Somehow, inexplicably yet inextricably, I knew that, given the precarious position we all now found ourselves in, I for once had the rare upper hand in this particular dialogue. By this point in my life, I had seen any number of films with damsels in distress, and to me, this sure looked to be that.

In a frustrated and defiant tone that was wholly uncharacteristic of my interactions with him up to that point in time, I shout-demanded of my father, "Who is that woman? What are you doing with her?"

His eyes went wide with anger, like he wanted to put me in my place, but immediately gave way to something more mellow. Something more paternal, more concerned. Something that told me that I was quite right in my suspicion that it was he, not me, who had the explaining to do here.

"Son, I don't know if you're ready for all this."

Doug raised his head and lifted his hands to his sides in defeat. "Ships sorta sailed on that count though, hasn't it? May as well fill him in. You got nothin' to lose."

"What ship sailed?" I snapped back, as if this was a real zinger, thinking prematurely that I had them on the conversational ropes and should keep swinging wildly— verbally, that is.

Jim shifted uneasily in place. I finally noticed that in his hand (the one without a Budweiser in it) was a small Glock pistol that he had trained on the hard luck woman in chains. Still, despite his steely-eyed resolve, even he seemed somewhat resigned to the situation. "You may as well tell him now. Otherwise you're gonna have to just let him explain what he saw to his mother. That a conversation you wanna have with her?"

My dad raised his voice, "Of course not!"

Doug smiled. "Then go ahead, *Ed.* No need to shout it out loud. He's tough enough. Right, buddy?"

"Right!" I assured them, knowing damn well I could not be more full of shit on that count. Then I asked, "Tough enough for what?"

Jim laughed, and I didn't care much for the sound of it, to be honest. The casual tone he assumed seemed wholly out of place in that moment. "To know what we are; what we do. *How* we do. And likely what—at some unknown time in the future—you will do as well."

I hesitated for a moment, then stammered out, "So...so what are you? Are you bad guys? Are you—are you like serial killer guys? Like that blond man who wears ladies' skin in that one movie?"

Jim shot my dad a look. "What's he talking about?"

My father rubbed his face and sighed. "I think he means *Silence of the Lambs.* Right? That what you mean, Pat?"

A blank stare from yours truly. Then, "Yes."

My pops frowned. "While I'm gonna be wondering just how the hell you ended up seeing that particular film after this, I can still assure you that that's not what we are, son. That isn't the score here."

I crossed my arms. "You're not? 'Cause it looks like that."

Doug gave me a warm smile and assured me that, "No. No! Of course not! No way, buddy. We only make trash outta the trash that's been made. We dump thems what needs dumping!"

The woman twisted her wrists above her head, tugging at her restraints, then called to me once again. "Please, boy. Please help me! These wicked, wicked men are going to murder me and I need your help, please!"

Her voice was a siren song that filled my stomach with butterflies, and I wanted so much in that moment to charge up into the container and let her loose. The only thing stopping me was worry about my father, combined with having no idea how to undo handcuffs in an expedient manner.

Doug glared at the woman and hissed, "We're not the wicked ones here. Don't listen to her; she's just more trash to take out. And take it out we shall!"

The woman twisted her wrists, and pleaded to me, "I'm not trash! My name is Beth and I'm scared that if you don't—"

Her words were halted by Jim taking his mostly empty beer can and throwing it at her head. It bounced off her face without doing much in the way of damage, but caused her to utter a low growl. Her eyes looked hatefully at Jim, but then her features softened and she returned her gaze toward the opening of the trailer.

In that earlier siren voice, she again addressed me. "Help me, boy! Please set me free. You're my only chance at living through this. Your father is evil, as is his constituency of dunces."

Jim waved the gun in the woman's direction. "Shuddup, bitch! You ain't got nothing to say to this little man over here."

But the look on my face and thoughts in my head were pointed in a different direction. "She isn't trash! She's a person. And she's scared. And so am I."

Hearing this, my father set down the duffel bag on the edge of the container's floor, took a tentative step toward me, and reached out his hand to comfort me.

I instinctively backed away and shot him a deadly look. "What is wrong with you, Dad? Are you a killer?"

"No." He shook his head, looking positively crestfallen at my accusation. I couldn't recall him ever looking that way before.

Jim straightened up from his leaning position against the interior wall. He took a single step toward me while keeping the gun trained on the woman. "He isn't lying. You got it wrong, kiddo. You got it all twisted around. We do take out the trash. More specifically, we take out the demons. Like this yapping bitch here with her sense-snaring rat-a-tat." Jim then took two quick steps in the direction of the woman and pistol-whipped her across her right cheek, immediately drawing blood.

Now, I had been absorbing myself in horror since the first time I found a black and white novelization of the *Creature from the Black Lagoon* in the Carbondale Elementary School library.

But nothing I had seen in my couple of years being fascinated with the genre made me believe my ears.

"Demons?"

Doug shrugged and put his hands up at his sides. "We're, uh, just...I guess you could say we're your friendly neighborhood demon cleaners. Yeah."

"I'm not a demon!" shrieked Beth from her precarious position.

Now it was Doug who tossed his beer at her. "Lick it up, ya wicked temptress! Lick it up! Ain't nobody trying to hear that ol' bullshit!"

Jim yawned and eyeballed Doug. "Doug, every other sentence needn't be a reference to a KISS song. Nor do they need to be non-sequiturs."

Doug laughed. "I don't think you know what a non-sequitur even is."

And Jim conceded, "You may be right."

The writhing woman in red suddenly stopped moving and violently cocked her head sideways in an unnatural way. That would've been unsettling enough, but then she repeated Jim's words back in the *exact same* voice he'd just used to say it.

"You may be right."

This had the immediate effect of shifting my perception of the woman standing before me. She reminded me of Linda Blair in *The Exorcist*. Unnatural and impossible to deny. Something was very wrong with this—not woman—

this…*thing* they had tied up. Whatever doubts I had about the veracity of their claims ceased then and there.

"She's a bad thing, isn't she, Dad?"

The relief in my father's eyes was apparent. He held out his hand again and I slowly approached him. I took his hand in my own, and for the first time that I could clearly recall, I knew that he was happy I was with him. He pulled me close and gave me a hard hug, then lowered his hands to my shoulders and looked into my eyes. "That's right, son. She's not what she looks like."

From behind him, the creature in the red dress called out in my father's voice, *"Not what she looks like."*

Over my dad's shoulder, I could only watch helplessly as an inhumanly long, pink appendage came shooting out the thing's mouth and flicked against my dad's head like the end of a whip. He was sent crashing out of the trailer's door and dropped like a sack onto the ground, unconscious.

I stared down, frozen in place. I wanted to dash to him and see if he was okay, but before I could, the tongue retreated into the confines of the container and likewise whipped Jim in the head. Knocking him to the wall, and as with my pops, to the ground soon thereafter. He looked dazed and confused, but not quite knocked out. The pistol dropped from his hand and hit the floor.

Doug's eyes went wide as ran to where the woman/demon had knocked Jim to the floor, reaching for the gun but missing it by inches. In less time than it took him to reach his friend, the demoness had turned her full attention to the diehard

KISS fan among us. Her long, slick tongue shot out and wrapped around his throat like a boa constrictor. He stopped reaching for the gun as his fingers came up reflexively to pry at the leathery pink whip choking him.

Mouth agape, I remained in place, an utterly horrified statue.

Doug tugged at his own throat just enough to temporarily loosen the grasp the tongue had on his windpipe. Between shallow gasps for air, he managed to call out to me, "The bag! *Ack!* The bag! Toss it here!"

Against all odds, my spell of passivity abruptly ended, and I did just that. I didn't think. I didn't wait. I didn't decide nor did I debate. I simply acted on bloodborne instinct.

As I propped myself up and lifted my body into the cargo container of demonic imprisonment, I snatched up the duffel, then tossed away. The dark green bag flew as straight and true as it needed to, finding swift purchase in Doug's outstretched hands. This while his face began to turn red from the grip of the demon's tongue.

In one motion his fingers unzipped the small duffel and ripped free a silver blade with a golden hilt. A short sword, as a matter of fact, with a large black diamond on the pommel. I pointed my Maglite at it, causing the hard steel to cast lines of reflective light all around the interior of the spacious shipping structure.

In one disco ball flash, he turned his body and swiped the sword upward, cutting straight through the slick pink appendage and falling to his knees.

Beth (if that's what this thing wanted to be called), yanked and yowled. She twisted and pulled at her wrist restraints as the severed stub of flesh recoiled into her howling maw, leaving unnatural purple drips of blood pouring onto her red dress. She screeched, and she bellowed, and she grunted like a wild beast. Her cries were guttural and deep—not at all like you'd normally hear from a person's mouth. More like the sound you might hear from dying animals being torn apart by some quadrupedal predator on one of those *National Geographic* television programs about the African Savanna. The kind of show with a parental warning after the commercial breaks.

My stomach churned at the godawful sound hitting my eardrums, and I cupped my hands over them to cut down on that terrible howl. Still, it persisted.

Purple fluid sprayed out from the severed tongue like a garden hose that had been pinched, and loosened its hold on Doug's neck. He dropped the sword and I rushed to him. My tiny fingers dug into the space between his throat and the severed tongue, unwrapping it in a matter of seconds. Doug inhaled deeply and leaned against the wall as he caught his breath.

The demon didn't stop. She spat and twisted. Cursed in some foreign tongue (puns be damned), and spat out purple blood.

After a minute that seemed like an eternity, Doug regained his composure, kneeled down to pick up the silver blade, and faced the creature. He waited only a moment—for her head to shoot out ahead of her writhing body—then struck true. This time, he cut horizontally through the air.

The ungodly sound from the thing was suddenly silenced by her head being cut clean off in one fell swoop. The dangling body went limp as her blonde, violet-smeared head rolled forward along the metal floor and came to stop a few feet away from the edge of the trailer's open doors.

Doug stood there for another moment, breathing deeply and slowly. Then his eyes met mine and he smiled. "Knew there had to be some reason for you coming with us tonight, buddy. Sorry your first time was this messy. Usually it doesn't turn into such a, I dunno, such a fucking…clusterfuck."

And in spite of myself, I laughed. "Holy shit! That was insane!"

Jim suddenly sat up and rubbed his ribs as he reached out and snatched the gun from the floor. He looked at the hanging body in the red dress, then eyed me for a good moment before mumbling, "Not bad, little man. Not too bad at all."

Outside, I heard my father stirring and breathed a cool sigh of relief. As I hopped out and did what I could to help my father to his feet, Doug helped Jim to his.

Blood trickled from a small cut on the side of my dad's right temple, and I exclaimed, "Oh my God, Dad, your head is bleeding! Are you gonna be okay?"

Semi-dazed but seemingly none too worse for the proverbial wear, he quietly muttered, "I'm okay. I'm okay. Little fucked up, but I'm okay. Are you…are you okay? Did they—" He slowly stood and peered into the container. Within a few seconds, he seemed to grasp what had happened. "Did she…" His voice trailed off, waiting for a reply.

Jim and Doug stood next to the limp body, still hanging by its wrist from the middle of the large metal box.

Jim pointed the gun at the body, but before he could pull the trigger, Doug reached out and motioned for him to hold his fire. "Don't, just…don't. Enough loud shit for tonight. Besides, if you do that in here, my ears will be ringing until next week."

Jim considered this, then clicked on the safety and slipped the pistol into his jean pocket. "Good point." Shifting his focus toward me and my father, he pointed. "Bitch got the drop on us, but little man delivered Doug the blade and he dealt her down to the devils below. Pretty tough in a pinch, that one you got there, Ed."

My pop's eyes went wide, then settled into bemusement. "You helped them take her out?" he asked without averting his wide-eyed stare.

I nodded. "I guess I helped a little bit."

Doug snorted and shot me a look. "Damn straight he did! No need for false modesty, bud. Kid's a natural."

My dad looked down at my face, speckled with nasty purple dots, and wrapped one arm around me. In his eyes was a pride that I had never before beheld. It was a look I would never forget, for it was in that exact moment that I knew that he was grateful I was his son.

And it was also then that I realized how cool he really was. My father and his buddies were demon slaying badasses. And now, I was one step down the long road to becoming one of them.

"Love you, buddy."

I smiled and looked into his eyes. "I love you too, Dad."

As I wrapped my arms tightly around my dad's waist, Doug began to whistle the melody to "I Was Made For Loving You" by you-know-who, and we all shared a collective, if somewhat strained, chuckle.

After they'd united the body and dragged it outside, Jim retrieved a long metal sled from a rectangular compartment on the side of the long haul truck's flatbed, just below the image of the big gold halo on the trailer's side. He pulled it around to the back and we loaded the body, the head, and the severed tongue onto it. Then, without too much chit-chat, I studiously followed them a few hundred yards through the darkness to a nearby drop off. The cliff's edge was long and impenetrably dark. Even in the ample moonlight, I couldn't make out the bottom. It may as well have been a bottomless ravine into which we all gazed.

I later came to find out that it essentially was just that.

Doug was the first to speak. "So here's where they all end up."

"Won't somebody find her?" I asked.

"Nah," my pops replied. "This thing is a long way down and drops into a crevasse. One time Jim repelled down about six hundred feet, but it emptied into some sort of cavern. We never hear them land, so it might go down forever."

"How did you find this place?"

Jim and Doug shot my father a look, and he turned to speak to me directly. "Some of these things are conveyed to us through dreams; sometimes our directives are more overt."

"Huh?"

My dad shook his head. "You'll understand with time, son. Hard to sum it all up succinctly in one night."

Not knowing what he meant, I decided to trust that he knew best. Still, I asked, "Where does it go?"

Doug piped up, "All the way down. To the grotto where the dead demons dive deep. It all goes into the chasm, and it never comes back. You can count on that."

I gazed down at the sled full of dead demon parts and suddenly noted, "Her tongue was so long!"

Doug grinned widely. "Oh yeah. Big, big tongues they got on 'em. Bigger than Gene Simmons', I can say that much from the many times I've seen KISS in concert. Not sure why that's such a common denominator with this breed of evil, but it's almost always the case." He turned his attention to Jim and leveled his tone to something more accusatory. "Which is precisely why we *always* make sure to duct tape their mouths, isn't it, Jimbo?"

Jim coughed to clear his throat and admitted sheepishly, "Yeah, yep. My bad. That one was all me. Sorry. Really, I should've been on top of that. I might have been distracted by those voluptuous boobs she had. Still, no good excuse and rest assured that it won't happen again."

I frowned. "So, does this mean…am I going to do this one day too? Am I going to be a killer?"

Pops patted my shoulder. "That's not exactly how I'd describe what we do. And I don't think that's gonna be a good thing to be telling your mother either, if you catch my drift. We aren't killers. These things are the killers. You'll know in time what I mean." He sighed deeply. "No, son, what we do is just and righteous and is the work of a higher power. One that, from time to time, needs some earth-bound help in dealing with these sorta malevolent monstrosities."

"So we're good guys?"

"Oh yeah. This is good work we do. And if nothing else, you can bet that it gets us an express shot to the front of the line at the pearly gates."

"Really?"

"Sure. One could say this sorta work is like a golden ticket to the great beyond."

"Like Willy Wonka?" I asked sheepishly (because I was young and sweet-ish and naive and mostly free of all innocence-robbing, bigger-picture know-how back then).

"You got it. Once we get to the front gate of heaven, it's entry guaranteed! No dropping down the bad egg chute for us! As a matter of fact, we are the ones who help ol' Willy sort out the bad eggs from the good eggs! But for the purposes of this admittedly strained metaphor, God is Willy Wonka, we are the Oompa-Loompas, and the bad eggs are demonic sons a bitches in human skin suits that we gotta kick into the proverbial dumpster. That's what we use this place for."

"Christ Ed," Jim chuckled. Doug snickered at my dad's explanation as well.

My father reached over and playfully swatted at Jim. "I'm winging this, guys. Gimme a fuckin' break."

"This is the end of the road." Doug pointed out toward the cliff face ahead of us.

I cocked an eyebrow. "So, this is your dump?"

My father continued. "Oh yeah. That's exactly what it is. The local dump site for the ugly little demons who walk amongst us mere mortals. A repository, if you will."

Doug replied, "Well, there is one thing we have to do first."

"What's that?" I asked.

Doug answered. "We gotta pour some holy water onto this beast before we give it the old heave-ho. Then, we pitch the bitch off the cliff and let the hole do the rest."

"Holy water? Like the thing that Simon throws at vampires in the Castlevania games?"

Doug looked at me with his own raised eyebrow. "If it's a game about greasing vamps, then I would assume so. But I don't think vampires exist. Guess we can't know for sure. However, as you've seen, these baddies certainly do."

Then I had a thought. "So isn't she—isn't *it*—already dead?"

"Dead is a relative term with these demonic types, ya see," Jim chipped in.

"Are they always women?"

All three men laughed, and my father answered, "No, in fact they rarely are. Usually it's a man. Every so often it's a lady. But the tongue thing is pretty universal. Isn't it, Jim?"

Jim smiled. "Said I was sorry, guys. Though, if I may be so bold, I gotta suspect that everything that transpired tonight happened for a reason. Don't you?"

Without skipping a beat, my father and Doug replied in unison, "Yeah."

I regarded them quizzically. "How do you know someone's a demon?"

My father bristled in the cold air and swiftly replied, "Let's get this done, son. Plenty of lessons for you to learn as time progresses. We'll teach you how to spot 'em soon enough. For now, let's finish our work here."

"Does the holy water seal their evil or something?"

Doug stepped forward, pulling a familiar small silver flask from his back pocket. Without hesitation, he turned the top and poured the clear contents onto the sled. The liquid began to rapidly dissolve away the body.

"Turns 'em into primordial slop, is what it does," he said as steam rose from the metal sled and the demonic corpse melted into a pile of pink and purple goo.

It smelled like cheese and I winced as I held my hand up to my nose. "Don't people put alcohol in those things?"

Doug smiled as he dumped out the rest of the flask's contents, shook it, returned the cap, and slipped it back into his back pocket. "I used to keep some cold gin in this flask that I would mix with Mountain Dew from time to time. But then I became more of a beer guy, so..."

Jim kneeled down long enough to tip one end of the sled over the cliff's edge, and the purple goo slid off into the darkness below.

And just like that, the whole harrowing evening had come to an end. We brought the sled back to the campsite, and my dad put me down in the van, where—against all odds—I immediately dozed off into a dreamless sleep. While I slumbered, I can only assume they cleaned out the container and finished off the case of Bud.

The next morning, we headed back into town for an early breakfast at The Village Smithy.

I had biscuits and gravy. They were fucking delicious.

I never told my mom anything about what had happened. Better she be kept in the dark, I figured.

As I grew, my role became clearer and I aided my fellow fiend fighters in their divine quest to rid the world of many other evil creatures, such as the one we haphazardly slayed that night. I even came to find out that we were hardly the only outfit of our type.

But that's a whole other story.

After that night up Thompson Creek, my pops and I didn't have much trouble getting on the same page or finding things to chat about. We could easily banter for hours on end, and my dad seemed to be much more willing to endure my endless pop culture prattling. Sure, fulfilling some holy, familial mission by decapitating demons with sacred swords and melting the purple-blooded remains with holy water may be an unconventional method of father-son bonding, but it is one of the many things that now binds us together.

And we think it's pretty darn groovy, if we do say so ourselves.

YUM-YUM

Jeff and Lisa Miller had been planning this particular chilled out, stress-free, wintery wonderland of a vacation getaway for months. Weeks upon weeks of phoning in reservations, making entertainment arrangements, filling up Amazon shopping carts, and voraciously browsing trip-planner websites had ended them up right here. Swaying precariously in the frozen afternoon winds from the thick, woven, interlaced steel cable of an old-fashioned, two-body chairlift running along the Western side of Buttermilk Ski Resort, just outside of Aspen, Colorado. Waiting for the lift to resume moving.

Meant in part to provide a snow-dusted escape from the humdrum drudgery of their workweek, it was also supposed to serve as an emotional reset for the both of them. A break in the unrelenting chaos of working together every single day at their small medical practice, as well as a welcome respite from the non-stop arguing and intermittent physical altercations that too often made up their daily routine.

But it was a stopgap, really. A flimsy way (in both their estimations) of repairing the likewise flimsy thread from which their nearly twenty-year relationship now barely hung. Dangling by a thread—just as their snowboard-strapped feet now dangled fifty feet above the hard snowpack below.

Even this planned excursion was of half-hearted effort, as they lived but a mere hour down the winding stretch of Highway 82 from here, in the gorgeous, albeit small town of Carbondale. The same place where they had set up their business, had two children, and everyday regretted their choice of spouse for the lion's share of two decades. For this trip, they easily could have afforded Milan, Belize, Napa Valley, or even Disney World. But as with nearly every other aspect of their dwindling relationship, they had instead opted for the easiest thing to accommodate the need, phoning it in just as they did with everything else that remained between them.

Neither expected it to be enjoyable.

This late in the day and this far west on the mountain, they were only seeing the rare skier or snowboarder pass underneath them every few minutes or so, often pausing long enough to gawk curiously at the unhappy looking duo, then smirking and continuing their icy slide down the snow-dappled slopes.

Clad in their premiere cold weather gear, the couple were nonetheless getting chillier by the moment, both figuratively and temperamentally. Both had been quiet for nearly five full minutes before a single frustrated complaint broke the silence between them.

"Christ, how long has it been now?" Jeff mumbled, his voice muffled by the collar into which his face was currently tucked in an attempt to keep the chilly breeze from freezing his dripping snot into icy tracks on his upper lip. His clothing was that of *wealthy ski-bum sheik*, positively resplendent in its nouveau-riche simplicity. Black jacket with silver piping, bearing a thick, rubber Volcom logo on the right breast. Matching silver snow pants, a black beanie, and Louis Vuitton goggles over a three day old beard-stache.

Saying nothing, Lisa rubbed her red, cold nose. She wore a likewise puffy black snow jacket with matching legging-shaped goose-down-stuffed snow pants and a tuft of dirty blonde hair tucked under a red Gucci ski cap.

Waiting for a reply that never came, Jeff finally followed up his own statement with a question. "What?"

Lisa kept her icy stare pointed down the slope beneath them, lightly swinging her board-bound feet to and fro. "I didn't say anything."

Jeff snorted. "Yeah, I know you didn't. Obviously. That's why I'm asking."

"Nothing. It's nothing."

"Nothing, really?" he pressed.

"No, nothing." Her head gave a quick swivel as her eyes surveyed the area around them. She sniffed softly, then cleared her throat, finally finishing, "It's just that this is complete bullshit, that's all."

"What's bullshit?"

"Being stuck up here like this. This situation is the shit o' the bull."

"Okay, and exactly how is this my fault?"

Lisa rolled her eyes and sighed loudly. "I didn't say it was, Jeffrey."

What he perceived as this type of cold serve standoffishness, as his wife was well aware, irked Jeff to no end. "No, no of course you didn't say it. You never say it outright, do you? But that's most assuredly what your whole *not saying anything* is actually saying, *isn't it?* Obvious enough to send a clear signal but also subtle enough to deny when I call it out?"

Lisa waited a long ten seconds before finally responding. "Make of it what you will."

"That's cute."

"What's cute?"

"Your steely silence coupled with those cheeky little quips kinda paints the picture, doesn't it?"

"I didn't say anything, Jeff. So please don't start."

"I'm not. You're the one who's already starting, aren't you?"

Lisa exhaled, watching her own breath dissipate as a white mist in the air before her eyes, then casually shot back, "News flash, Kimo Sabe: Bitching at me won't make the chairlift start again."

"Right, see—and there you go, per-fucking-usual. You always turn the shit around just like that when I try to confront you on your passive hostility bullshit. Then you shift the subject as soon as you can because you can't win the argument on its merits, and therefore, you have to divert."

"Whatever you gotta tell yourself, sweetie. I couldn't care less. Maybe what you should do is go tell your butt-buddies at the next medical conference about—"

"Wait, wait. *Butt buddies?* What the fuck does that mean?"

"You heard me, big man. Butt buddies! Your buddies in butt. Your claptrap collective of capricious, knuckle-dragging cuck-lord cohorts. Your posse of pud-pulling pussies—"

Jeff snorted, interjecting, "Always with the alliteration! Always with the five-dollar word bullshit. And always trying to sound smarter than you really are. When are you gonna stop trying to get waived over to the cool kids' table, Lisa?"

"When you grow a pair and locate yourself a clue. Just save it, Jeff. Go bitch and moan to your conference pals, *dude*, and spare me the earache."

Jeff's rising volume betrayed his attempt to maintain the conversational upper-hand. "Oh, should I? Is that what I should do, Lisa?"

"You should. I beg of you, for everyone's sake. Or maybe bend the ears of the pay-for-play girls I can only assume you bring back to your hotel rooms. Sure they would happily buy into your bullshit for the right price, bucko."

"What girls? There are no girls. Less than zero girls. You see, unlike you, I've kept it in my pants for all these years.

Lord knows why, at this point. Not that I haven't plenty of opportunities…"

"I'm sure you have."

"Oh, you know I have. Yet it is *you* who's stepping out on *me*."

"Maybe I have, and maybe I haven't."

"Hah! You know you have. And I'm the dipstick who actually took our wedding vows seriously."

"Yeah, right! I'm calling bullshit on all that noise. If you've been chaste and faithful all these years, then I'm Daffy fucking Duck."

"Quack away then, bitch! Just quack the fuck away. 'Cause there have been no other girls, toots." He took a deep breath, lowered his volume, and mumbled loud enough for Lisa to hear, "Though if wishing made it so."

Lisa smiled, knowing she had struck a nerve. "Just so long as that limp cock's worth something to someone."

"You can't fucking talk to me like that, Lisa!"

"And yet I just did. And so I still shall! Fuck you, Jeff."

"Well, that would be a refreshing change of pace now, wouldn't it?"

"Fuck you."

"Okay."

Lisa shifted uneasily in her seat, trying to come up with something fresh, something that cut deep, and yet ultimately resigned herself to playing the classics—the phrase she'd said a million times since their wedding day. "Fuck you."

Jeff smiled and said, "Is there a dim-witted echo out here? Or...'

"No, Jeff; no echo out here. Just me and the limp-dick choad I allowed to knock me up twice is all. But no echo."

"You make it sound so glamorous, my dear. Spoiler alert, it really, *really* wasn't. I was having better sex back in high school."

"Fuck you."

"Honestly, I'd sooner stick with my own hand, thanks."

"And so you shall. But, you know, instead of choad-goading me like the smarmy little prick you seem so set on being, maybe you could use your phone to call somebody."

Chuckling, Jeff asked, "Call somebody? *Call somebody?* Like who?"

Rolling her eyes, Lisa shifted her head and replied, "Like who? Like the fucking ski patrol, maybe?"

Fishing a small cellphone from his right jacket pocket, he pulled his face up out of the collar and said, "I don't have any bars."

"Or balls, either. But you should still try to reach someone."

"Why don't you try with your phone?"

"I left mine back at the lodge."

"Well, who's fault is that?"

Without warning, Lisa reached over, snatched the small Motorola phone from his black-gloved grasp, and heaved it as hard as her cramped arm would allow into a nearby cluster of lodgepole pine trees.

Patrick Quinn Kitson

He watched helplessly as it disappeared into a three-foot-high column of glistening powder. He met her eyes as Lisa glared at him and whispered, "Whoops."

"Fuck, Lisa! Why did you do that?" Jeff yelled, disbelieving.

"Because *fuck you*, chucklenuts."

"Okay, fine. That's—that's real, real nice, Lisa. Real charm school shit. Classy all the way. You better believe I'm taking the cost of a new phone out of your monthly bonus."

"Like I fucking care."

"You should, you know. You really should. Because if we end up getting a divorce, I am not gonna be paying you a monthly bonus anymore, if I pay you at all."

"If we get a divorce, I'll take half ownership of the practice and we can dissolve it. That's what your doe-eyed insistence on no prenup gets ya in the end, smart boy. And that'll be all the payday I need for the foreseeable future."

"You'd do that, wouldn't you? Just throw away everything I've built over the last decade because of some imagined sense of—"

"That *you've* built!? Don't you mean that *we've* built?"

"No, I don't actually. I said exactly what I meant. You didn't build shit. You barely do shit. I put down the deposits, I paid for the lot, I installed the new shelves in the waiting room, and I developed our client base. I'm also the only one who went through medical school and got my doctorate at twenty-four."

"Oh, and I did nothing? That's what you're saying?"

Jeff rubbed his stubbly face and scoffed. "Pretty much. I mean, let's be real here, cupcake; you're a glorified surgery assistant and part-time interior decorator. I could replace you in an instant with a third-year med student."

"Fuck you, Jeff."

"Oh, fuck me? *Fuck me?*" He angrily shoved her shoulder with his own. "You are nearly as useless in an operating room as you are in bed! If I could find a nurse that gave a decent enough blowjob, I would just—"

"Sorry to interrupt you two," a voice suddenly called up at them from the ground.

They both sheepishly fell quiet, wondering how long this person had been there, listening in on their nasty little squabble. Moving their respective boards aside and looking down between their legs, they saw a young, handsome man in his early twenties with a mop of dark black hair, aviator glasses, and wearing a red, white, and black Aspen SkiCo snow jacket with red pants astride a pair of white skis.

He pointed one of his black ski poles up at them and said, "I just wanted to give you an update on your situation."

Lisa elbowed Jeff in the ribs, causing him to double over in pain, and affected a sweeter tone than she had previously been using with her husband as she shouted down, "Oh, thank God! Yes, please! Do you know what's happening with this rickety old chairlift?"

The man below rubbed his head and looked around. "Yeah, they have paused it for a moment. They were just doing some routine safety checks on the cable. Can't be too careful, ya know? That said, out of abundance of caution, we are disembarking all remaining riders to the nearby far western lift which will take you back to the top."

Lisa and Jeff exchanged curious glances, which quickly resolved into their stock hostile glaring at one another. Jeff hollered down to the young man, "Uh, I've been here like a thousand times and I don't know about any far west chairlift. Do you mean the eastern lift? The main lift?"

"No, sir; I mean the far west lift. It isn't for use by the public just yet. We are opening up a new section of the mountain and it'll be another month or two before riders can utilize it. But for now we can use it to transport you guys back to the primary runs."

"How come we haven't heard anything about this supposed far west lift?"

The young man shrugged. "SkiCo is playing this one pretty close to the vest, I guess. The public doesn't know about it yet."

Lisa pushed her suspicions aside and jumped in. "Okay, so you're getting us down? 'Cause we would very much like to depart this death trap of a ski lift."

"Hey, no worries. We'll have you down in a jiffy."

Lisa glanced over her shoulder, seeing no one in the six or so chairs further up the cable. "Where is everyone else?"

The man on the ground surveyed the lift line in either direction, then returned his gaze to the couple. "Who else? I think you two are the only ones on this lift. We stopped boarding folks after you got on."

Again, suspicious glances shot between the two star-crossed squabblers. Lisa shook her head and shouted down to the man, "Really? That's odd, isn't it?"

The young man paused as if to consider his response, then relented by saying, "Above my pay grade, I'm afraid. But don't you fret ma'am, we will meet you down at the bottom and drop you off where you belong."

Jeff cocked an eyebrow and asked the young man in the SkiCo jacket, "Who's 'we'?"

Without answering, the man turned to head down the slope, flipped up his jacket hood, and as he began his descent to the lift booth just a few hundred yards ahead, called over his shoulder to them, "We'll see you at the bottom!"

They watched him slide down the slope away from them, and Lisa half-whispered to Jeff, "That guy is giving me creeper vibes."

Jeff snorted. "Everyone gives you creeper vibes."

"Fuck you, Jeff."

"Right, and there's the old pepper. Why do I even bother?"

"Because you're an idiot."

Affecting a baby-like cadence, Jeff mumble-garbled, "Said the *widdle-biddle* pot to the big, bad kettle."

"Think you're so clever, don't you, bucko? News flash, you're an imbecile. And also, fuck you."

"Okay," Jeff replied, somewhat satisfied. And he just might've kept at it in the interest of good sport, but for the fact that, at that moment, the cable shimmied and the chairlift began to move once again.

The rest of the ride was filled with a tense silence between them. Both knew that, one way or another, this was likely to be their final vacation together.

Nearing the bottom, they spied the small, outdated box of loosely nailed together boards that made up the lift control booth of the West Buttermilk lift. Next to it, they saw the man pulling off his skis and resting them against the outer wall of the booth. Standing beside him, sans skis or board, was a stunningly attractive and slender woman in her thirties with long raven hair hanging down over a two-piece ski suit of pure white.

Disembarking the lift, the unhappily married couple were surprised as the man swiftly dashed into the booth and hit the kill switch inside, stopping the cable at once. The dark-haired woman came around the corner and, as they attempted to hobble-hop over to her, they caught a glimpse of a small black object in her right hand, training straight their way.

It was a pistol. A Walther P38, to be precise. The very same gun that was directly issued to the Wehrmacht as a replacement for the Luger P08.

Lisa gasped and Jeff instinctively put up his hands.

The younger man came out of the shack, smiling as he saw the color drain from the duo's faces at the sight of the firearm.

The wind whistled between the nearby trees and along the slope as Lisa stared at them, and then quietly asked, "Uh, so what the hell is this shit now?" She scowled. "Uh, dude... SkiCo guy—I'm sorry, I didn't get your name."

The man in the SkiCo jacket walked over to where the woman in white stood and pulled his hood down. "Oh, yeah. My name's Lawrence and this here is Misty. And we will be your guides from here on out."

"So what's with the gun?" Lisa asked. Jeff remained silent, still with his hands raised.

Misty raised her gun and pointed it directly at Lisa's nose. "We can't have you two running off, now can we? Besides, we have a little surprise for you."

"Do you now?" Lisa asked.

"We do. See, we need you to come with us and help out with a little problem we have. Won't take but a few minutes." Misty nudged the nose of the gun at a nearby grove of lodgepole pines, bisected by a narrow, barely noticeable footpath. "Now, click out of your cheeky designer snowboards and start walking toward the trees over there. When you get to the yellow tape, just duck under it and keep going. We will be right behind you."

Lisa tossed a glance at Lawrence as if to confirm that the woman in white was serious. He smiled broadly, then swiftly replied, "I'd listen to the lady with the Glock, if I were you. She's a regular sharpshooter with that old thing."

"Now wait just a goddamn minute—" Lisa's words were cut short by the sound of her snowboard taking a single round along its length. She glanced down and saw a bullet hole near the NeverSummer logo, not a foot away from her bindings. It was a hole big enough to fit a thumb through. Her body tensed up as she peered up at the two.

Next to her, Jeff did nothing but stare forward with his hands up. Then, absent any vocalization, he slowly began to kneel and undo the bindings from his right foot. He stepped out as a glazed-over look enveloped his eyes.

Lisa waited, and after a few seconds, Misty raised and retrained the gun onto her head, cocking back the hammer. "Let's get this show on the road. Daylight's a wastin'."

Lisa pulled at her bindings and freed her attached foot, then looked over at Jeff. "Are you gonna do anything, you putz?"

Jeff said nothing, but began to walk in the direction of the footpath.

Lawrence and Misty walked over, placing themselves behind the other two, and Lisa started to follow her husband into the trees. Crossing between them, they followed the path for a few minutes until they saw a band of yellow tape blocking the path. Hanging from the line was a metal sign, emblazoned with big red lettering that read:

ABANDONED MINESHAFTS AND DEADLY HAZARDS LIE AHEAD. DO NOT CROSS THE YELLOW LINE UNDER ANY CIRCUMSTANCES. PROPERTY OF ASPEN SKICO, WHO COMPLETELY AVAIL THEMSELVES OF ANY AND ALL LEGAL LIABILITY SHOULD YOU CHOOSE TO TRESPASS INTO THIS AREA.

YOU WILL NOT RETURN ALIVE.

HAVE A NICE DAY.

As if in a trance, Jeff walked straight through the yellow elastic tape line, and after a moment of tugging, it snapped at his waist. Lisa followed with the other two close behind them.

After another couple of minutes, they arrived at a clearing. Near the center of it lay a large circular hole, maybe twenty feet in diameter.

Lisa suddenly realized that the day was rapidly headed in a direction that she would rather not go, and fast. She pivoted on her heel and raised her arm up, as if to strike down the nearest person following her. Her movement was met with the blinding sensation of the gun butt crashing down onto her head. Spots dotted her vision and she fell to the snow.

Lawrence laughed and brought his boot down onto her arm. She felt it crack underfoot, then shrieked and yowled as Lawrence leaned down to pick her up.

"You motherfucker! You just broke my arm! Motherfucker, I will sue your ass!"

As he helped her to her feet, Lawrence pulled her arms behind her, eliciting more pain. "Unlikely, lady." He then casually called over to Lisa's husband, who might've kept walking straight into the hole but for the sound of Lawrence's voice. "You can stop there, Jeff."

He stopped at once.

Misty walked past Lawrence and Lisa, putting the gun up to the back of Jeff's head. "This is the place. No need for pleasantries. Into the hole you go."

Lisa struggled in Lawrence's grasp. She called out to her seemingly catatonic man. "Jeff!"

He remained as he was, with the gun muzzle against his skull.

"Jeff, say something! You—you fleece-brained, flat-footed motherfucker!"

Nothing. His pale, ice-kissed face was now a blank slate—void of any emotion, vacant of all conscious thought. Wherever his mind has gone, it was no longer anywhere near the snowy slopes of Buttermilk Mountain.

Misty pushed the gun muzzle into the back of Jeff's head and he mindlessly began to march ahead, gaze seemingly fixed on nothing. As she led Jeff's body forward, she snickered at Lisa's pleas. "Honey, I wouldn't waste a whole lotta your words or thoughts on this'un right here. Going into a fugue state near the end isn't as uncommon as you might think."

"The end?" Lisa asked as she was nudged in the direction of the black chasm before them.

"Oh yeah. You two are mighty fucked. Food for the hungry."

Out of the hole came a voice, a deep, inhuman voice that mumbled from the depths below. "*Hun-gry!*"

Lisa's eyes went wide. "What the fuck was that?"

Ignoring her, Lawrence softly cooed in response. "Hey there, big boy. You been a good boy since we saw you?"

From the hole came the unearthly voice once again: "*Gooooood boy.*"

Lawrence grinned. "Don't you worry, Yum-Yum! We got a couple of fresh flesh sacks for you to floss your big, dopey teeth with."

A low, hollow sound like a knuckle rapping along a bored-out tree trunk called up to them from the dark, "*Big teeth not dopey.*"

Laughing while holding Lisa's now fractured arm with one hand and running the fingers of the other through his black hair, Lawrence shook his head and smiled. "Aww, you know I don't mean it, big guy. You know you're the handsomest guardian of the mountain anyone could ever hope for!"

From the hole, the deep-rumble voice sounded up to them: "*Yum-Yum guard mountain good.*"

Misty smiled and shouted down to the beast, "Yes you do, big buddy!"

"Whoa, whoa!" Lisa feebly tried to wriggle free to no avail. "You chucklefucks won't be feeding us to anything—certainly not some fucking thing in a damp, dirty hole—you understand me? That was not on the itinerary and I give you no such permission! Do you sons-a-bitches even know who we are?"

Misty grinned as she kept the gun trained on the back of Jeff's unmoving head. "Sure, we do. You're Lisa and Jeff Miller of Carbondale, Colorado; formerly of the Denver-metro area. You have two mean-spirited kids in college, a small medical practice, a yappy little shar pei that you've shamefully named JWOWW, a net worth of just over eight million dollars, and you two regularly kill people on the operating table."

Lisa hissed through her teeth, "We did not agree to be fed to any large—Wait." She paused, then shouted, "Wait, did you—you said we kill people? What people? We don't kill people!" Lawrence and Misty stood silently and just watched as Lisa took in their accusatory looks, then shook her head. "I don't know what…I mean, it's not that… I'm saying that we don't… Look, people die sometimes; it's the sad truth of our chosen profession. People die. That's life. But we do *not* kill people."

Misty mockingly quipped back, "You say *po-tay-to*, we say murder. It's all a matter of perspective, I guess."

"You guess? What the—what the fuck does that mean?"

Misty dropped her head momentarily, then swung it up in one swift motion. "Should I just shoot her before we toss her down?"

Lawrence pulled her arms tighter, giving Lisa another flash of pain in her arm. "Maybe. She is a mouthy one, I'll grant you that."

"Don't shoot me!" Lisa pleaded.

Misty countered, "Okay, then go jump into the hole and save us the effort. Otherwise, I'm gonna put one between your eyes and kick your corpse on down. Either way works for me."

Lisa pushed through the pain and pulled her arms away suddenly. Surprisingly, Lawrence allowed her to break free.

She passed Jeff and slowly stepped backward to the edge of the black chasm, then stopped to address her two assailants. "What is this? Why are you doing this to us?"

Lawrence answered her. "Because long ago, a prehistoric prophecy was fulfilled, and a primeval pact was made in secret. This was before man, before our perception of time, really— or so I've been told. Just like so many of the other mountains in Colorado, this place is the ancestral home of a slumbering guardian. A fanged beast from time immemorial, who lies and rests within the subterra beneath our feet. I've been told he does something to ensure snowfall, but I'm not sure it's true. Anyway, doesn't matter. As part of the ancient agreement with the spirits of the slopes, we must feed the creature, or he will spring forth and leave a trail of bloody rampage in his wake. No one would escape his hunger, nor his unbridled fury."

The ground beneath all of their feet trembled as two hard smacks of the creature's fist rocked the wall of the grotto from which its voice called up. "*Big fury! Me hun-gry!*"

Though shocked and shaken, Lisa still kept up her tone of incredulous defiance. "What the fuck are you two assholes blabbering about? What's down in that hole?"

Lawrence's face went flat as he replied. "Uh, I just told you. It's the guardian. Our guardian. The guardian of Buttermilk. I mean, in practical terms, he's a forty-foot-tall Yeti that we all affectionately call Yum-Yum. But yeah, the guardian. Weren't you listening to what I said?"

Lisa's eyes narrowed, mouth agape. "Listening, yes. Believing you, no. Why do you call it Yum-Yum?"

Misty yawned and checked her watch, still training the pistol on Jeff's head. "Oh Christ, can I shoot her yet?"

"Wait, wait, wait! Don't! Please don't! I just— Can I just… Please, we have money—"

"We don't want your money, lady," Lawrence replied. "We must satiate the guardian, and that is damn well what's about to happen. See, this sorta thing used to be the sole purview of a long bloodline of protectors, a family who had been here since the time of the ancients." He cracked a wry grin, then continued, "But once the last one of his familial line died of a cocaine overdose back in the early seventies, it fell to the Aspen Ski Company to take up this sacred charge."

"You're serious?"

"Sure I'm serious. Deadly serious. The same kinda serious you and your husband are all too acquainted with."

Lisa stood there dumbfounded. After a bit of quick mental math, she still found herself at a loss. She knew, way down in her gut, that somehow, some way, these two maniacs knew what she and Jeff had done. Had been doing, really. Against all odds, they knew that the eternally-squabbling pair of vacationers had let folks die whilst under their care. Because, you know, shit happens sometimes.

But also, because, you know, *money.*

Isn't money the answer to ninety-nine out of one hundred questions?

And it was true that she and Jeff had allowed several patients to die on their table. Not because of any sick, sociopathic, angel-of-mercy-type need to kill others or satiate some bloodlust.

No, never that.

The truth was, in point of fact, much lazier and more banal. It was simply because sometimes it was easier and a whole helluva lot more expedient—to say nothing of much more profitable—to let them go than to trudge through all the hard work of making sure they survived.

What can you do? You can't save everyone, she thought grimly.

And certainly not when she had figured out a nifty little trick o' the bookkeeping, allowing them to collect lucrative copays without rendering the full amount of treatment which they had billed out to the various insurance companies.

Naturally, they pocketed the difference.

Looking over the two SkiCo employees once more, she saw that the two well and truly meant and believed in everything they had said to her. She could hear it in their voices. She could see it in their eyes.

Lisa sighed and made a feeble attempt to force her own eyes to well with tears, yet to no avail. Even the crocodile tears she'd easily pulled forth throughout her life were impossible to produce at this point. Frustrated, defeated, broken, and finding nothing left in herself but to acquiesce and accept the cards she'd been summarily dealt by harrowing fate, she quietly asked, "Before I go, can you—can you please tell my children I love them?"

Misty laughed malevolently. "No, probably not." She shot Lawrence a quick look and he grinned back at her, shaking his head

Whatever energy had possessed her up until now had truly run its course. Lisa slumped her shoulders and, still disbelieving what was happening, made one last request of her armed captors. "Okay, well then. Can I just at least say one last thing to my husband, please?"

As Misty and Lawrence nodded their heads in cautious approval, Lisa slowly raised her own hung head and cast her steely, hate-filled gaze onto the expressionless face of her still catatonic husband.

With her last bit of will remaining, she softly hissed at him through gnashed teeth, "I fucking hate you, Jeff."

Lawrence smirked, but said nothing as he stepped forward, clamped one gloved hand onto her shoulder, and unceremoniously shoved her into the abyss below. She tripped as she fell forward and was sent sprawling into the hole, end over end. Tumbling a good forty feet, she wailed all the way down.

Just as they heard the hard thud of Lisa hitting the stone floor of the cavern beneath their feet, Misty likewise shoved Jeff from the back and he went in after, headfirst. And while they could hear Lisa groaning from her hard landing (likely breaking one or both of her legs upon impact), the audible crack of Jeff's spine snapping told them he had landed much less fortuitously than his wife.

Lawrence shot Misty a look. "Know what always comes to mind when we do this?"

"What's that?"

"That Aerosmith song, 'Eat the Rich.' You know?"

"No. Don't think I've heard that one."

"It's like the first track on their seminal nineties album, *Get A Grip*. Great fucking song."

Turning away from the hole, Misty clicked the safety on the Walther P38 pistol and slipped it into the waistband of her white snow pants. Looking at Lawrence, who was already turning back toward the narrow path between the lodgepole pines that would lead them back to the Buttermilk base lodge, she yawned and began to stretch her arms as she asked, "Well, personally, this shit always makes me hella hungry. Where should we go for dinner, my love?"

Lawrence shrugged as he trudged back the way they had come. "I dunno. Somewhere good. Maybe we should stroll over to the Red Onion."

Misty shook her head as she followed him. "Nah. Not really in the mood for cheap burgers."

"How about we hit the chili bar at Bentley's?"

"We were there two nights ago."

"Okay, fine. What about the J-Bar? They got tasty drinks for days."

"Uh, no; no way, José! There is a whole lotta that shit not gonna happen, ya feel me? I want something tasty, and their food is straight-up crap, you know that. Sure, the drinks are decent enough, but the food is just utter yuck. Also, not that this is neither here nor there, but I met Luke Wilson there last week, and he was a total prick to me."

"Really?"

"Yeah, no, I'm fully serious. I didn't tell you about this? He was getting drinks with his brother Owen at the J-Bar and was rude as shit to Penny and I for absolutely no reason whatsoever. Owen was really nice, but Luke is a fucking asshat."

"Oh. Okay. That's random. Well then, how's 'bout the ol' Hickory House?"

Misty clapped her hands together joyously. "Oh, hells to the yeah! Now you're talking, baby! I could definitely chow down on some fresh cornbread and sloppy-ass BBQ short ribs. That sounds fucking delicious right about now."

While Lawrence A. and Misty B. of the Aspen SkiCo casually walked away from the hidden hole in the frozen ground, the reverberating screams of Lisa and Jeff Miller heightened in mortal terror, then slowly began to die down. As the loud crunching of bones, along with the wet slapping of torn flesh being chewed into digestible bits tapered off, so did the surrounding area fall into relative silence. All around, shadows began to swallow up the shimmery white earth as the failing light of day retreated wearily into the western horizon.

After a long minute of nothing but the sound of air whooshing down the side of the mountain and through the nearby trees, the tranquility was shattered by a booming belch traveling up from the snowy hole, followed by a deeply satisfied declaration from the hairy hoofed creature within its darkened depths.

"*Yum yum!*" it bellowed skyward, to no one in particular.

HEADLINE

What happened in Colorado?

Mystery, frustration, and conspiracy theories still surround the near destruction of a small Colorado mountain community, forty-five minutes from Aspen.

By Adam Rudd, Associated Press Contributor

COLORADO, USA, December 22nd (AP). After two weeks of deliberate press obfuscation, unexplained military quarantine, and exhaustive investigation, federal agencies, along with local and state law enforcement organizations, remain largely quiet about the violent and bizarre events that unfolded in the small town of Carbondale, Colorado at the beginning of December.

Despite extensive interviews with eye-witness survivors, worldwide news coverage of the event, and attempts at reconciling the cause of the damage that has left the town all but uninhabitable in the wake of the tragedy, law enforcement has remained wholly obtuse in their interactions with the press. It has been claimed, though not yet corroborated, that the White House, in conjunction with the Federal Bureau of Investigation, has stepped in and advised all other federal, state, and local agencies to withhold any pertinent information from the public. This has led to an explosion of mass media speculation and online conspiracy theories about the events surrounding the destruction of the otherwise quaint and, until recently, little-known mountain town.

Carbondale sits at the feet of Mt. Sopris, located in Garfield County and situated roughly within Colorado's western slope. It lies along Highway 82, between the more familiar communities of Aspen/Snowmass and Glenwood Springs.

All 507 confirmed survivors have been sequestered by the authorities and none have been granted availability to the media. When recently pressed about the uncommon degree of secrecy surrounding the investigation, Todd Deekholder, spokesperson for the Colorado Bureau of Investigation, stated that, "Given the scope and severity of the tragedy that has unfolded, we are inclined, and frankly legally obligated, to hold off on any further comments until we can conclusively say what transpired during the evening in question."

This lack of disclosure has understandably fueled a cacophony of outcries from lawmakers, the public, and press outlets at large. In scathing rebukes of both the media blackout as well as the military occupation that has cut off the area from outside contact, pundits and legislators on both sides of the aisle have vented their frustrations to the administration, as well as the press. This week, James Comer, chairman of the house committee on oversight and accountability, put forth a motion to effectively force the agencies involved to disclose any and all information about the events that occurred the night of December 1st in Carbondale, Colorado.

President Donald Trump has recently barred all press from the White House and has not taken any questions since the days immediately following December 1st. As such, he has been incapable of focusing on or furthering his so-called "America First" agenda that has been the lynchpin of his tumultuous and sometimes chaotic second term in office.

In her single meeting with media outlets on December 8th, Trump's press secretary Karoline Leavitt spoke on the front lawn of the White House, saying in part, "We are focusing on helping the community and its residents reconcile the tragedy that has befallen them. As always, our administration, as well as President Trump, are first and foremost focused on the safety of the American public. We are deeply committed to accountability as well as transparency. As such, it would be premature to speculate or comment on the matter in any detail until we sort out the information we are receiving from our agencies on the ground. All our efforts signal our dedication to get to the bottom of all of this. What we can say is that the facts are coming in. It is our hope in the coming weeks to be able to end all the unfair and unjust rumor mill nonsense that you, the media, have taken it upon yourselves to engage in since this devastating development occurred. Quite frankly, it is embarrassing that you are putting your need for information above the safety of the American people, and it is this administration's belief that history will judge you unfavorably for your irresponsible actions in the wake of this event."

After her prepared statement, she declined to take any questions from the various media outlets in attendance.

While news organizations and the public have remained in the dark, the outcry has done little to hinder the administration from heavy-handed enforcement of the quarantine zone surrounding the town. Some fifty or so persons have been arrested and detained without any legal representation for trying to gain access to the area in the last ten days. These persons have been likewise hidden from the inquisitive public. However, this has not stopped the press or online sleuths from attempting to unearth the truth about the fate of townspeople and the incident in question. Drones, leakers, and "hacktivists" from several nations have laid siege to the attempted media blackout and some narratives have begun to take root.

Editor's note: The following section contains information garnered from several persons familiar with the investigation who wish to remain anonymous and should be thusly afforded some degree of skepticism.

Initial reports of a domestic terrorist attack, as originally reported by several media outlets, have been vehemently denied by the authorities. This, despite several of the surviving population purportedly (according to several anonymous police sources) claiming that the events of that night were the result of a malicious collection of bad actors. So far, the information available does seem to detract from this narrative. Details about any group action are vague and often do not corroborate one another. The earlier speculation by the media about a dirty bomb or small thermonuclear device have been disproven, both by the scientific community and a handful of our sources in the Pentagon.

Neil deGrasse Tyson has led an effort to allay the public's concerns about any type of large explosion causing the destruction of the town. Speaking to a crowd of thousands at a conference in Los Angeles this week, he said, "Well, what we don't have are any of the easily detectable markers of such a detonation. Our satellites rely on sensors to monitor radiation from nuclear explosions. Such blasts always produce gamma rays, X-rays, and neutrons in unbelievable quantities. Nuclear explosions release a massive burst of X-rays that occur repeatedly with an interval of less than one microsecond that could be detected by any number of global satellites. So I am personally inclined to lean away from the nuclear narrative. Rather what we have here is something much more sinister. I hesitate to paint such a tinfoil hat portrait, but this level of secrecy is wholly unprecedented in this sort of Orwellian time in human history. A time where everything is photographed and everyone is watching. I doubt the crumbling facade of this puzzle will last long."

To that end, in the last week, the hacker group Anonymous has claimed to have infiltrated several secure government websites and databases in a search for answers about the incident. According to various posts from the clandestine organization, they've been able to access surveillance footage and video recordings from the night of December 1st. Furthermore, they have stated that the clips and footage they have illegally acquired seem to show several common, albeit hard to believe denominators.

First, that there was in fact only one aggressor responsible for the event in question.

Second, that nearly six thousand people were killed in a matter of hours while the town was laid siege to by said individual.

Third, that the relatively few survivors are all residents who lived in the areas outlying the town proper.

And lastly, and perhaps most troubling of all, that this perpetrator might still be at large.

Editor's note: A person identifying themselves as a member of Anonymous has sent us a detailed communication, including screenshots, and have disclosed that they plan on releasing all obtained videos within the next twenty-four hours.

While most outlets (including the AP) have had little cooperation or confirmation from the various agencies involved from which to draw a clearer picture of what some in the public space are now labeling a "cover-up," there have been several others in the upper echelons of the armed forces who have spoken to us privately on the matter.

A credible and verified high-level military source, speaking on the condition of anonymity, sat down with the Associated Press and was candid in their assessment of what they know about the incident: "As far as we can tell, the whole fiasco was perpetrated by a single individual who has yet to be identified. This person was the sole reason the town was effectively burned to the ground."

When asked for further clarification, the same source confided the following:

"Crazy as it may sound—and believe me when I say, this is about as fucking nuts as any situation can get—it appears that some blood-crazed maniac in what could only be described as a high-tech suit of some type was running around town blowing up buildings, setting fires all over, and getting into several brief firefights with local law enforcement. I say 'brief' because the police department of Carbondale, brave though they surely appear to have been, was not even remotely prepared for such an assault. I've seen footage and the whole thing is nightmarish. This guy, if you want to call him that, was able to leap from building to building and create chaos on a scale that is truly unprecedented. From some of the more recent images I've seen, the perpetrator had metal implements on his hands, and was seen from various doorbell cameras and security feeds tearing into people like, I don't know, a wild animal or something.

"Again, I cannot stress enough how little I would believe any of this had I not seen it with my own eyes. When the cops fired on him, it was completely ineffective at slowing the aggressive onslaught. The few that managed to directly engage the perpetrator were unsuccessful in stopping it. He tore them to pieces, figuratively and literally. John Rambo didn't have shit on this evil mother, trust me. And the crooked loon even seems to be laughing in a few of the clips I've seen of the firefights with local law enforcement. And I've seen some ugly stuff in my time, but I've never seen anything like this. Frankly, I hope I never do again. To say it was shockingly brutal would be an understatement."

These allegations, extraordinary though they may seem, are in line with some of the claims made by several other sources, as well as Anonymous, which include the assertion that a sole individual committed the acts that transpired on December 1st and that the suspect engaged with well-armed residents and police alike.

Aside from the aforementioned violence, the mentions of a "high-tech suit" were expounded upon by the same military source:

"We've had several meetings just about that suit, if that's what it is. The helmet, the fire, the claws—we have analysts working around the clock trying to pin down a country of origin, because frankly, it's way beyond our technology in the

States. Whoever it was, they seemingly leapt from building to building like they had boots that were capable of safely vaulting them about. As though they had springs on their feet. And the helmet this individual wore was capable of emitting, for lack of a better description, fireballs. And yes, I mean that exactly like it sounds. Those very projectiles were the source of the hundreds of fires that all but turned the town to cinder. When this person, about an hour into the siege, accessed a small explosives cache located near the police department, things really got ugly fast. It was those explosives that were responsible for the destruction of the police department and the adjacent buildings, as well as the large flash that was reported by nearby airports that evening. We suspect that came from some oil storage tanks on the southern side of the town, along Highway 133."

When inquiring about this supposed individual specifically, the source seemed unsure how to characterize the suspect:

"We know next to nothing about the who and why in this case. One group in the Pentagon has been tasked with the theory part of it. So far, they've come up with essentially nothing, which plays directly into why the media has been kept in the dark. There is one thing that has come up a couple of times, but it's fairly ridiculous if you ask me."

The source then seemed to consider whether or not to speak upon this further, eventually relenting and disclosing that, "It's an absurd kind of thing. But there is one historical item that has consistently popped up in a few briefings and reports from the Pentagon team. Supposedly there was another time in history when something occurred that bore eerie similarities to the tragedy in Carbondale. Albeit, it was in the mid 1800s, so documentation was hard to come by.

"I suppose they have classically described it as some form of humanoid cryptid, but really it's a spotty story from English folklore during the early Victorian era, in which a masked marauder laid a similar siege to villages in the English countryside. This guy matches the description of our suspect in the Carbondale incident, right up to the laughter. They called him Spring-Heeled Jack. It could be a bunch of malarkey and is, likely as not, completely unrelated to what we're seeing here. Though I will be the first to admit that there are some disconcerting similarities in both appearance and modus operandi of the two situations. It's why I mentioned the spring foot thing earlier. This devil guy from English folklore had claws, a helmet, and a propensity for setting buildings ablaze. Supposedly he was able to vault about rooftops using spring-loaded lifts affixed to his boots."

After doing some quick digging, the Associated Press was able to construct a summary to corroborate the source's claims. There was, in point of fact, a spate of incidents in Great Britain dating back to the mid-1800s through the early 1900s which do bear a striking resemblance to the information given to us by both Anonymous and the high-level military source we spoke with.

The first confirmed report was in London in 1837. Tales of a masked madman seducing women, stealing livestock (specifically sheep), and burning villages were often thought to be large-scale hoaxes or fanciful creations to explain away responsibility for the victims of other crimes. However, as sightings and incidents continued to persist among the body politic of the day, newspapers and even the government began to take interest.

Several testimonials—including a series of vividly detailed accounts from the counties of Somerset, Dorset, and Devon in 1855—lend some credence to the myth. One such notable report came from a group of soldiers with the 2nd battalion of the British Army, stationed at Aldershot Garrison in 1877. According to their account, a few sentries engaged with a person matching the earlier descriptions of Spring-Heeled Jack. The following year, another group of soldiers (a detachment of the King's Royal Rifle Corp) who were held up in the winter of 1878 at Aldershot exchanged gunfire on several occasions with the fabled humanoid creature. Many of these officers claimed that they were given extra ammunition and advised by their commanders to "shoot the night terror" on sight.

Another account from 1877 at Newport Arch in Lincolnshire spoke of a group of citizens engaging with "a man wearing sheepskin, brandishing long metallic claws, and able to escape by jumping over high walls."

The last reported sighting was in 1904 in Liverpool.

Since its inception within the public zeitgeist, the character has appeared in penny dreadfuls and was the subject of several pamphlet publications. However, the only known copies of these three pamphlets, claiming to be "factually-based, historical records of Spring-Heeled Jack" were reported to have been destroyed along with the British Library during The Blitz (the German bombing campaign of London during 1940 and 1941).

After speaking with this military source, we contacted other media outlets to ascertain if they'd heard anything about a military grade weapon system for individuals involved in the event. While hesitant to disclose their own information in full, we can report that after speaking with their own sources, tales of a suit, a historical figure, and mention of a single perpetrator were all but confirmed.

We now await the release of the information by the hacktivists involved, and express our admiration for their ability to hold this administration accountable for the lack of transparency in this matter.

Editor's Note: After the Associated Press was given the aforementioned information, we reached out to the White House press office for comment before posting the feature on our website. In what could be construed as an act of intimidation meant to silence us, our colleagues were afforded little courtesy and, in point of fact, were told in no uncertain terms that the publication of this well-sourced article would be "effectively tantamount to treason" and would bring forth "severe legal and criminal charges."

Following this call, we were immediately contacted by Kash Patel, director of the Federal Bureau of Investigation. Claiming to have clear directives from the president himself, Mr. Patel threatened to send agents to our offices to prevent publication of this article. However, when our colleagues disclosed that several other media outlets had been given some of our information, that our story included descriptions of a single individual burning down the town in a suit resembling descriptions from old English lore, and that videos from the investigation had been taken from their servers to be made public by the hacker group Anonymous in the next twenty-four hours, Mr. Patel seemed to abandon his former stance and accept that the media blackout was nearing an end. The FBI director then hurriedly ended the call, claiming he would have to contact us at a later date.

FROM THE AUTHOR

To all who have graciously journeyed this far into the literary shadows with me, I wish to thank you for reading *BONEDALE*. I hope you enjoyed reading the stories as much as I enjoyed writing them. This was a labor of love because Carbondale is not only my hometown, but has also been instrumental in making me the person I am today.

With a vast and varied, yet perfect blend of people, culture, nature and a mellow lifestyle that is unlike any other, Bonedale represents everything that I find wonderful about our all-too-brief time in this life. For me, it is nothing less than true north, and I fervently (perhaps biasedly) believe it to be the greatest place in the world.

(This, despite the dark undercurrent of terror, rampant nocturnal creatures, varied monsters–both human and otherwise–to say nothing of the greedy grotesqueries and nascent ne'er-do-wells that stalk about it's gorgeous landscape).

Before you take your leave of this many splendored tome, I have prepared a little something for you in the following pages. Call it the literary equivalent of a post-credits scene.

Continue reading for an exclusive sneak peek at the prologue of my next book, *TALENTED*, set to be released later this year. The synopsis is as follows:

"When 24-year-old Caitronia Smyth signs up for a four-day writer's conference in Nashville, Tennessee to garner interest for her first short story collection, she has zero intentions of making friends or getting too involved with anybody else attending—far from it, in fact. Little does she realize that something else has descended upon the convention. Something sinister which seeks to rob others of their autonomy and inspiration. Before the weekend is through, she'll need to face down her own self-destructive behaviors and reluctantly employ the assistance of some newfound literary acquaintances to survive a veritable gauntlet of firing-squad pitch sessions, vulpine publishing agents, militant furry-fetishist conventioneers, legions of Ray-Ban bespectacled, black-suit clad demon subjugates, one badly prepared mass murderer to say nothing of a charismatic succubus with a global reader base, just to come out the other side in one piece. All this, while trying simply to get someone to read her damn manuscript."

Until we meet again, boys and ghouls.

Patrick Quinn Kitson

TALENTED

"Writing is the hardest work in the world. I have been a bricklayer and a truck driver, and I tell you—as if you haven't been told a million times already—that writing is harder. Lonelier.
And nobler and more enriching."
— Harlan Ellison

"Okay, so I write overblown, purple, self-indulgent prose. So fucking what?"
— Angela Carter

PROLOGUE:
In Medias Res

People do not explode in the way you'd expect them to, based on what you see in movies and video games. As of ten seconds ago, this is something I now know first-hand.

There are rare and powerful moments in your life when you know precisely what you have to do. The mind achieves a sort of crystalline clarity as time slows to a crawl. The many possible choices that lay before you fall away, leaving one clear and often daunting path of action down which you must proceed, or swiftly perish.

And yet you'd still really rather not.

You'd rather flee the scene, find a cozy bed, click on another video of soothing beta wave ASMR fodder to zone out to, pull the covers over your head and attempt to forget that this Kafkaesque nightmare ever occurred. Praying you wake up to a new and better day, realizing that it was all a fleeting, albeit wildly vivid dream.

But that doesn't happen, you see. Dream sequences are for dullards and hacks, so you better believe this harrowing shit is live and in stereo, baby.

Such moments are the fabric of what ultimately defines most of us. When the rubber meets the proverbial road and one is faced with the unenviable task of putting it up or shutting it all the way down. When actions damn well better match words. Otherwise, you need to do the world a big fat fucking favor and just pack up the stage setup, the lighting equipment and the instruments, cancel the remaining tour dates, wipe off the makeup, disband the group, and release your greatest hits album.

Action talks. Bullshit walks.

I'm staring down the metaphorical double barrel of such a moment as people run screaming in all directions. The blood pooled on the floor at my feet is thick and dark against the filigree-patterned carpeting, looking more black than red. It has also, as I'm noticing for the first time in this oddly slow-motion moment, stained my dress. Which is some real shit. You'd think this would be nary impossible with black satin, but apparently it's a thing.

Had I known earlier in the evening that I would be splashed with gore, I would have worn my miniskirt. *Should* have worn my miniskirt.

For that matter, had I known how the weekend was going to culminate, I would have been better prepared, and at minimum, packed a weapon in my suitcase. Any weapon. A stiletto knife, or a Taser, maybe a nice kneecapper—whatever. Not quite the high-caliber artillery that the nutjob in Room 908 was packing earlier today when he initiated his brief and ill-fated attack on the hotel—but something. *Anything.*

Truth be told, a gun might not help me much right now. Not with that fiery-eyed, crimson-skinned, grinning-mad demon staring daggers at me from across the room. Can it even be killed? Who knows?

We're in uncharted waters here for sure, with nary a compass in sight.

I could run, though I doubt I'd get very far. Several of the demon's henchmen are eyeballing the exits, then me, and the exits again. Steely-cheeked and suited out in the same clandestine, albeit vaguely formal regalia you'd most readily associate with secret service agents, they are surely waiting for me to make a dash upon which they can readily pounce and thusly trounce.

Despite eyes hidden behind aviator sunglasses and amid a fast-fleeing mob of literary professionals, their laser focus on me remains undeterred. Said sheeple run past unmolested, clamoring over one another like swarming ants as they frantically scatter through the Big Birch Ballroom's double door exits. Away from the white-linen tablecloths, the ritzy catering bars, the well-groomed wait staff—and now the erstwhile bodies freshly exploded into a blackish-red goo.

Spilling out into the open ten-floored atrium of the Embassy Suites hotel like stampeding, evening-wear-clad bison, hundreds fill the glass-paneled space with startling speed and reckless abandon. Any feeble attempts by the staff to quell the raucous exodus or ascertain a source for the commotion are swiftly dashed. No sooner do the employees come out from behind the front check-in desk to investigate the din rising from the ballroom, then are they forced to quickly retreat behind it. All to avoid being trampled by the frightened horde of authors, and publishers, and editors, and agents, and money-focused clingers-on that pour out in a frenzied cascade of flesh and fear. The egress of panic unbound.

Terrified voices screaming for someone to call the police, while others are already dialing 911 and wailing into their smartphones. Shouting women holding their hands to their mouths as they dash through the sliding glass doors of the lobby entrance. Scores of men—normally self-assured and overtly masculine, now having rapidly devolved into wide-eyed, semi-dazed, lip-quivering wrecks—clamoring past one another like linebackers aiming for the opposing team's QB. Bodies crashing against the padded chairs that line the lobby, knocking over merch tables, tumbling into the basins of large fountains filled with copper coin wishes, and smashing through walls of one another in a bid to find escape through the automated exits.

Back in the Big Birch Ballroom, I realize everyone at the nearby tables have left (who can really blame them?), with the exception of my four new friends in this fresh literary hell.

My peeps. My tribe.

They all remain, watching me for an idea of what to do next, while the rest of the room chooses flight over fight. As if I have some stratagem pre-planned for this very predicament. As if I have a goddamn clue.

I smile back to reassure them that I do in fact have a plan, though the one idea jumbling about in my brain at present is arguably a bit psychotic and/or possibly suicidal if carried to fruition.

Arguably.

The local bluegrass/new jazz band hired for the final night of the Killer Nashville International Writers Conference (The Blue Notes, I think?) has stopped playing and now cowers on the stage, not far behind the demon.

A white-bearded man in a tan collared shirt, black bowler hat, and blue strap suspenders holds up his banjo in a defensive pose.

A large, trembling, potbellied gent in blue coveralls sits behind the drum set holding his sticks up in the sign of a cross, his head turned away from the unholy sight.

The keyboardist—a long-haired fellow in a blue vest—hides behind his electric ivories like a World War I trench soldier awaiting an incoming mortar hit.

Behind the standup bass, a slender brunette woman uses the big wooden body to hide the whole of her figure. Not doing too bad of a job, either, if we're being honest. I can barely glimpse her strapless blue dress behind that big stringed instrument.

The horned succubus's clothing has fallen away to the floor, revealing something fearsome, freakish, and almost biblical in form—though admittedly not of the pearly gates variety. Its wings, appearing as though fashioned from leathery tarp, arc up and out. While I'm generally not easily frightened, seeing this unholy being extend them skyward, I'm completely horrified.

Cards on the table: I'm as scared as I have ever been in my life. I'm even more scared than I was just before Bruno left this mortal coil. I'm scared for my newfound friends and I'm terrified for my father. The prospect of him missing me—or worse. My fear for them hurts my heart for the briefest of moments, then starts to rapidly mutate into something else. Something less defensive, less passive. Something like anger.

No, more than anger. Something worse.

I *hate* this monstrous bitch.

Through gnashed teeth, I utterly seethe toward this duplicitous, devilish demoness and her dapper devotees. Not just for what this wretched thing is or what it represents, but for what it has already taken.

For that which it still sought to take.

This overinflated, gargoyle-looking piece of evil has now, on top of all the other sins committed over the past few days, ruined what was otherwise a really, *really* nice and elegant awards dinner.

(Lemme tell ya, the food was spectacular. Chicken cutlets marinated in a balsamic reduction, roasted garlic fingerling potatoes, fresh sautéed veggies, and pecan pie to polish it off. Damn good.)

The now-cowering band had been deftly laying down the jams and the upscale ambiance had possessed all the trappings of the rich and quasi-famous whilst the event's founder (and tonight's moderator) had read off the winners in each category to a varied gaggle of literary constituents.

A cocktail bar, free to all attendees. Clapping every sixty to ninety seconds. Bubbling champagne and red bowties. Cowboy hats and Vera Wang dresses. Glad-handing. Networking.

And now this. Blood and demons.

The night-wrecking devil of our collective discontent now raises its foul hands; wretched, withered, wrinkled, knotted and gnarled tendrils hanging from a witch's knuckles. It growls at me and my tribe through the alabaster knives protruding between its cracked black lips. Pointing a single, crooked finger our way, it cackle-hisses, "I'm not gonna miss this time, you little shit! You would've done well to keep your mouth shut and take the early hint!"

I can't help but grin and call back, "Not really my style, ya know? You're probably thinking of some other bitch. Got your number now, so your time is well and truly at an end!"

The cooky idea bouncing about in my head would rely on a gamble, a dash, and a prayer.

The gamble is that something magical and good still exists in this cruel and lonely world.

The dash would be toward the demon without being splayed down the middle with its razor-tipped claws.

The prayer is that I have enough strength to do the deed once the instrument of this evil being's destruction is firmly in my hand.

A lot of variables to go wrong here.

And yet, the choice is the right one. The only one. A single card to play, and no time like now to play it.

Looking back on it now, there was really no other way the wild weekend in Music City could have unfolded. We can move around within the flow of a raging river, flapping about wildly as we fight the current, yet it still guides us through the land of life as it has predetermined. Destiny is time-chiseled into the bedrock beneath the rapids long before the currents carry us past them.

This was the endpoint of a journey that had been filled with fury and fear, friendship, fiction and fun. It was arguably the greatest moment of my entire life.

And it all started five years ago, with me killing my best friend.

Transmissions From The Campfire is Colorado's #1 original horror podcast. Spooky and irreverent, humorous and homebrewed, each episode is a horror / sci-fi tinged trip into the dark underbelly of the Colorado landscape. Written by Patrick Quinn Kitson, and produced, mixed and edited by Daniel Kelley, episodes feature many stories set in and around the Roaring Fork Valley as well as the odd interview with the genre's top-tier storytellers/celebs of middling import–it's quite literally the best way you can spend your time on the internet.

"With a Stephen King feel and a knack for quickly hooking you into a story, Patrick Kitson is a compelling storyteller with a very bright future."

— Tom Barber, author of the *Sam Archer* thriller series

KILLER NASHVILLE
CLAYMORE
TOP PICK

BE SURE TO PICK UP THE FIRST TWO SHORT STORY COLLECTIONS BY PATRICK QUINN KITSON, AVAILABLE WHEREVER BOOKS ARE SOLD.

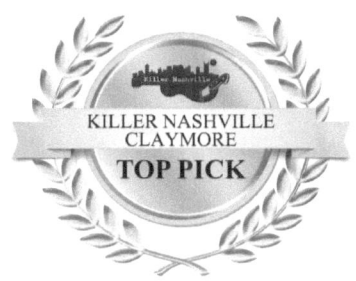

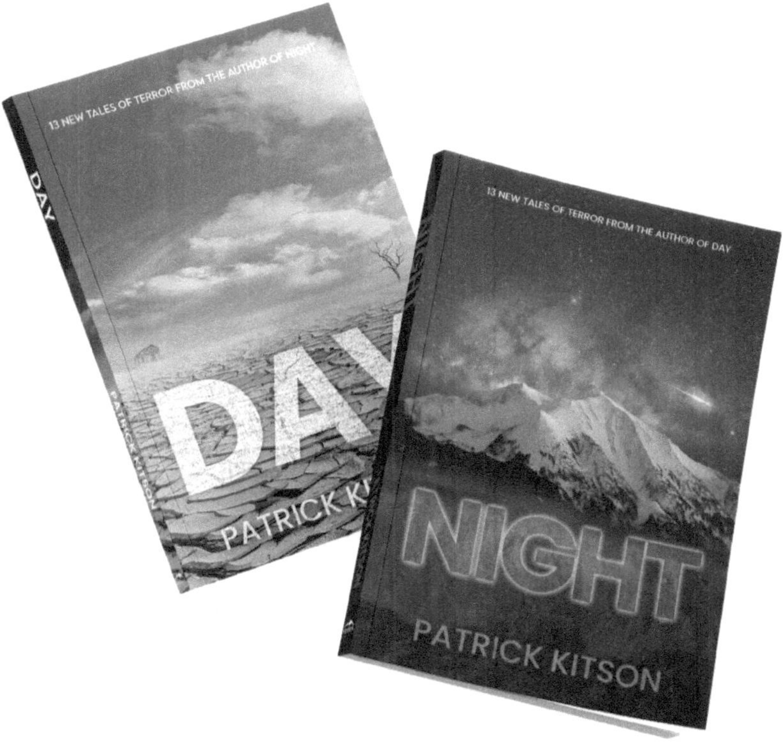

ABOUT THE AUTHOR

Purveyor of dread, bon vivant, and scribe of middling import, Patrick Kitson has been a lifelong student of the macabre, the satirical, and the intellectually dubious. Born and raised in The Roaring Fork Valley, he's coined the term, "Valley Horror" in reference to his particular brand of homebrewed speculative fiction which largely takes place in and around the snowy climes of Colorado.